D0046444

Lethal Vintage

ALSO BY NADIA GORDON:

Sharpshooter
Death by the Glass
Murder Alfresco

a sunny mccoskey napa valley mystery

Lethal Vintage

nadia gordon

CHRONICLE BOOKS

SAN FRANCISCO

Library of Congress Cataloging-in-Publication Data:
Gordon, Nadia.
  Lethal vintage : a Sunny McCoskey Napa Valley mystery / Nadia Gordon.
     p. cm.
  ISBN 0-8118-5801-4
  1. McCoskey, Sunny (Fictitious character)--Fiction.
  2. Napa Valley (Calif.)--Fiction. 3. Wine and wine making--Fiction.
  4. Restaurants--Fiction. 5. Women cooks--Fiction. 6. Cookery--Fiction I. Title.
  PS3607.O594L48 2009
  813'.6--dc22
                              2008035388

Manufactured in the United States of America.

Typesetting by Janis Reed

10 9 8 7 6 5 4 3 2 1

Chronicle Books LLC
680 Second Street
San Francisco, CA 94107
www.chroniclebooks.com

For my mom, with love.
And for the Good Twin of Crooked River,
may he prevail and prosper.

Strange to say
those whom I treated
well are those who do
me the most injury now

— Sappho, Fragment #77,
translated by Mary Barnard

Heat dulled the morning air. No breeze, not a cloud; the early sun blazed in a thin blue sky. Sunny McCoskey thought, in the chaotic days that followed, that if only it hadn't been so hot, perhaps none of it would have happened. She might have spent the afternoon pulling weeds in the back garden at Wildside, her little restaurant in St. Helena, as she had planned to do. Instead, when Anna Wilson, an old friend, called out of the blue with an invitation to have lunch and swim, Sunny had accepted without a second thought, no matter that they hadn't spoken in years.

If it hadn't been so hot that day, they might not have lingered so long by the pool or had so much to drink. Anna, the girl everyone always wanted or wanted to be, might have gone to bed early that night and woken up the next morning. She might have opened her eyes to the dawn light blazing on the vineyard and delighted in another day of a life most people would consider one long vacation. But it did happen and nothing could change that reality, no matter how Sunny tried to will it away later, returning again and again to the pointless hope that it might all be a dream or a mistake, that somehow the plain facts might shift and change and suddenly reveal themselves to mean something quite different from the obvious and undeniable, that her friend Anna was dead.

I

Skin tacky with sweat, Sunny stood in front of enormous double doors, their mahogany polished to an amber glow. She wondered what kind of person lived in a place that looked more like a resort than a home, and what Anna was doing staying there. She made eye contact with a tiny black bubble that she assumed was a camera, wiped the sweat from her face with both hands, and rang the bell. A smiling, blue-eyed woman answered the door in an apron and led the way through the house, her blond ponytail swaying as she walked and a string of friendly, Australian-accented chatter trailing behind her. The cold air inside the house revived Sunny pore by pore, and she looked hopefully toward a living room full of art and inviting places to sit.

"Everyone's down by the pool," said the woman, opening glass doors.

Sunny stepped back outside into the heavy heat to the low thump of house music. Down a terraced walk, a rectangle of blue water flicked bright needles of light. The view stretched across acres of vineyard, all the way down the Napa Valley to the Carneros and beyond. Light green squares of vineyard and dark green forested hills and finally fuzzy, distant blue stretches where the valley flattened out to delta. On the slope next to the pool, grapevines baked in the midday sun.

From the patio, a swath of lawn extended to the right, so lush it made the air around it moist. A path stepped down to the pool. Young olive trees broke the view here and there, and sunlight filtered through an old live oak. A fieldstone wall held back the terraced hillside. There was an arbor with wisteria still heavily in bloom and a glass table and chairs, and a hot tub with a fieldstone fireplace rising up at one end. At the far end of the pool, under an ochre umbrella, lay Sunny's friend Anna Wilson. She was wearing a white bikini and black sunglasses and holding back her long dark hair with one hand as she spoke to the busty girl sunbathing next to her. When she saw Sunny, she leaped up and came bounding over.

Same Anna as always, thought Sunny, embracing her with a kiss on each cheek. She was still as leggy and light on her feet as a half-grown housecat, and had the same playful tendency to saunter and pounce. Slightly more taut, perhaps, thinner and more muscular, as though the tendons had been tightened a quarter turn and the soft spots worn fractionally away. But still beautiful and radiant in that way she'd been famous for around San Francisco back when they used to run into each other at art openings. She and Sunny had known the same people and gone to the same parties and liked each other's company in their early twenties. Then Anna went to Europe with her boyfriend and Sunny moved to Napa to open her restaurant. They'd hardly spoken or seen each other in the years since.

"Same Sunny!" exclaimed Anna, taking off her sunglasses. "Except the short hair. That's new."

Sunny put a hand to the line of bangs cut high across her forehead. Lately, she wore her auburn hair as short as a man's, much to her mother's dismay, and had it cut at the barbershop in St. Helena.

But it wasn't ugly, she was sure of that, and it was easy, and cheap, and showed off her eyes, which she considered her best feature.

"I cut it off after I opened the restaurant," said Sunny. "Four years ago. When was the last time we saw each other?"

"My twenty-eighth birthday party," said Anna. "December four years ago. You cooked those enormous crabs and we all sat around cracking them open over newspaper. I'll never forget it."

"At your father's studio," said Sunny. "Does he still have that place?"

"Always. He'll live there until he dies. It's literally covered in his paintings, for one thing. We'll have to tear it down to get them out."

Anna's father was the charismatic Czech painter David Novak, a man with green eyes like a prophet, who said he came to San Francisco because it was the only European city where no one had heard of him. As he himself had once told Sunny, he met, married, impregnated, and separated from Anna's mother, an accomplished poet named Sylvia Wilson, all in less than a month. "It was the seventies," he said gruffly with a shrug. She left their North Beach apartment for a farm in Marin County, changed her own and her daughter's last names back to Wilson, and raised Anna around back-to-earth intellectuals, organic farmers, and artists. Anna was blessed with her father's green eyes and her mother's lavish mouth, a long and shapely affair—"like the flying lips in the Man Ray painting," her father had said one night, holding her face between his hands—as well as the considerable talents of both parents, at least as far as Sunny could judge from the work she'd done in college and the years immediately after. Since then, despite having demonstrated talent and earned a number of accolades as both a writer and an artist, Anna had spent most of her time entertaining an A-list of wealthy and powerful men and skillfully evading their proposals.

She was still strikingly beautiful, though slightly dimmed, thought Sunny, and there was something about her eyes that gave the impression of disengagement. The natural brightness of her face with its wide smile and gemlike eyes could mask all but the most subtle indications of what was going on underneath, but the signs were there for those who knew her. She was troubled, and deeply so, if Sunny was not mistaken.

Anna held Sunny's wrist as though taking her pulse and smiled. "I am so glad I was able to reach you. When I saw your name in the paper this morning, I laughed out loud. I knew it was a sign. The only time I've picked up the *Napa Register* in my entire life, I see your name. You were destined to be here today."

Sunny's name had been in the paper all too often lately, thanks to her role as a material witness in a sensational local murder trial. At least the publicity was good for business—her restaurant had been booked solid weeks in advance since the story hit—but it wasn't exactly the sort of notoriety she wanted.

"Destiny or not, it's great to see you," said Sunny. "And in such an outrageous place. Does one person own all this?"

"It's pretty amazing, isn't it? It belongs to my boyfriend."

"Who is he, some kind of royalty?"

"California royalty," laughed Anna. "Oliver Seth. He used to be a VC. Made a fortune in the tech boom. Beyond millions. I think it might actually be a billion or two. Silly money from Sili Valley. It's ridiculous. You can buy anything and not make a dent in it. You should see the place he has in London."

"Did he retire?"

"Hardly. He's got a hedge fund and a bunch of businesses. Software, finance, intellectual property. I can't keep track." Anna pulled a chaise closer for Sunny. "Come sit down. Do you want a drink? Wine? I'm having Campari orange and we have mojitos, but we can make anything, whatever you want. And you have to meet Jordan."

Sunny took the glass of wine Anna poured for her. Lying next to Anna, Jordan looked like the sexpots they put on promotional posters for dance parties. She lifted her sunglasses when Anna introduced them and offered a girlish hand, small and soft, nails painted hot pink with a gold star in the middle of each. She had narrow hips and buoyant, round breasts barely contained in a shiny gold bikini. It was hard to say if she was Asian, Latina, or possibly even Persian. She reminded Sunny of her sous chef, Rivka, who was half Guatemalan and half Eastern European Jew. They both had strong features, black hair, and golden skin. Rivka had her Mayan nose and almond eyes, whereas Jordan had the tilted dark eyes Sunny associated with veils and saris. Wherever her parents had come from, she looked like Hollywood now.

"Jordan is a great photographer," said Anna. "Oliver has some of her work. Fantastic stuff. I'll show you later. Right now you have to tell me about your life. What would you have been doing today if you hadn't come here?"

"Today? I was going to go to the restaurant and pull weeds in the back garden. Not very glamorous."

"It sounds perfect to me," said Anna. "You don't know how much I miss having a life. Fixing up a house. Working. I have my gallery bit, but you couldn't call it a job. And I haven't painted anything in months. We've just been bouncing around. I've seen everything, of course. It's been amazing. We were in Egypt and Syria and all over Europe, but I haven't *done* anything, you know what I mean?" She looked around as if momentarily lost in the familiar surroundings. "I'm so glad you're here. You've always been so grounded, you know? I could use a little of the McCoskey common sense about now."

"*Grounded* sounds like a nice word for dull," said Sunny. "Like *sensible.*"

"Listen, there is nothing wrong with being sensible." Anna stood over a side table and lit a cigarette. "I could use a little sensible about now."

"What's going on?" said Sunny, thinking she was right about Anna. There was something wrong.

"Oh, I don't know. We can talk about it later. Jordan is probably tired of hearing me psychobabble. It's the usual stuff. Boy meets girl. Girl makes chaos in her life to be with boy. Boy meets another girl or possibly girls." She waved the cigarette. "I hope you don't mind. We've been going out nonstop since we got to California and I'm back in the habit. That's why we came up here. To get away from the city and just relax. And here I am, smoking more than ever." She gave Sunny a dazzling smile that might have swept everything away a few years ago. Now it wasn't entirely convincing. "Anyway, I guess it's not technically a problem of *monogamy*, so to speak. I wish it was that simple." She stared off for a moment, then snapped back, smile in place. "Enough of my little woes. Tell me about you. I need the vital stats. Married? Children?"

"Neither."

"Boyfriend?"

"Sort of. Well, yes. I have a boyfriend. I guess what I'd say is that we're still getting to know each other."

"Warning lights," said Jordan, flashing her fingers. "That doesn't sound too promising."

"He's a great guy," said Sunny. "Incredibly sexy. Extremely good looking. Great style. I love it when we're together. But we have very different lifestyles. Sex and cooking are about all we have in common. I live like a nun. I like my work and my garden and that's it. I go to bed early and get up early. He doesn't sleep. He's always out and he can't understand why I don't want to go. And then I wonder the same thing. What's wrong with me? Why am I so, you know, sensible."

"Men never sleep," said Anna. "Oliver doesn't sleep. He thinks it's a vice, like gluttony."

Jordan remained expressionless behind her sunglasses.

"Why don't you change into your swimsuit?" Anna said. "You're making me feel hot."

Anna lifted a bottle from an ice bucket (1997 Groth Chard, noted Sunny automatically), found it empty, and poured her a mojito from a pitcher on the table. Lolling in the heat, the sun hanging motionless in the sky, they waited, each on her teak chaise, three shiny bodies dotted with beads of water, unmoving. Bright sun, blue sky, sparkle of water. Sunny adjusted the fabric of her swimsuit and sighed. She watched the branches of an olive tree bounce gently on a breeze. When the water had dried and her skin was slick with sweat, she stood up and saw stars. The sudden cold of the water made her gasp. She swam silently, breaststroking through the still water, the only sound an endless track of club music from hidden speakers. Jordan dove into the deep end and swam back to the stairs, where she sat flicking water on Anna's toes.

Anna swirled the pitcher of mojitos and called up to the house. "Cynthia?"

The woman in the white apron came out onto the patio. "More drinks?"

"And fresh glasses, please."

Sunny pulled herself out of the pool and sat down on the cement. Next to her, Anna had lain back down. She had a Band-Aid on her knee. Things don't change much, thought Sunny. Anna always had a

Band-Aid somewhere, or worse. One night when they were leaving a cocktail party at what was then the new SFMoMA, she missed the curb, fell off her spike heels, and sprained her ankle bad enough to need crutches. For weeks, all the best-looking guys in town took turns carrying her shoulder bag and opening doors for her.

Cynthia arrived with a fresh pitcher of mojitos. She put a Campari orange in front of Anna, who held up the drink to admire its layers of red, orange, and yellow. "Looks like the sunset we saw at the Dallas airport last week. Sunny McCoskey, this is Cynthia Meyers, Oliver's personal chef. You two might have something in common. Sunny owns a restaurant in St. Helena."

"Oh, really? Which one?" said Cynthia.

"Wildside," said Sunny.

"You're kidding! That's my favorite secret spot for when people visit. I've eaten there a dozen times."

"I thought you looked familiar." From her station in the kitchen, Sunny could look over the zinc bar into the dining room. It had to be that way. She would never want to cook where she couldn't see what was happening in the front of the house.

"We'll have to talk shop later," said Cynthia. "Meanwhile, are you girls ready for lunch?"

"Whenever you are," said Anna. "Oliver should be home any minute. And we should have Troy and Franco as well."

"Good. I'll have everything ready in fifteen minutes."

"Perfect." Anna turned to Sunny. "You're going to love Cynthia's cooking. She's amazing."

Cynthia went back up to the house. Opportunities sometimes came along for Sunny to leave the restaurant business and become a private chef. There had been offers, and she'd occasionally been tempted. Watching Cynthia, she wondered what it was like, if she enjoyed it, if it was easier than restaurant life. No doubt. But how did it feel to have Anna Wilson in her white bikini ordering up drinks from the pool? About the same as customers doing it at Wildside, thought Sunny.

"Does she work full time?"

"She lives here," said Anna. "Oliver built her a place right next door. It's not the most comfortable arrangement for me, but Oliver is extremely attached. And I think she's in love with him, in a maternal way at least. She gives me dagger eyes every time I come here." Anna looked over her glasses and winked at Sunny.

"Who cares if she's in love with him," said Jordan, face down. "The woman can cook. I'd sleep with her if that's what it took to keep the oven on."

"Speak of the devil," said Anna.

A guy in khakis and a white shirt with the sleeves rolled up jogged down the stairs and walked over to them. If he was older than thirty, it couldn't be by much, thought Sunny. His eyes dodged around the scene, taking a host's inventory of empty glasses and wet towels. He picked up a towel from the ground and draped it over a chair. "Who's Crowley sleeping with now?" he said.

"Don't you wish you knew," said Jordan.

"All the time," he said, leaning down to smack her behind.

Jordan stuck a pink tongue out at him.

"You girls are a sight," he said, frowning at the glare off the pool. His build was slight but muscular. He had light brown hair cut just right and a cocky look to his brown eyes.

"Go change and join us," said Anna.

"I don't want a swim until after lunch." He pointed at Sunny. "McCoskey, right?"

"That's right."

"The cook."

"Right again."

"What kind of restaurant?"

"Oliver has a way of interrogating people he's just met," said Anna. "He doesn't realize it's rude."

"I'm sure she's capable of describing her own restaurant without undue strain," he said, giving Anna a mirthless smile. "Besides, we haven't met yet. Oliver Seth."

Sunny stood up to shake his hand, a gesture that always seemed a bit stiff to her and felt utterly ridiculous in a bikini. Oliver checked his Rolex and looked at Anna. "Is lunch late? Aren't you hungry?"

"Cynthia's setting it up now."

"Good. So, your restaurant."

"It's called Wildside and it's in St. Helena. We serve lunch Monday through Friday in an elegant yet intimate setting. *Intimate* being euphemistic for very small. The food is California-style Mediterranean. Tuscan, Provençal, with Basque and North African influences."

"What about dinner?"

"No dinner."

"And weekends?"

"No weekends."

"What is that, a joke? How do you survive?"

"Modestly. I keep my overhead low."

"Meaning you do everything yourself."

"I have some good people helping me."

"Do we always have to talk business?" said Anna. "It's Saturday."

"I bet McCoskey enjoys talking business. Entrepreneurs are obsessed with their work or they wouldn't do it. Am I right?"

"You're both right," said Sunny, in an effort to defuse the tension. "I love my work, and I love not thinking about it for a few hours each week."

Oliver's cell phone buzzed and he excused himself to answer it. A man walked up from behind them wearing trim black trunks of the sort seen more in Europe than California.

"Did someone just say something intelligent?" he said. "I thought I caught a whiff of distinctly un-American moderation in the air. But I could have been dreaming."

"Sunny McCoskey, the Italian accent is Franco Bertinotti, wine-maker and eavesdropper," said Anna.

"Sicilian, my dear. From the belly. Italians talk way up here like their shoes are too tight."

He lifted his sunglasses, revealing blue eyes so pale and bright they gave Sunny a jolt. She waited while he cast them over her from her eyes to her toes and back again, taking everything in. Apparently satisfied, he nodded to himself and lay down on a chaise, running his fingers through his short white hair and over the tanned skin of his chest and stomach. He wore a gold chain around his neck, which skimmed the top of a patch of white chest hair. The skin of his abdomen was tanned the color makers of fine leather goods call whiskey or cognac. When he was situated, he closed his eyes, idly grazing the upturned pads of Jordan's fingertips next to him. Cynthia arrived with a bottle of chilled white wine and glasses.

"Charming man," said Anna, abandoning her Campari and lifting a glass from the tray in front of her. "I wouldn't invite him if Oliver didn't insist. He is apparently indispensable at the winery. Can you hear me, Franco?"

"Every word, darling. I am charming and indispensable."

Sunny decided she would leave as soon as lunch was over.

2

They dined under the wisteria. Cynthia served roast beef, garden greens, and couscous, all expertly presented.

"We're casual today. Serve yourselves," she said cheerfully, setting down pitchers of ice water filled with branches of mint and slices of lemon and cucumber. "There's more of everything inside, so don't be timid. We also have a chocolate torte with raspberries for dessert. Let me know when you're ready."

"Thank you, Cynthia. Everything looks beautiful," said Anna, looking up at her from under a white straw hat. Midday sun shot through the vines overhead. Anna's cheeks were pink from the heat and her eyes were green like bottle glass held up to light. It was this Mediterranean light that changed everything in the Napa Valley from mundane to extraordinary, particularly in summer. A slice of lemon glowed. A floppy straw hat transformed a girl from beautiful to breathtaking.

Franco the Sicilian sat down next to Sunny in his swim trunks and gold chain. He had on a linen shirt, open. All three of the women wore the sheer tunics with embellished collars that were the ubiquitous trend of the season, Sunny in Moroccan blue, Anna in white, Jordan in black. Soon they were joined by a very tall, well-groomed man in a linen shirt and baggy linen trousers who plunged in with the confidence of the life of the party. He crushed Franco's shoulder and kissed the girls on the lips, including Sunny, introducing himself afterward.

"Keith Lachlan. I'll sit here next to you if that's okay."

"Keith is Oliver's lawyer," explained Anna. "He spends more time with him than I do."

"I prefer *enforcer*. When you have this kind of money, somebody's always after it," said Keith, looking over his shoulder. He spoke in a deep, rich voice with a slight accent, vaguely British, mostly American, and something else Sunny couldn't quite put her finger on. His head was completely bald and covered in smooth brown skin.

"Where are you from?" asked Sunny.

"West Indies, my dear. Barbados. But a long time ago, before you were born."

Sunny looked at his face. No lines, no beard. He might not even need to shave. At first glance he might be thirty, but now she guessed closer to fifty or even sixty. He leaned around behind her to ask Franco about some business to do with a deposition. Her head felt suddenly heavy, as if she could put her chin in her hand and fall soundly asleep. She stared dreamily at the pitcher of ice water in front of her. The yellow of the lemon rind and the green of the mint leaves and cucumber were as bright and fresh as anything she'd ever seen in her life. She filled her glass. No doubt it had something to do with the mojitos and wine, and the heat of the perfectly cloudless day, not to mention the decadent surroundings and the prospect of being served instead of rushing to cook, serve, eat, and be ready with the next course, which was what she usually did when she tried to relax, since she rarely ate alone. Whatever the cause, the water tasted sublime. The heavy feeling vanished, replaced by what could only be called ecstasy. It was an odd feeling.

Things weren't right between Anna and her boyfriend, that much was clear. And she felt no immediate kinship with the others in their party. And yet the surroundings were so pleasant and her head so dull, she didn't bother to give much thought to why Anna had called her. She was utterly swept up and engulfed in the sweet and tang of the flavored water, and the scent of garden tomatoes coming off the bowl of couscous in front of her.

Oliver Seth came from the kitchen with a bottle of wine tucked under his arm, hands loaded with glasses.

"Anna says you know something about wine." He pulled the cork, poured a glass, and handed it to Sunny.

"Like everyone in Napa." She took a sip. "Syrah?"

"You got it."

"Very nice. Your own?"

"How'd you guess?"

"I saw the marker on the vineyard on the way in. And you hold the bottle a little too carefully."

"Oliver would bring cases of the stuff to bed with us if I let him," said Anna.

"This vintage is our first production after five years of blood, sweat, and tears." He splashed wine into the other glasses and passed them around. "It's a bit raw, but it won't kill us. We have a couple of nice Pinots I'll open in a minute."

Keith Lachlan raised his glass in an enormous hand. "When you started consorting with this guy"—he nodded toward Franco—"I thought for sure we'd find you anchored to the bottom of the bay before it was over. But you guys did it. And you're still here to drink it."

"We did it," said Oliver, touching his glass to Keith's and then Franco's.

The lawyer quaffed the glass and asked Sunny what she thought. She thought it wasn't bad. He looked at her, an assessing look she couldn't decipher. He was taking her measure, but in what context? As a wine expert? A woman? Or simply a conversationalist? The whites of his eyes looked jaundiced next to his white teeth, and Sunny wondered if he was in good health. Like everyone at the table, he drank too much, and even his baggy linen shirt couldn't hide the roll above his waistline. His skin was smooth and brown, from his glossy bare head to the big, sharp-nailed toes that nicked Sunny's ankles under the table.

Oliver Seth emptied the bottle and set it down in front of Sunny, turning the label toward her. It featured a painting of a bull charging into a frothing sea, a girl in genie pants half reclined sidesaddle on its back, holding on to the horns gracefully. The name of the vineyard, Taurus Rising, was written in Roman-looking letters across a stormy sky. Below the illustration it said *Estate Bottled Napa Valley Syrah.*

Jordan took the bottle. "Is that the rape of Europa?"

"Exactly," said Oliver. "From the Greek myth. But I'd call it more of an escape. She doesn't look too concerned to me. This version is nineteenth-century Russian. I have the original in my place in London. It's better than Titian's, which is the one you usually see. Besides, I own the rights to this one. The rights to the image come with the painting. Isn't that amazing? Think of all those museums selling postcards and posters of the paintings they own. The artist doesn't get a dime. Imagine if you bought a car and the rights to the image went with it."

"Why Taurus Rising?" said Sunny.

"I've always liked the symbol of the bull," said Oliver. He laid slices of roast beef on each of their plates as he spoke. "I was born under the sign of Taurus. The first time I saw the term *bull market,* I knew I would make my first million on the stock market. I was in third grade."

Franco handed Sunny the bowl of couscous.

"We had a class hamster," Oliver continued. "On weekends, somebody always got to take him home. His name was Roosevelt because he was a teddy bear hamster. I took him home and started cleaning his cage. One of the layers of paper lining the bottom turned out to be the front section of *The Wall Street Journal.* I read every word, including the advertisements. That's how I found out about the *Robb Report.* I sent away for a subscription and my sister had to pay for it with our Christmas money. But I knew it would pay off. I knew even then if you want to make money, you have to understand how rich people think."

"I read somewhere that a huge percentage of history's dictators have been Tauruses," said Anna. "Hitler, Lenin, Pol Pot. Saddam Hussein, Machiavelli, Robespierre."

"And most damning of all, Barbra Streisand," said a lanky, dark-haired guy approaching the table. He kissed Anna and pulled up a chair next to her.

"Sunny, this is Troy Stevens. Troy, this is my dear, long-lost friend Sunny McCoskey. We used to hang out in San Francisco together ages ago."

"Delighted." Troy shook her hand with mock formality, then started dishing up his plate.

"What happened to the hamster?" said Jordan.

"My best friend's mom made him keep it in the garage and it froze to death."

Sunny held up her glass to Franco. "Nice work."

"This one is not technically mine," he said. "I begin with last year's harvest. That one is quite good, though not exactly in my style. Too fruity and agreeable. I like more earth, more herb, more gaminess. You should taste a little bit of leather and spice, not just plums and blackberries. We will get there eventually, if Oliver's grapes cooperate."

"I don't care if we ever get a wine we can release," said Oliver. "If we get something we can drink at lunch and pour on the ground for ablutions to the ancestors, I'll be happy. My citadel will be complete."

"Your ancestral sins are your affair," said Franco. "I will commune with the grapes and see what they have to tell us. You won't want to pour it on the ground, I guarantee that much."

Despite her plan to leave after lunch, Sunny agreed that a digestive nap was in order, then that a dip to cool off was a good idea, and finally that one more glass of wine wouldn't hurt. Time stopped. The sun never moved. The bottle of chilled wine they'd brought from the table became mysteriously empty. Gradually, the group scattered. Anna went into the house with Troy Stevens on some errand and didn't return. Jordan lay motionless, her nose in the seam of a paperback copy of *Memoirs of a Geisha*. Franco the Silician took up his same chaise and closed his eyes. Oliver and Keith went off to Oliver's office, talking business. When Cynthia offered to give Sunny a tour of the house and garden, she put on her tunic and sandals.

The kitchen had everything any cook could want, professional or otherwise, including natural light from a wall of south-facing windows. There was a full-size wine cabinet, a prep island, a wall of German appliances, a steamer, the definitive ultra-modern Poggenpohl cabinets with refrigerated drawers, and a mysteriously inferior espresso machine defiling one of the sleek countertops.

This is what money can do, thought Sunny. She had almost forgotten. Money had the power to make everything beautiful, at least on the surface. With money, she could cook in a shining, perfect kitchen like this, instead of sweating the way she did at Wildside, where the kitchen, an oily sauna by the end of each day, was little more than a maze of stainless steel work benches squeezed into a space so small she couldn't open the oven door without moving to one side. If it weren't for the desire to be her own boss, she could stand on a sublimely chalky limestone floor like this one instead of the black rubber mats at Wildside that had to be hauled out and hosed down every night. But they were different animals altogether. A picture-perfect kitchen like this was fine for dinner parties, but it would never survive the fiery mosh pit that was a daily way of life at Wildside.

"I keep asking Oliver to invite more people up," said Cynthia. "I never get to really cook. He has one or two people in for lunch or dinner on the weekends and that's it. We put in a full outdoor kitchen down by the pool and we've never used it. It only makes sense for a big party."

"I didn't see it."

"Did you see the fireplace by the hot tub? The grill and the rest of it are around the back of that stone wall. I put in a garden last year and I've been giving away bags of produce all summer. The neighbors are eating well."

"I'd love to see the garden."

"We can go down there after you've seen the house. It's my little paradise. We have vegetables, herbs, chickens, and a pig. It will be a pleasure to finally get to show it off to somebody who's interested in food. Nobody cares much about these things around here, not even Oliver, though he pretends he does. As long as the food is on the table, they don't care how it gets there. I don't think Anna knows the garden exists."

She gave Sunny a conspiratorial smile and led her down a luminous white hallway to the living room, where an enormous Rothko in shades of crimson hung on one wall. Another large canvas—Lucien Freud? Sunny's knowledge of modern art was limited at best—hung above the couch, offering a portrait of several women, all naked, variously reclined. Cynthia opened a few doors on bedrooms done in spare modernism on a grand scale, executed in wood, stone, and shades of cream, eggshell, putty, gray. One room featured king-size bunk beds with white and chrome ladders.

"He must love houseguests," said Sunny.

Cynthia smiled and closed the door. She led the way past a staircase leading down. "Sauna, workout room, racquetball court, et cetera."

They went back the other direction. The north wing of the house was darker, not just because of the lack of southern exposure. It was clearly designed for night games. Another living room looked out on the lawn but was decorated in shades of black and sand, with primitive statues in the corners and canvases of Rousseau-like beasts and eyes peering from jungle darkness. *Paradise*, written in garish red neon script, covered an entire wall. Other rooms held a pool table, a lounge facing a flat-screen television, a library lined with shelves but no books, more bedrooms, and, off the master suite and adjacent lounge, another hot tub and outdoor fireplace. (By Sunny's count, the house had at least seven fireplaces, including one in each living room, one in each of two master suites, one in the lounge, and two outdoors.) An extensive glassed-in wine closet held bottles cataloged with the care and precision of treasures at the Smithsonian. A floor-to-ceiling case held Armagnacs and whiskeys arranged by year, some quite old. Across from them was a long, low wall covered with gritty black-and-white photographs of edgy-looking party people doing drugs and making out. Sunny wondered if this was Jordan's work.

On the way back to the foyer, Sunny detoured into a heavily mirrored bathroom with no windows and the same limestone floor that ran through most of the house. Instead of a light switch, there were at least a dozen buttons on a pad just inside the door. She pressed one and the fan went on. Touching it again made tiny footlights along the wall appear, but did not turn off the fan. She pushed another button and the fan got louder. She studied the pad and the tiny screen above it to no effect and chose another button at random. The lights went out but the fan stayed on. In the end, she closed the heavy door and peed by the murky glow of two recessed halogens over the distant marble vanity. Between the long mirror above the sink and a floor-to-ceiling mirror covering the wall opposite, she had an overly generous view of herself *in situ*. Out of the corner of her eye, she saw Sunny McCoskey as though in a movie, flushing the toilet, washing her hands, running her fingers through short hair, hunting in bathroom drawers for hand cream, lip gloss, hair gel, anything to smooth her rumpled post-swim appearance. The drawers were empty except for a blow dryer, its cord still neatly bound by the manufacturer's tie. The cabinet under the sink held a supply of toilet paper and nothing else. The house seemed hardly to have been used. Earlier in the day, she'd used the same bathroom to change into her swimsuit and left her bra and underwear rolled up in a hand towel on the edge of the vanity. Now they were gone. The work of overly fastidious domestic help, no doubt. Hopefully Cynthia could help her look for them when they came back from the garden. She checked her appearance one more time in the enormous mirror and pulled up the sleeve of her tunic to observe the new scar on the inside of her forearm, a band of purple skin where she'd caught an upset pan of pork loin coming out of the oven. One among many. A few futile punches at the controls on the way out only made the fan louder.

Out in front of the house, Anna's friend Troy Stevens slumped in his tight black jeans and laceless Converse, talking to Cynthia.

"Do you two know each other?" asked Cynthia. It occurred to Sunny that Cynthia didn't know much more about Anna's guests than she did.

"Just from lunch," said Sunny.

"I'm Anna's chaperone," said Troy. "They let me hang around as long as I don't get in the way."

"He's one of Britain's leading artists, here to install a new piece Oliver just bought," said Cynthia.

"Which one?" said Sunny. "I'd like to see it."

"So would I," said Troy. "It's still in transit, apparently. Or else they've lost it and aren't ready to admit it yet. Not that I don't enjoy hanging around watching Anna sun herself, but it's getting a bit nerve racking." He jostled Cynthia playfully and she pushed him away, laughing.

"We're off to the garden," Cynthia told him. "Join us?"

"Not I, said the art guy," said Troy. "I'll check on the damsel in distress."

Troy went inside just as Oliver and Franco came up the path.

"I can give them a call on Monday," Franco was saying to Oliver.

"Don't call them," said Oliver, holding Franco back. He looked in his eyes. "And don't take a call. Send a certified letter, and mail a copy to me and one to Keith. Force them to put everything in writing."

"You think they'll negotiate?"

"Of course. Everything is negotiable if you position yourself correctly."

"Nothing is left to chance, eh?" said Franco.

"Never." Oliver smiled, then turned to Cynthia.

"I'm showing off the garden to my fellow chef," Cynthia told him. "Come with us?"

"The extended tour," said Oliver. "You go on ahead. I need to make some calls."

"Franco?" said Cynthia.

"With pleasure."

Situated on the other side of the road behind a tennis court and a tall oak tree, the garden and chicken coop were easy to miss on the way in, and Sunny had. Now she saw what an ambitious setup it was. The garden, enclosed by a fence that would be the envy of any neighborhood, contained everything a cook could want. The summer chaos was just beginning to hit its stride. Tomato plants had overgrown their cages, squash blossoms lay in a tumble of vines and leaves, corn was nicely on its way, sweet peas were reaching above their guides. A tidy but not obsessive order prevailed. The herb garden had all the usual suspects, plus lemon verbena, three varieties of mint, and four of basil. In fall there would be blue potatoes and Yukon Golds and rosy reds and fingerlings. Nearby was a newly constructed outbuilding with tools and supplies, as well as living quarters for at least two dozen chickens of various breeds, some shiny black, others white with mops of feathers on their heads, others like the red hens in storybooks, and the majority of them, unfortunately and unexpectedly, said Cynthia, young roosters, who strutted the loose soil whooping and flapping. A large pink pig flopped in a far corner on the other side of a fence.

"Recycling at its best," said Cynthia. "He turns scraps into ham, sausage, and bacon."

"You wouldn't," said Franco.

"I already have. This guy is pig number two. Piggy number one is all hung up to dry in the cellar."

Franco raised his eyebrows.

"Prosciutto doesn't grow on trees, you know," said Cynthia with a mischievous smile that made one eyebrow go up.

"I am well aware," said Franco. "I just never saw such a pretty butcher."

Cynthia pushed a strand of blond hair behind her ear. "Well, I didn't actually do it myself. I know some people up in Sonoma who raise hogs. They came down and got him. But I went with him all the way and I stayed to the bitter end. If you're going to eat a pork loin, you have to be able to face the truth about what that means. I'd feel like a hypocrite otherwise." She looked at Sunny.

"I couldn't agree more," said Sunny. "If everybody knew where their meat came from, we'd eat much less of it and enjoy it more. And a lot fewer animals would suffer."

"Amen to that," said Cynthia.

"How did they do it?" said Franco.

"One shot in the head with a rifle, then they cut the throat to bleed it. It was not a very nice scene, but there's no way around it. That's where meat comes from. If you want to eat meat, somebody has to die."

"I thought they stunned them electrically," said Franco.

"In the big places. These guys are small time. But they do a good job. It all happened very quickly."

The three of them stood looking at the spotless outbuilding, the foraging chickens, the garden, and a little farther off a large composting bin and a heap of manure and lawn clippings waiting to be added. It was an enviable arrangement. To have endless means and nothing to produce but a few luncheons on the weekend must be a kind of heaven for a cook, thought Sunny. No payroll, no workers' compensation, no customers asking for ketchup and Tabasco, no taxes, no busboys calling in sick ten minutes into their shift, no headaches.

Sunny picked up another glass of wine on her way down to the pool. Anna was back on her chaise, smoking and talking into her cell phone. The club music had been turned off and a wide-open quiet enveloped them. She stopped to listen to the tick of dry-land insects, the tender slosh of water in the pool, the distant hum of a plane overhead. Jordan was in the pool, swimming laps with her face and hair out of the water. Sunny sat down and nearly missed the chair. It was definitely time to switch to water.

"I'm thinking of moving back to California permanently," said Anna, putting her phone down. "You think after a few years you'll settle into a new country and start to feel like you belong, but you never do. I've been living in Barcelona on and off for almost five years and I'm still a foreigner. I always will be. I used to like it that way, but now I want to feel like I belong somewhere." She looked at Sunny. "I admire the life you've built here. Everything I own fits in a suitcase. A *small* suitcase."

"That's not such a bad thing," said Sunny.

"In Barcelona it looks like I have a life. I have an apartment and a job. But it's all pretend. It's really just a room I rent in Troy's apartment. I have a commission sales job in a gallery that lets me come in whenever I like, do my deals, and leave. It's a nice life, but it's completely ephemeral. There's no there there."

"What about Oliver?"

Anna leaned closer and lowered her voice, her expression playful, then serious. "That's what I'm here to find out. Oliver has been a very enjoyable distraction for years, but now we want to try to make it real. At least I do, or did, until last night, anyway." She smiled as though she'd said something amusing. "Who am I kidding? I couldn't live here, anyway. Oliver's place in the city is so, I don't know, nice, it's like living in a museum, and this place is gorgeous, but it's in the sticks, which might be okay if I had work and friends up here like you do. For me it's too lonely. Realistically, what am I supposed to do up here all day, hang out with Cynthia and the gardener? Both of whom resent the hell out of me just for being here, invading their privacy. You'd think they owned the place. I'm the one who always has to pass on all of Oliver's instructions and complain for him when things aren't exactly perfect— and believe me, they'd better be perfect—so of course they can't stand me. I have to tiptoe around the place. It's fine for Oliver. This is his world. But I'm just a guest. I can't deal with living like this anymore. Not to mention Oliver's sister, who has nothing better to do than try to fix him up with her friends, even when I'm *here*, for God's sake." She stopped herself with a little laugh. "I'm a piece of work."

Sunny tried to think of something to say, failed, and said nothing, her face betraying her confusion.

"Don't worry, I'm just venting," said Anna. "Let's change the subject. Tell me about this boyfriend you mentioned." She gave Sunny the ten-thousand-watt smile. "I love hearing about someone else's romance. It's a refreshing diversion."

Sunny took a breath. "Well, he's very eligible. The village hotty. Like everyone else in a fifty-mile radius, I had a huge crush on him, but then we ended up cooking together at a big charity event one night and it turned out he liked me, too. That never happens, right? It was all very dreamy." Sunny paused. Jordan was at the other end of the pool with her elbows over the edge. Anna waited while Sunny chose her words carefully. "I wish he was right for me. I want him to be right for me. But sometimes I get the feeling it's not going to work out." She heard the words as if someone else had spoken them. Her stomach lurched as she recognized the truth she'd been trying to avoid. Or was she only afraid that it might be the truth?

"So he cooks, too?"

Sunny nodded. "He owns a restaurant in Yountville."

"Then invite him over. It's salad days around here."

"He'll be at work until late tonight."

"Have him come over after. We'll be up, I'm sure. Some other friends might turn up."

"I would, but I should get going myself pretty soon," said Sunny.

Anna sat up. "Get going? You can't! We've hardly even talked. You can't leave, Sunny. Stay to dinner at least. For me. Honestly, if you only knew. You can't leave. Promise you won't."

Sunny studied her friend. "I'll stay. For another swim at least."

"Good."

Anna lit another cigarette and blew a plume of heavy smoke. Sunny looked at the pack. Something French without a filter. Sunny had not smoked anything in over two months and it felt great. Better every day. She looked again. Today was turning out to be one of those days when you decide to ditch all the rules and just enjoy life for a few hours, thought Sunny. All signs pointed to as much. If not, why was there a perfectly chilled, perfectly balanced glass of Rhône Valley Marsanne on the table next to her when she'd already had two cocktails and at least three glasses of wine? Or was it four? Her ordinary routine on a Saturday was to work on the restaurant, work on the garden, plan for work, catch up on work, rest for work, unwind from work. And now with her twenty-five-year-old sous chef, Rivka, getting more ambitious every day and insisting they do the farmers' market on Friday mornings and nagging to open the restaurant on weekends or nights, or God forbid both, it was only going to get worse. Today was a stolen moment, a cameo appearance in someone else's charmed life in which there was nothing to do but sit by the pool. Rationalization complete, she took a cigarette and leaned over Anna's outstretched hand, steadying herself above the flame with some effort. After all, she thought, inhaling, the body should be able to take a bit of abuse from time to time. Something to give the immune system some practice. She had been the picture of discipline and good health for weeks, working out at the gym, swimming laps, squeezing in classes at the fascist dictatorship yoga studio up the road, and even swallowing a spoonful of flaxseed oil and two of glucosamine chondroitin without gagging every morning, as if to punish herself for good deeds. Sunny McCoskey deserved a day of parole for good behavior, she told herself, even if it entailed behaving badly.

She let the back down on the chaise and flopped over onto her belly, feeling the warmth of the sun on her back and the heat of the cigarette on her fingers. She hadn't even reapplied her sunscreen. Now she made the conscious decision to expose her cells to the full force of the day's ultraviolet A and B rays, though not for more than an hour. Selective debauchery was one thing, sunburn quite another. She heard Jordan pull herself out of the water and felt a spray of droplets on her calves as she walked past. Sunny closed her eyes and listened to Anna and her friend gossip about their acquaintances.

After a while, Keith Lachlan, the lawyer, came and sat by the edge of the pool with his linen trousers rolled up and his feet in the water. Oliver himself emerged from the house in his swimsuit and gold aviator sunglasses, BlackBerry in hand. He stood in the water in front of Keith and they talked about the booming Shanghai economy and the real-estate portfolio they were building there.

Keith said he had a local contact who was showing him new parts of town slated to explode in the next few years. Sunny checked her phone. Twenty-three minutes of unprotected sun left. She got up and dove into the pool, staying underwater. The restaurant had lost money again last month. Not a lot, but losing money was not what she had had in mind when she started a business. Barring catastrophe, and if she kept the menu reasonable, she would make it up by the end of August, as she had other years, but it was still worrisome. She surfaced and treaded water drowsily. Oliver Seth had taken her chaise and was rubbing lotion onto Anna's back.

"Molly called," he said. "Apparently she has some new boyfriend she wants us to meet. I told her to come over and bring him so we can have a look."

Anna looked up. "Do we have to? We just got here. Can't we just relax for one day?"

"It'll be fine. She's blissed out on the new guy."

"Did you tell Cynthia there will be more of us for dinner? Keith said Marissa is coming later, too."

"I told her we'll be ten. She said it's no problem."

Anna counted. "We're only nine."

"Cynthia has to eat, too," snapped Oliver.

Anna pushed herself up and looked over her shoulder. "Sunny, you're staying for dinner, right? You have to. Cynthia is so excited to have people to cook for."

Sunny treaded water, trying to think of an excuse. It was still several hours until sunset.

"Of course she's staying," said Oliver. "We won't let her leave."

3

Oliver Seth's sister, Molly, arrived a few hours later in a new Jaguar coupe. They knew because she stormed through the house insisting everyone come out to look at it, and they did. She'd just picked it up from the dealer and was taking it on its maiden voyage along with her new boyfriend, a guy with a model's good looks and toned physique dressed in long, silky basketball shorts, an outsized tank top, and spotless white high-tops.

Sunny stood with everyone else admiring the black sports car with its honey-colored leather seats and wood-panel interior. Molly gripped her boyfriend's hand. Her blond hair swooped and tumbled over her shoulders so that she had to push it back every few minutes with a manicured hand heavily ornamented with gold rings and bracelets. She had a wide, white smile and thoroughly made-up eyes separated by two vertical creases. She wore a narrow black skirt and a snug blouse and blazer that showcased bronzed cleavage. Her boyfriend introduced himself as Jared Bollinger.

Anna came out of the house in a white sarong, carrying a cocktail. She kissed Molly on each cheek.

"Anna, I want you to meet someone," said Molly. "Jared, this is Anna Wilson, my brother's girlfriend. Anna, this is—"

"Any relation to the tennis racquet?" interrupted Jared.

"None." Anna took a sip of her drink, studying him over the glass. "You look vaguely familiar. Like someone I used to know a long time ago. Did you ever wait tables?"

"Not since college. You?"

"Never. I don't think I'd be very good at it. I'd end up pouring soup over somebody's head."

Jared laughed. "I'm sure they'd get over it."

Molly looked at Jared, who was staring at the ground and smiling, then back at Anna, whose eyes betrayed an act of mischief. The furrow in Molly's brow deepened. She seemed about to say something when one of the garage doors went up, revealing the backsides of a black Ferrari and a blue BMW convertible. Oliver came out carrying a chamois and a black bottle.

"You need to take this thing back to the dealer and tell them you want the finish done right or they can keep it," said Oliver. He squirted wax on the chamois and rubbed at what he said was a scratch on the front fender.

"I can't even see what you're talking about," said Molly, walking over to him.

"Look, if you don't mind buying a used car, that's fine, but when you use my money to do it, that's a different story. When I buy a new car, I like it to be new. As in pristine. A new car should not have a scratch on it." He rubbed the car fiercely. "They're not doing us a favor. We paid for a new car and they should deliver one. Or did they give it to you?"

Anna stood in the dressing area of the master bedroom she shared with Oliver and picked through the contents of her overnight bag. Sunny perused the bedside reading. Under Oliver's glasses were

Plutarch's Lives, The 48 Laws of Power, The Economist, and the poems of Cavafy.

"I don't have any actual proof," said Anna, leaning toward the lighted mirror to apply her mascara. "Nothing tangible. Just a feeling. But I know I'm right. I know he's not being honest with me."

Sunny lay down on a padded bench behind her. Anna's clothes hung in the mostly empty walk-in closet. There were three dresses—one white, one sandy brown, and one black—a sunflower-yellow blouse with the Balenciaga tag still on it, a pair of jeans, and a pair of gray trousers with wide legs and a fat cuff at the bottom. Underneath were two pairs of high heels, one Prada and one Jimmy Choo, and a Chloe handbag. Thousands of dollars' worth of clothes and it would all fit in a carryon. Anna never wore ordinary clothes. No sweatpants or T-shirts for as long as Sunny could remember. Her only makeup was lipstick and mascara. She wore little camisoles instead of bras and didn't seem to own a pair of underpants. She was the place where minimalism and luxury met.

Anna turned around to look at Sunny. "I'm no saint. I used to see other people when we were apart. It's no secret. There were no rules, and we were fine with that. But things are different now. We used to just meet places for vacations. It wasn't a real relationship, it was just for fun. It's only recently that I've been coming here to be with him in his day-to-day life and we've started talking about really being together. He has a house in San Francisco and one in London. For the last few months, we've been traveling and going back and forth between them. He says he wants to be with me, that he wants to get married. And I want to believe him. I want to let go and let myself finally fall in love. I'm not interested in dating anymore. But lately I get the feeling he's not the man I think he is."

"You think he's seeing someone else?"

"I don't know. There's an old girlfriend he says is just a friend. I know they talk and e-mail all the time, and I think he might see her sometimes when he says he's away on business. Whether it's her or not, I just can't shake this feeling he's involved with someone else. You know me, I'm not a jealous person. But if someone lies to you, lies outright when you ask them a direct question . . . Anyway, that's a problem I can at least comprehend and deal with, one way or another. Now there's a whole new issue on the table. That's why I called you."

Sunny sat up. "Well, are you going to tell me or not?"

"Yes, I am," she said with some difficulty, as though trying to convince herself. She sat down next to Sunny. "Last night I found something very strange. I probably should have told you before I even invited you here. I guess I'm in denial. I know what it means, or what I'm afraid it means, but I don't want to know, you know?"

"Not yet I don't." Sunny stared at her friend. Anna had always been prone to theatrics and drama. But now there seemed to be something genuinely wrong.

"Last night, after we went to bed, I woke up around two. I couldn't sleep. I've never been a good sleeper. So I got up and went into Oliver's study. There's a wall in there that retracts. Behind it is a big screen that's hooked up to the computer and satellite TV. I was fiddling around with the buttons, trying to get the wall to retract so I could watch a movie or something. Apparently I hit the wrong button because a different panel opened and there were a bunch of little TV screens behind it. Feeds from surveillance cameras all over the property and the house. There's one at the gate, one at the front door, one right over there." She waved a hand toward the bed. "But they're also in the guest bedrooms, even in some of the bathrooms."

Sunny remembered the big mirror in the bathroom and how she'd felt as if she was watching herself in a movie. "What did you do?"

"I completely freaked out. I tried not to say anything, but I couldn't. I woke him up. He was very calm. He said it's just for security. Because he's gone so much, and sometimes he lets people stay here he doesn't know very well, and a bunch of people who clean and keep the place up when he's gone have keys, and there are valuable paintings and objects lying around."

"That makes sense."

"It's bullshit. I don't buy it. Sunny, it gave me chills. It's not just some rich guy getting his ya-yas watching people have sex in his guest room." She closed her eyes and took a breath. "Sunny, what is your impression of Oliver?"

"I'm not sure I really have an impression. I hardly know him."

"Sunny, please. I need honesty right now."

"Okay. He seems arrogant, but he has good reason to be. He's extremely accomplished."

"And?"

Sunny sighed. "There doesn't seem to be much warmth between you two."

"Well, that's the understatement of the year."

"What do you like about him, anyway?"

"It's hard to say. His . . . composure."

"Composure?"

"He's in such control. It's like living with God. Everything he wants, he gets. He just makes it happen. It's intoxicating to be around that kind of power. I can't make a plane reservation without changing it three times. He's my counterbalance. I guess, in a way, the same arrogance I can't stand is also what draws me to him. He's utterly confident. He is absolutely certain that he is right at all times, and he usually is. But that's also what frightens me. He's one of the most aggressive, shrewd, cutthroat businessmen I've ever known. Obviously he would have to be, or he wouldn't be where he is."

She paused and for a moment the distressed look that had been on her face since they started talking disappeared, replaced by a smile as genuine and glamorous as everything Sunny remembered about the old Anna Wilson.

"A few years ago, I helped him buy a particular painting by a very famous artist. That's how we first got to know each other. He outbid the Tate. It was pocket money. And he started with nothing. There's something thrilling about that kind of competence, but it's also intimidating. And it gets old. It's tiring to make sure you always have the best of everything."

"Maybe it's the money itself that's freaking you out," said Sunny. "It's freaking me out and I hardly know him. This closet is actually bigger than my living room. By about two hundred square feet."

"That's part of it. If you can have everything you want, with no limits, ever, it ultimately starts to get a little confusing. Like, why me? And then you start to wonder if maybe you're using up so much luck that it will run out. That maybe one day God will look down and say, 'That's enough for you, Miss Smarty Pants.'" She smiled wearily. "Anyway, all I know is I didn't sleep last night after I saw those cameras. I couldn't get back into bed with him. I pretended to accept his explanation, but my skin was crawling. It still is. I have to know the truth. I know there's more he's not telling me. I put my life on hold to follow him around the world and try to find out if this relationship is going to work or not. That part is over, I guess. I have to face it. Now I just want to know who he really is, and then I want to go home, wherever that is."

Sunny watched her. For the first time she saw that Anna was not just upset but scared. "Where do I come into it?"

"I guess I just don't want to be here alone with him. I hope you don't hate me. I saw your name and all of a sudden you seemed like the antidote. Honest, real, straightforward, totally grounded Sunny McCoskey. I just needed a little taste of what that's like, you know? You see through people like Oliver. I think I even imagined if you liked him, I'd know he was okay."

"I don't know him. You know him. Is he okay or not?"

"I wish I could say for certain. Last night I imagined all kinds of things, even that he might be dangerous. I'd love to just leave, but I can't right now, not until I iron out a few details. You'll stay tonight, won't you?"

"You mean for dinner?"

"Or stay over until tomorrow? We could really catch up and do a nice brunch on the patio in the morning. It's beautiful here in the morning."

Sunny hesitated.

"Just think about it," said Anna, "that's all I'm asking. You can decide later. I don't want to pressure you too much. But you'd be very comfortable. We have plenty of guest rooms. Everything is all set up. Franco is staying here, and so is Troy, and I think Jordan will stay tonight. I'd really love it if you did, too. This house is so much more bearable when it's full of people."

They walked down to the pool, where Troy had taken over as DJ and was playing music he had picked up "hanging out in Ibiza," he said. The thumping beat was gone, replaced by a sweeter, lighter sound that went well with the fading day. It was pleasantly warm, not hot, and the light was soft all around. Jordan and Anna laughed and danced around in the grass and Troy picked up Anna and twirled her. He tossed her over his shoulder while she screamed and laughed. Her sweep of black hair fell across his chest and her long brown legs kicked the air. He pulled her around in front of him as easily as if she were a child, tossing her and laughing. Anna's body still had the willowy resilience of a young girl's, and she laughed and bounced like a plaything. After their romp they lay panting on the grass, Troy roughing up his mop of dyed black hair. They walked back to the pool to pick up their drinks and Anna seized Troy's hips.

"You are skinny like a lizard," she said. "I'm going to start calling you Lizard Boy until you gain some weight."

Troy lit a cigarette and flicked his tongue at her. "You should talk. Besides, I don't like eating. I could live on bubbly water and lime. I'd just get lighter and lighter, like the misty essence of a Tanqueray and tonic floating around the pool."

"How can you not like eating?" said Sunny. "That's like not liking breathing."

Troy flopped down onto a chaise in his black T-shirt and jeans. "It's kind of disgusting if you think about it. Sitting around chewing stuff up. All that salivating and excreting."

"You should take vitamins if you're not going to eat," said Anna. "Your bones probably look like Styrofoam." She had a miniature Leica out, like a camera for a spy or a doll, and she photographed him while she talked.

Troy offered a cheesy smile. "And you should tell your future sister-in-law her boyfriend is a retread before all hell breaks loose."

"Shh!" Anna ran over and covered his mouth with both of her hands. "Do not say a word about that. Not a word. Molly already hates me. Besides, it's been years. And he seems to really like her. Promise?"

"It'll only be worse if she finds out you didn't tell her."

"She can find out, just not today. It's not the appropriate moment."

"Just tell her you've met before. You don't have to tell her he was your boy toy."

"Just let's not tell her anything today, okay? You'll only be hurting her, not me."

"Why would I want to hurt you? I'm your bodyguard, remember?"

Sunny looked at Anna with raised eyebrows. "What's going on?"

"Jared, the guy Molly brought. He's an old friend. An old boyfriend of sorts. From a few years ago."

"That's a funny coincidence," said Sunny.

Anna stared off. After a moment she said, "Troy is an extremely gifted artist. Oliver has several of his pieces. There's one outside the house, near the entryway. Very phallic, but interesting. Did you see it? The *Times* gave the show a great write-up last year."

Anna went into the house to take a phone call and didn't come back. Sunny put on sunscreen and Anna's white hat. It seemed like she'd been at the pool for days, weeks, months, and still a mild late-afternoon light prevailed. Franco the Sicilian winemaker had returned to his chaise, inanimate. His short white hair, nearly a crew cut, and black trunks reminded Sunny of Dr. Quest about to dive into the ocean to save Jonny and Bandit. The thatch of white hair on his chest stood out against the tan skin. He spoke to her with his eyes closed.

"What about you, Ms. McCoskey, are you also an artist, like everyone I meet in California?"

"I cook for a living."

"I remember now. The restaurant. In Sicily everyone cooks. It's not a job, it is part of enjoying life."

"And are the restaurants staffed by volunteers?"

"Don't be a joker. You should get serious and go to Sicily. It's like your wine country, but with history. Americans can't appreciate history. It means nothing to them. A cook from California has no roots. You're like a caveman—excuse me, cavewoman—who just discovered the potential of the wheel, while over in Europe we're driving Ferraris since you were born. But our Ferraris are out of gas, metaphorically speaking. The energy is greater here. You should take your youth and your energy and graft yourself onto a place like Sicily so you can draw from deep down in the earth."

He rolled onto his elbow and reached for a pack of cigarettes. Everyone was smoking like it was the fifties and cigarettes were as good as vitamins. And in California! Where you can get arrested for smoking, thought Sunny, where no one even thinks it's cool anymore, except maybe in the food business. Ironic that a habit known to kill your sense of taste and smell would thrive in the restaurant business. Of course, it was also known to ease the mind after the high-speed endurance test of a night working the back of the house. Franco offered the pack to Sunny. When she accepted, he pulled it back. "Don't smoke. It's very bad for your health. Seriously."

"What about you?"

"I'm an old man and a European. The rules are different."

"The rules are different for me, too, at least today." She lit one and held it without smoking it and studied the pool, the white pavement, the tiny blue tiles shimmering under the water. "What would I eat in Sicily?"

He lifted his eyebrows thoughtfully. "Nothing special. Marinated olives. Anchovies in oil. Eggplant with tomato sauce. Fresh riccotta with honey. Fava beans. Stuffed peppers. Cured meats. It's not what you eat, it's the total experience of a culture and a landscape that culminates in each bite. You could go into a restaurant in the worst part of town in Palermo or even over in Reggio Calabria, sit down at an old card table under a fluorescent light, and order anything off the menu and it would change your life forever."

"You sound like a man who misses home."

The music suddenly got very loud, drowning out whatever Franco might have replied. Anna came down to the pool dancing around, her head tipped back to the sky. She seemed high on something. It wouldn't be the first time, thought Sunny. The girl always loved a party. She didn't seem stoned. Cocaine, probably. Once there had been a rumor of heroin. Could it be true? Or was she just getting drunk? Whatever the cause, when the hostess started spinning in circles on the grass and laughing hysterically, it was time to leave. Sunny would wait until her head was reasonably clear of wine and then go. Tomorrow she would call Anna and apologize for not staying for dinner and see if she and Oliver had talked things through. She had a hunch they would. Anna was probably overreacting. A penchant for technology-driven voyeurism was the least of Oliver Seth's faults.

4

The hazy orange light of sunset lingered over the pool and turned the lawn dark green. Troy Stevens sat hunched up at the foot of the chaise. "Don't leave now," he said, looking at Sunny accusingly. "What's the point? You have to stay for the sunset. After that you might as well stay for dinner. If you leave now, you'll get home to your lonely little miserable house with no one around to talk to and it will suck. Why are you in such a hurry to leave, anyway?"

"It's not miserable. And I'm not in a hurry. I've been here since noon. Anna's not even awake anymore."

"Anna isn't the only person here. Besides, she'll get up for dinner. You should stay. We need you for ballast. You're the only one who isn't all uptight about something."

"What are you uptight about?" asked Sunny.

"Me? I'm always uptight. I exist in a state of perpetual anxiety. But I mix it with perpetual torpor so I'm reasonably functional."

"Why do you live in Barcelona? You're British, right?"

"Guilty. Barcelona is a great city. Great art scene, great nightlife, good weather. Not like fucking London. I can't take that freezing rain all winter."

"And you share a place with Anna?"

"She uses my place as her Euro–crash pad. We used to live there together for real. Now she comes through town once a month, writes me a check, and opens her mail."

"You mean you were a couple?"

"Two years."

"What happened?"

"She met Oliver."

"You mean this Oliver?"

"The very same."

Sunny took the bottle of wine from the table between them and poured herself another glass. He was right. She might as well stay for dinner. By the time she was sober enough to drive, it would be dinnertime, anyway. "Does Oliver know? I mean, that Anna was with you?"

"Of course. I introduced him to her."

"You're kidding."

"Definitely not."

"So Anna lived with you in Barcelona until you introduced her to Oliver, who brought her back here."

"It wasn't that simple, but that's the gist."

"Somewhere along the way she dated this guy Jared, who is now dating Oliver's sister. I guess it's not that many men to have dated in a lifetime, but it's a lot to have dated at one dinner party. It's sort of odd that you've all stayed friends."

"We're not friends. I can't stand Oliver, who is a shit of the highest order in my opinion. Jared seems like an okay guy. I met him in South Beach at Art Basel with Anna a couple of years ago. But I don't really know his story."

"What about Keith?"

"You mean Oliver's lawyer? I just met him a few days ago." Troy gave her a look, as if deciding whether to divulge a secret. "I'll tell you something I haven't even admitted to myself. Until I got here, I didn't know she was shacked up with Oliver again. He's bought a couple of my pieces, thanks to her, mostly. One just last month. The one in transit that I'm here to install, if it ever arrives. I thought she wanted me to fly out here to make sure he didn't put it in the bathroom, and to do a little performance as the eccentric artist. That's included in the price. Instead, I seem to be here as some kind of handler."

"What do you mean?"

"Haven't you noticed? Anna likes to travel with an entourage."

"And Oliver doesn't mind. I mean you being here."

"I assume he doesn't have a choice. Anna does whatever she wants." Troy pulled himself up. "I'm going to go get a shower and change before our grand repast."

Sunny went in after him and stood in the kitchen, not sure what to do. She could hear soft exchanges from distant rooms, a door close, water coming on. The oven was on, baking a tray of herbed potatoes. Cynthia came in talking on the cordless and checked the potatoes.

"Shower?" mouthed Sunny.

"Downstairs," whispered Cynthia. "Any room that's free."

The first room she went in was as posh as any swank hotel room she'd ever seen. The shower was big enough for four people and made of little one-inch tiles that faded from sandy brown at the bottom to rose to pearlescent to luminous white toward the top, like dip-dyed fabric. After a long shower, she put back on the clothes she'd arrived in, with one annoying exception. She'd forgotten to ask Cynthia about the bra and underwear she'd left in the bathroom upstairs. They were probably in the laundry, wherever that was. The bottoms of her swimsuit were still wet and she resolved to go without. Womankind had survived millennia without panties.

And men went regimental all the time. Wade Skord, vintner on the mount, had never worn a pair of skivvies in his life and proudly said so to anyone who noticed. Still, Sunny went up to dinner feeling half naked because she was half naked.

Upstairs, Anna sat in the living room wearing the white dress and sandals Sunny had seen in the closet earlier. The skin of her arms and legs glowed with the day's sun, and her face wore a tranquil expression. A slender oval of gold sat on the ring finger of her right hand. A matching necklace with a thin gold disk lay on her chest. She looked like the queen of an empire.

"Intellectual property is the next big land grab," said Oliver, holding his wineglass like a trophy. "We've consumed all the real estate. Now it's time to colonize the estates of the imagination. The Information Age isn't about facts. It's about perception. Perception is reality. The next wave of wealth is going to be made from intellectual property—attitudes, ideas, instructions, code—and the wars waged to protect it."

"What does that mean?" said Anna. "I never know what you're talking about."

"Code is the new gold. DNA, encryption, genetic engineering, software. It's all code. Instructions for making a hidden world function. That's the next Gold Rush. That's why video gaming is so huge now. Code. Finding the secrets that keep the game advancing. In the not-so-distant future, ideas are literally going to shape reality. Real life will be nothing more than where you plug your game in."

Dinner was over, the plates cleared. Oliver had pulled a few of his favorites from his wine collection, but no one could taste anything anymore.

"Even the old-school guys selling tangible products will have their paradigm rewritten in the context of intellectual property. It's the unintended consequence of globalization. In a global marketplace, brand is everything because you have no other context for a product. Look at a brand like Mouton Rothschild. They're not selling wine, they're selling the idea of France, wealth, art, Grand Prix, beautiful women. The wine itself may or may not be the best value for the money. It doesn't matter. The perception of the product is the actual value proposition. And in a world where perception is largely dictated by the Web, what gets posted has a tangible and sometimes tremendous effect on the value of your product. So you've got all these companies leaving their most valuable asset out in the parking lot with the keys in the ignition. All I have to do is set up a Web site saying Mouton Rothschild is actually just a lot of rotten grapes. The bloggers pick it up, mainstream media covers the blogs, and the share price takes a hit. Next thing you know, sales are down and the competition is moving in. We've known this for a while. Now we need to figure out what to do about it."

"You're talking about work," said his sister. "You promised you weren't going to talk about work tonight."

"Somebody better change the subject or we'll be in the office writing press releases all night," said Keith.

Oliver ignored them and his voice grew louder. "We all thought the Internet had settled down into this nicely indexed tool designed to turn loose the inner librarian. Wrong. This has been the calm before a storm that's going to reorganize the global economy before half the people know what's hit them. It's going to be fucking Armageddon, and TR Enterprises Ltd. is going to be driving the flaming chariot that rips the sky apart."

Silence followed and Cynthia stood up. "We have chocolate torte for dessert. Anyone?"

Oliver smiled and seemed to forget all he'd been saying so passionately. He turned to Sunny. "Cynthia is the best pastry chef in the valley, hands down. Her chocolate torte is second only to my personal favorite, lemon meringue pie. You didn't happen to whip up one of those, did you, Cynthia?"

Cynthia smiled and shook her head. "Not tonight. But I'll see what I can do."

They stayed a long time at the table under the stars and wisteria. After his pronouncements about the future of the global economy, Oliver didn't say much more and eventually excused himself to attend to some urgent matter from his cell phone. Franco told stories about his childhood in Sicily, and Keith countered with his about growing up poor in Barbados. Finally the air cooled enough to drive them indoors and Oliver returned to pour cognac and port. Keith's girlfriend arrived dressed in capri jeans, sandals with four-inch heels, and a lacey camisole. She came from Guam and looked like one of Gauguin's Tahitian subjects. Her name was Marissa Lin. She gave Keith a kiss and went to Anna's side, holding her hand and snuggling up to her the way some girlfriends do. Sunny had taken the comfortable chair, slightly distant from the others, and put her bare feet on the ottoman. Keith sat down on the edge of the ottoman and took up one of her feet, which he began to massage.

"You look tired."

"A little. I got too much sun." Sunny watched him rub her foot as though in a dream. She should stop him, but it felt too good.

"You look good with some color on that skin."

"Thank you. What time is it?"

"It's early."

"Is it?"

"Relatively," he said, switching feet.

Across the living room, Anna, Jordan, and Marissa were arranged like a liquor ad on the sofa, all legs, heels, and cocktail glasses. They were undeniably beautiful, each in a different way, though all with dark hair. Anna was tall, with golden skin and green eyes. Jordan was voluptuous, made up, and sexy in a Hollywood way. Next to them, Keith Lachlan's girlfriend, Marissa, looked even more petite and delicate than she was. Nestled in among them was Oliver Seth, handsome in a boyish way, looking exactly like a man enjoying the hard-earned realization of his childhood fantasies.

Keith returned her foot to the ottoman and stood up. "Can I get you a drink?"

"I think I'm good for now."

"You need a bump?"

"A bump?"

"A pick-me-up."

"What do you have in mind?"

He gave her a knowing smile. "You like coke?"

"Lowercase C?" She shook her head. "Afraid not. Not my thing. Sensitive nose."

"You're kidding. Aren't you in the restaurant business? I thought foodies lived on blow."

"I'm more the double espresso type."

"Good for you." He went to join Oliver and the girls and Sunny left to prowl the house. She found Franco Bertinotti looking through the glass at the wine collection. He'd changed out of his black trunks into jeans and a linen shirt.

"This bastard really knows how to buy wine," he said. "If somebody has to be as rich as Seth, I'm glad it's him. At least he knows what to do with it."

"Do you know how he made his money?"

"The usual way. Rob, pillage, and plunder."

"Seriously."

"My dear, I am being serious. No one achieves the rapturous decadence of your current surroundings without a great deal of compromise, on everyone's part."

Sunny followed the faint sound of talk punctuated by laughter. Franco, whom she'd been talking with for the past half hour, had gone to bed. The others had vanished. Now she tracked them to the double doors off the lounge with the red neon. Outside, a fire was burning in the fireplace next to the hot tub. From the doorway, she couldn't see who was in the water, just outlines against firelight.

"Sunny! Come in. We're getting warm," said Anna.

"No bathing suits allowed," said Keith. Someone giggled.

"Hush! It's dark, anyway," said Anna. "We won't peek."

"Don't stay out in the cold, McCoskey," said Oliver. "There's plenty of room."

"We'll make room," said Keith. Again a feminine giggle, presumably from Keith's girlfriend, Marissa.

Sunny hesitated. Having grown up in Northern California, she'd seen a fair number of hot tubs and bare bottoms. The fireplace and the water certainly looked nice. And the only men seemed to be Keith and Oliver, both of whom would be kept in check by their girlfriends.

"Back in a minute."

She left her clothes on the bed in the first room she came to, then took a towel from the bathroom and wrapped it around herself. No one took any notice when she stepped out onto the patio. She draped her towel over the rock wall by the fireplace and found an open spot in the tub, mortifyingly aware of the bare elements on display by the murky glow of underwater lights until she could take cover in the froth. Oliver, soaking opposite, broke hot-tub etiquette and stared openly, watching her lean over and step into the water. Jordan, breasts buoyant as tub toys, sat next to him with a thick twist of dark hair clipped high on her head.

"You must work out," said Oliver. "I was watching you swim earlier. You have great muscle definition."

"Thanks for noticing," she said, hoping he would catch the sarcasm.

She sank into the hot water and leaned her head back. Even with the glow of the lights under the water, the stars stood out in the black overhead. She closed her eyes. The water felt wonderful. When she looked up, Keith and his girlfriend had their heads together, whispering and laughing softly. Marissa had delicate features except for rather full lips that the dim light accentuated. Her delicate hands touched Keith's head while they talked. Across from them, Anna, Oliver, and Jordan were discussing whether there was anything useful to be gained by reading newspapers. Oliver thought not, and Anna accused him of hypocrisy, since he read several daily. The only people missing were Franco, who was in bed already, Troy, and Oliver's sister, Molly, and her boyfriend, Jared.

Sunny closed her eyes again, and when she next opened them, she saw that Keith had pulled Marissa onto his lap and was kissing her. Not a playful kiss. Mouths were open, heads were tilted, and, there it was, the hand moving to cup a bare breast. She looked away. Across from her, Anna was nibbling Oliver's neck. Someone's toes came to rest on Sunny's calf. While she'd been soaking up the night air, some silent signal had been given, some gate lowered, flag waved, light changed from red to green. Now Jordan was taking a turn kissing Keith while Marissa sucked on her ear. The girl from Guam locked eyes with Sunny and smiled, Jordan's earlobe clamped between white teeth.

None of this should have been a surprise, and yet Sunny was surprised. This wasn't exactly hippie heaven. Was everyone on some drug she forgot to take? Suddenly she felt extremely naive. There had been plenty of hints as to what was to come. Was that the real reason Anna had wanted her to stay? Was all that talk about trouble with Oliver just a ruse to make sure she hung around until the fireworks started? No, of course not, thought Sunny. In Anna's world, anything could happen. She could decide her boyfriend was some kind of monster, then take him to bed with a friend, or two, or three. What would it be like to live in that world? Anna's fingers took her hand underwater and Sunny decided not to find out. She pulled herself out of the water and grabbed a towel.

Inside, she found the bedroom where she'd left her clothes and opened the door, revealing a shadowy tableau of acrobatic flesh. She closed the door. Jared Bollinger had a well-toned backside and muscular shoulders. Also, Molly Seth kept her bra on during sex. Sunny thought with a pang of her lovely blue tunic and the new skirt she'd left on the bed, now almost certainly under siege. Apparently everyone was going to get some action tonight but her, including her clothes. She stood outside the closed door, barefoot and dripping in her towel. This was exactly what she deserved for hanging around this place all day. Now what was she supposed to do? Drive home in a towel? She should have known. She did know. This was precisely the sort of predicament any association with Anna Wilson was bound to produce. She was lucky she wasn't in jail.

Sunny trudged downstairs to the bedroom where she'd showered earlier. All was silence except for the thump of house music from upstairs. She rinsed off in the shower and turned down the bed. The decor offered plenty of understated luxury, but the room was otherwise empty. Nothing to read. No radio, no television. Her cell phone was out by the pool. And now she didn't even have any clothes. And she'd passed up a golden opportunity to become a swinger. Rivka was going to have a good laugh when she told her. She looked around at the mostly bare room. There was too much alcohol and not enough reading material in this house. Her beach bag was here, but there was nothing much in it unless she wanted to read the label on a tin of Altoids, which she did, only to find the room lurched and heaved like a rowboat at sea. Thoroughly sauced. Far too sauced to drive home. Thanks to her own doing, she was a prisoner of Oliver Seth's country house until morning.

French doors at one end of the room opened onto a tiny patio enclosed by a low hedge. She closed the curtains and hunted for her watch in her beach bag. One-fifteen. She put it on the night-stand, lay back on one of the pristine pillows, reflected that she was probably the first to have done so, and fell asleep.

Sunny woke up suddenly, not sure why, listening. The muffled sound of loud voices came from upstairs. A door slammed, then slammed again. More raised voices. One high, one low. Sunny went to the door and stuck her head out into the hallway, where the house seemed perfectly silent. She went back inside, pulled open the curtains, and opened one of the French doors. The voices sounded like they were just a few feet away. The master bedroom Anna and Oliver slept in would be almost directly above hers. Anna was saying, "I can't believe I trusted you," over and over. Finally she shrieked the words one at a time.

"Keep your voice down. We have guests," said Oliver.

"I don't care who hears me."

"I do. If you want to make a scene, do it somewhere else. I won't have a hysterical display in my house."

"If you think I'm going to keep quiet about this, you're crazy. I forwarded copies of those e-mails to myself and I intend to share them. I don't see why your precious ex-girlfriend, for one, shouldn't know what you're up to."

"Are you threatening me? You may want to take a moment to consider who you're dealing with."

"Even the all-powerful Oliver Seth can't control everything," said Anna. "You can't control me. I'll do whatever the hell I want, and there's nothing you can do about it."

"Anna, be serious." His voice was forceful but calm. "There's plenty I can do about it. You have no idea. Among other options, I could sue you for invasion of privacy and extortion. Do you have money—not counting my credit card, of course—to defend yourself?"

"This is what I think of you and your credit card and your sleazy lawyers." There was a thump and a crash, then silence.

"Invasion of privacy, extortion, and willful destruction of private property. That piece was worth more than you've made in your lifetime."

"Get away from me."

"You need to calm down," said Oliver, adopting a soothing voice. "This is all getting way out of control. You're tired, you've had too much to drink. You'll see, in the morning it will all make sense."

"I'm not tired and I'm not drunk and if you touch me I will scream loud enough to wake everyone in this house. You think I'm going to just walk away? I'm not. You're sick. I can't believe I fell for your lies again."

It sounded like someone fell or kicked over a piece of furniture. Oliver said, "Anna, don't make me call the police."

Anna was crying. "Just leave me alone."

After that, the voices got quiet. She could hear them talking to each other, but it was too soft to make out the words. Sunny pushed the door closed and pulled the heavy curtains together. She went to the door to the hall, then came back and sat down on the edge of the bed. Was she supposed to go up there? And break up a fight? Was Oliver really dangerous? Anna said she had invited her over because she needed help. What was Sunny supposed to do, run upstairs like a one-woman SWAT team and save the day? Wearing what, a bikini? Or perhaps a towel would be more intimidating. She tried to remember Anna's exact words. She said that last night after she discovered the surveillance cameras she had imagined all kinds of things, "even that he might be dangerous."

What exactly was going on in this house? Last night Anna discovered the Peeping Tom stuff and confronted Oliver. He said she was overreacting. This morning Anna saw Sunny's name in the paper and called her for help. Tonight she was kissing Oliver in the hot tub as if nothing was wrong, and now this. Was she afraid of her boyfriend or not? Was this all just the drama of people with too much time on their hands, or was Anna in a deeply manipulative relationship? How much of a hold did Oliver have on her? He certainly sounded angry just now, but Anna was the one smashing things. He didn't sound out of control. Could certain men become violent without losing control?

Upstairs, they were arguing again. Sunny paced, unable to hear the conversation or shut it out. She wondered if she should go up there and see what was going on. But how could she? In addition to not wanting to interfere, it was hardly her place. Anna was a grown woman who could take care of herself. As long as their quarrel sounded like any other heated argument between ill-suited lovers, it was none of her business. Unpleasant for everyone involved, yes. But Anna could and should handle her own unpleasantness on her own. For all Sunny knew, this was how their relationship worked. With that decision, she went back to bed and quickly fell heavily asleep.

The next time she woke up it was four o'clock in the morning. The room was freezing. She hadn't latched the French doors and an icy draft was coming through the space where they stood ajar. As she got up to close them, she heard a thump, and another, as though something heavy had been dropped on the floor above. Someone—it sounded like a woman—was sobbing. It had to be Anna, though the lurching, animal sobs sounded nothing like her. She listened, wondering again if she should go up, see if she was okay, try to comfort her. But what if she didn't want comforting? What if she just wanted to be left alone? What if she wasn't alone?

Sunny stood at the door, trying to decide what to do. She put herself in Anna's place. Would she want a friend there? No. She would want to be left alone to cry it out. She stood a long time, wondering if that was the right decision. Anna was still sobbing when Sunny once again resolved that it was not her affair to put her nose into, closed the French doors, made sure they were latched this time, and climbed back into bed. She jolted awake one more time before daybreak but heard nothing and didn't look at her watch.

Daylight. Sunny's face pressed hard into the pillow. Far away, or so it seemed, she could hear serious-sounding male voices and purposeful strides. She groped the nightstand for her watch. Nine-fifteen. She turned over and lay listening to whatever was going on. Someone heavy jogged down the stairs, keys jingling. A knock at the door. *Merde!* thought Sunny.

"Hello? Anyone in there?" said a husky male voice.

"Just a minute."

She got up and pulled the sheet around her. Her stomach lurched. She had a crease down her cheek and her head was pounding and her mouth felt like a day-old scone with a nicotine addiction. This promised to be a genuine hangover, not that she didn't richly deserve it. Drink and smoke all day and into the night and this is how you feel the next day, no mystery there. The big question was who had the courage to knock on any door in this house at this early hour on Sunday morning. Could it be a rude call to breakfast? She hobbled over to the door hopefully, thinking of freshly squeezed orange juice, and opened it. On the other side, dressed in his neatly pressed uniform and looking distinctly displeased, stood Sergeant Steve Harvey of the St. Helena Police Department. If he was surprised to find Sunny, as he certainly must have been, he maintained his composure seamlessly.

"Sunny."

"Steve?" It was difficult to speak. Her voice came out deep and scratchy.

"Sorry to wake you. We need everyone upstairs in the kitchen as quickly as possible."

She nodded. "Will do."

5

Sunny closed the door. She listened to Sergeant Harvey walk down to the next door and knock. Why on earth was he here, rousting people out of bed on a Sunday morning? It had to be because of Anna and Oliver's fight. Somebody must have called in a domestic disturbance. Not Anna. She wasn't the type to think calling the cops was a cute way to get the upper hand, and despite his threat, Sunny couldn't picture Oliver resorting to state-sponsored backup. He would handle things himself or call a lawyer, not the cops. Could it be a drug bust? Maybe something valuable was missing and Oliver had called the police. The house was full of art, intoxicants, and strangers. It was a tempting combination. A theft! That was it, thought Sunny. After his fight with Anna, Oliver stayed up late watching his security cameras and he spotted a breach. Thus the early-morning raid. She shuffled into the bathroom, sheet dragging behind her. As long as somebody produced an omelet, bacon, a side of waffles, and a pitcher of fresh OJ, she didn't care if the FBI stormed the house.

The McCoskey look was seriously impaired. Punk-rock hair. Eyes glazed and puffy. Shoulders and, she suspected—confirmed—bottom and backs of calves sunburned the color of strawberry sorbet. And where on earth were her clothes? She thought for a long, foggy moment and finally remembered the passionate embrace of Molly Seth and Jared Bollinger. Sunny cursed them and their blossoming love. What to do? The room might look like a suite at the Ritz-Carlton, but it lacked certain key amenities, for example, the all-important terry-cloth robe. She checked the closet and behind the bathroom door. Nothing. There was little choice. She hitched up the sheet and headed upstairs, passing two more police officers on the way. Both sternly avoided eye contact.

The set of doors opening onto the north-wing hot tub were easy to find. She retraced her steps to locate the door where she'd left her clothes. It was closed, naturally. Molly and Jared were no doubt entwined inside, mingling their bodily fluids over Sunny's best dry clean–only shirt. She racked her brain to come up with a better plan than knocking on the closed door of a known love nest. There was no choice. Bracing herself for the invasion of privacy, she knocked softly, waited, and knocked again. Someone moved around inside. A high voice murmured tenderly. Sunny knocked once more and said, "Sorry, you guys, I need to get my clothes."

There was more movement behind the door, and more soft, high words, followed by husky low ones. Sunny waited. She was just on the point of giving up and resigning herself to a police interrogation while wearing a sheet when the door opened and Sunny's boyfriend, Andre Morales, stood in front of her, handsomely rumpled, naked to the waist, towel around hips. He gaped in surprise. "Sunny! What on earth are you doing here?"

She tried to speak but couldn't. Her voice would not come. She coughed and cleared her throat and finally croaked out, "When did you get here?"

"Late last night, after work. What about you?"

"Earlier."

"I see that." He glanced at the sheet. "Have fun?"

"Not as much as you, apparently."

Marissa, Keith Lachlan's Polynesian princess, the same last seen sampling Jordan Crowley's earlobe in the hot tub, came up behind him in her camisole and panties. She held Sunny's clothes in one hand.

"Yours?"

Sunny took them. Marissa wrapped her arms around Andre's waist, pressing her head to his chest. Andre scrubbed at his hair. He put one arm around Marissa's shoulders absentmindedly, which he let drop when he looked at Sunny.

"Listen, I know this is, uh, awkward. Why don't you come in for a while and relax. Whatever the hell is going on out there can wait a little longer."

"Excuse me?" said Sunny.

He licked his lips. "Look, Sunny, I'm not saying this is an ideal situation, but it's happened, and now we have a choice. You have a choice. You can storm off and we can do the whole drama crisis thing. Or you can come in and we can talk things over, and you'll see it's not as big a deal as it seems."

Sunny looked at him, then Marissa, who gave her a smile and the look a cat wears when it's settled into the best chair in the living room.

"Don't storm off," he said, reaching for Sunny's wrist. "Come in. You'll see. There's no need to get all upset."

Sunny glared at his hand and he removed it. She walked back through the house to the room where she'd slept. There she took her time getting dressed. The image of the two of them—Andre wearing a fixed stare like a man focused on a distant goal, Marissa looking sweetly content, both of them rumpled and rosy cheeked—burned itself into her memory with such force and clarity that long afterward she could study them like an image in a book. She could see the position of Marissa's slender hand on Andre's ribs, and the dip of flesh above his collarbone where Sunny had formerly liked to place her lips when they were the ones who woke up in bed together.

———————————

"You don't look so good," said Sergeant Harvey, handing Sunny a mug of black coffee.

"I've had better mornings."

"You're not the only one."

His tone silenced any further exchange. She went over to the counter, where a collection of half-empty bottles from last night had accumulated. A bottle of Stag's Leap Artemis Cab was open and hardly touched. That would be Stag's Leap Wine Cellars, thought Sunny, not to be confused with Stags' Leap Winery or the Stags Leap District. How many hundreds of thousands, perhaps even millions, of dollars did the lawyers get to sort out that tangle of suits and countersuits? And, in the end, it all came down to the placement of an apostrophe. The place where one stag leaps versus the place where multiple stags leap versus the declarative statement that multiple stags are inclined to leap around these few acres where very good Cabernet Sauvignon grapes are grown. If Oliver Seth was right, the great battles from here on out would be fought over such ephemeral issues, over ideas themselves. Intellectual property. The ownership of an idea and the subsequent wealth it generated in a global marketplace. What else was wine, anyway, other than an idea? Could they really tell which plot of land had produced the fruit to make a particular wine? People paid more because they liked the idea that the grapes for their wine came from a certain piece of land that they considered prestigious. They drank it for the idea of relaxation, indulgence, pleasure, luxury, superiority, heritage. She poured a splash of the red wine into her coffee and sat down at the kitchen table, hugging the mug with both hands.

Spotlight consciousness, thought Sunny. The hangover was limiting her ability to see the big picture. She could see the elephant's trunk but not the elephant, and certainly not the field the elephant was standing in. The entire morning seemed unreal, like she was watching someone else's life. Had she really seen her boyfriend in the arms of another woman? Were the police really here, setting up camp as though they planned to stay? Was she really thinking about wine and intellectual property in the global marketplace when she should be wondering what the hell was going on? And where was everyone else, most notably Anna and Oliver? Were they hiding in a bedroom while the police swarmed the house?

Sergeant Harvey sat down across from her, his already impressive physical presence augmented by his uniform and the creaking belt and holster strapped around his waist. His crew cut was groomed to honor-guard perfection as usual.

"Sunny, you're the last person I expected to see this morning," he said. "What brings you here?"

"I could ask you the same thing, Steve," she said, and took a sip of coffee.

His expression turned serious and he shook his head. "I'm not making conversation. I need an answer."

She put the cup down. "A friend I hadn't seen for years called me yesterday and said she was in town staying at her boyfriend's weekend house and I should come over for lunch." She gestured to the surroundings. "I came over, lunch turned into dinner and cocktails, and I ended up spending the night. They have plenty of room."

"Your friend's name?"

"Anna Wilson."

He nodded. "Sunny, I'm afraid I've got some bad news for you about your friend. This morning at seven twenty-five, nine-one-one got a call from a guy named Mike Sayudo. Mr. Sayudo is employed by Oliver Seth in the capacity of landscape gardener and outdoor maintenance man. He said he came out early this morning to make sure the drip system was functioning. Apparently it's been a problem and he's been keeping an eye on it."

"The drip system."

"That's right." Sergeant Harvey glanced out the window. "I guess I don't know exactly how to tell you this except to come right out with it." He looked back at Sunny. "This morning Mr. Sayudo found your friend. Oliver Seth identified her body a few minutes ago."

"Her *body*?"

"She died sometime early this morning."

"She overdosed," said Sunny softly.

"What makes you say that?"

"Nothing specific. Just, you know . . . "

"She was doing drugs."

"I don't know for sure. It seemed like it. Or maybe just drinking too much. I don't know."

Sunny stared into her coffee. It was hard to feel anything. The whole morning, the whole day yesterday, felt like a strange dream. "If she didn't overdose, how did she die?"

"It looked like she fell out of one of the second-story windows onto the patio. The hill slopes away, so it was a pretty good drop. Fifteen feet or so."

Over time, Sunny had come to know Sergeant Steve Harvey pretty well. He prided himself on accuracy and chose his words with care. "What do you mean, 'looked like'?" she said.

He hesitated, glancing around the room. One of his lieutenants was lingering in the hallway off the kitchen. They could see him through the floor-to-ceiling glass. No one else was around.

"Sunny, we've known each other quite a while. We have a certain rapport, wouldn't you say?"

"Definitely."

They'd worked together, in a manner of speaking, on three murder investigations in the valley. Thanks to some unusual associations, a little too keen a nose, and a tendency to roam around at night, Sunny had landed in the middle of three of the valley's most notorious crimes in years. Naturally, Sergeant Harvey would rather see her cooking lunch than out digging around in his jurisdiction. Still, no matter how irritated he might be at her involvement, he was always respectful, if a bit stern and intimidating. He had a weight lifter's body and used it to full effect, wearing his shirts tight and standing arrow-straight. Now he spoke in a low voice, poking her forearm with a burly finger after each phrase.

"I don't know how you managed to turn up in the middle of this"—*poke*—"but if I were to tell you something about a case"—*poke*—"based on that rapport we have"—*poke*—"and I tell you it is absolutely vital that you not share this information with anyone"—*poke*—"in a situation like that"—*poke*—"I assume I could trust you implicitly to keep such information confidential until such time as I choose to reveal it to others at my sole discretion."

Sunny moved her arm. "I would take a situation like that very seriously."

Sergeant Harvey stared at her. "I'm sure you can imagine why I would take such a risk."

She could not. She had, specifically, not the slightest idea. He continued to stare at her until the fog began to clear. "Because things are going to get messy?" she asked finally.

He nodded. "That's right. I don't know exactly what we're dealing with here, but I've seen plenty of people with head injuries. Car accidents. Drunks falling down. Fights. You name it. This one doesn't look right to me." He shook his head. "Something's just not right. We won't know for sure until the coroner's report, but I'd bet my badge on one thing." Sunny waited. Sergeant Harvey gritted his teeth. "The funny thing about what happened to your friend Anna Wilson, Sunny, is that it's hard to fall out a window when you're already dead."

6

The situation demanded an emotional response. Tears, ideally, and lots of them. Uncontrollable sobs. Collapse. Something to indicate she was human and felt human grief and compassion. Sunny McCoskey had never been the type, as much as she would have liked to be. She knew it was strange. It felt strange even to her. One of her oldest friends was dead and her eyes were dry as cork. Nothing. Not even a tingle. She'd always been this way. Emotionally powerful situations rendered her calm, cool-headed, and oddly devoid of emotion in direct proportion to the severity of the impact. The more serious the incident, the calmer the state of mind. After the crisis passed, and usually at an oddly irrelevant moment, she would finally feel the punch of grief, doubling up with sobs over a particularly moving beer commercial or the sight of a dog locked in a car.

It was an effort to keep still. Her pulse was racing. She wanted to sprint up the dry trail behind the house, to run and claw and pull herself through the scraping bushes all the way to the top. She wanted her lungs to pump air until they burned and her legs and arms to work and sweat until they quivered with exertion. The worst was having to sit in the kitchen with a cold cup of coffee and wait. The police had asked them not to talk to one another, not to go anywhere, not to contact anyone, not to use their cell phones. An officer was left to watch over them while one by one they went into the improvised police headquarters set up in one of the guest rooms to tell their stories.

It was a relief not to have to talk. Franco tried to discuss the situation, but the officer guarding them asked him to refrain from unnecessary discourse. He resorted to sighs and the occasional disgruntled expletive as he settled and resettled himself in the chair. Once he glanced over at Sunny with a look of such penetrating sorrow that she almost got her wish. Her throat tightened and it took a great effort to arrest the welling up of tears.

They sat around the kitchen in a grim parody of the previous day's festivities. Troy Stevens, looking even paler and more disheveled than yesterday, slumped in the corner of a built-in seat in his black T-shirt and jeans, staring out the window. In the other corner, Jordan cried quietly but profusely. Every few minutes she took a wet ball of tissue from the pocket of a terry-cloth tracksuit and blew her nose. Sunny, Franco, and Jared sat at one end of the kitchen table. Molly stood outside the sliding glass door in her black skirt and heels, smoking, and Jared watched her. Cynthia sat at the other end of the table staring at her hands. Andre and Marissa occupied two of three barstools at the island, leaving one empty between them. Andre kicked back and forth on the stool, checking his watch. Sunny had heard Marissa tell Franco that Keith had returned to San Francisco late last night. Oliver had been in the guest room with the police giving his statement for more than an hour. Sunny's stomach growled. On cue, a cop arrived with a pink box full of doughnuts and a jug of reconstituted orange juice. The stuff confessions are made of.

"She was murdered, obviously," said Franco, squeezing sunscreen into his palm and rubbing it over his face and neck.

They were out by the pool, waiting. It was almost two o'clock. Sunny, like the others, had described her experiences of the day and night before to the police in detail, though one could argue that she'd left out the juicy bits. She had skipped Keith Lachlan's offer of a pick-me-up. She left out the late-night hot-tub session and interrupting Molly and Jared in flagrante delicto, as well as her surprise upon discovering that Andre Morales had joined the party after she went to bed. The manic energy she'd felt earlier had worn off and now she was in a daze. She stared at the water of the barely rippling pool as if she was watching television. Her hangover had probably, she now reflected, clouded her judgment. The events she had skipped over would come out eventually. Even if she didn't mention getting into the hot tub, someone else would. The police were going to come back to her and she would have to explain. At least by then her stomach wouldn't be lurching and sloshing like hide tide at the boardwalk. At the time of the interview, none of it had seemed terribly relevant. She thought describing the seedier aspects of the night would only embarrass her and shock Sergeant Harvey, who had seemed to grow sterner and angrier with every question. It was hard to say how much such stories offended him. Where did drugs, sex, and rampant affluence fall in his moral universe? Well outside, she assumed. Sergeant Harvey liked rules, and not just because he was a cop. He was order and regulation and discipline from his neatly trimmed nails to his gleaming black boots.

Franco moved on to his chest and shoulders, rubbing the lotion in with brisk, glancing blows to his deeply tanned skin.

"You must learn to face it," he said, "because this is not going to end today. We are all in for a bit of trouble over this poor girl's death."

Sunny was silent.

"Do you think I'm wrong?" he continued. "They interrogate us, keep us here like we are under house arrest. I am not to leave the country or even this town until otherwise informed or else they will find some way to make my life difficult."

The police couldn't keep them from leaving, but they had firmly suggested it would be better if everyone stayed until they were done gathering as much preliminary information and evidence as possible. It was a polite and hospitable prison, but a prison nonetheless. Out front, it looked like a major operation. The police had moved their headquarters to the "command van" parked in the driveway, and a truck had arrived in addition to several police cars. Officers were busy removing items from the house and loading them into the truck.

"It is quite clear the police have decided little Anna's death was no accident," said Franco. He settled into his chaise. "I hope Oliver has a good lawyer."

"He has Keith," said Sunny.

"I mean a criminal lawyer. Keith is a businessman."

"Do you think they will accuse him?"

"They always accuse the lover. Besides, you heard them fighting. Everyone heard them. It doesn't look good to people."

"How well do you know Oliver?"

"Well enough."

"Do you think he loved her?"

"Anna? Of course. But I'm not so sure she loved him."

"She thought he was unfaithful to her."

Franco chuckled. "Who knows? And was she faithful to him? I find it difficult to imagine." He looked at Sunny with the alarming blue eyes that had startled her when they first met. "Faithfulness is overrated. If the love is there, that's the important part."

She felt her face flush with embarrassment. So, it was known. Everyone must know by now. Everyone except Keith Lachlan. He was back in San Francisco, blissfully ignorant of both Anna's death and his girlfriend's unfaithfulness. Now she and Keith Lachlan had something in common.

"That is an interesting philosophy," said Sunny. "The European approach to relationships, right? I don't think it would work in America."

"It is the old man's approach. Believe what you want, people are nothing more or less than human. But if the love is not there"— again, he looked into her eyes—"then it doesn't matter, does it? A husband and wife should be first in each other's hearts. After that, you just live and hope and try not to hurt each other."

"But Anna and Oliver weren't married."

"They would have been eventually. He talked about getting married. I told him to marry her, or choose someone else. I don't agree with this American propensity to delay adulthood. What is so great about adolescence? Only in America do they prolong it to middle age. Everywhere else in the world, young people can't wait to grow up. To make their own decisions and become independent. All the best pleasures of life happen to adults, and take it from me, they're better enjoyed in youth. To be the young husband of a young wife is the greatest pleasure in the world. To be a young father, a young mother. To buy your first house, take your first vacation as a family. I honestly do not understand why Americans work so hard to avoid adulthood. Are movie theaters and nightclubs so much fun? You would think they would die of boredom by the time they're thirty."

He offered her a cigarette and she shook her head. No more of that. Yesterday she'd let go of her own better judgment from start to finish, thinking maybe someone else knew better. Maybe all those rules could be broken and everything would still be fine.

Franco looked at her. "How old are you?"

"I'll be thirty-three in a week."

"Too old to marry in Italy and most of the world. In America there's still time. This guy you're with now, he's nothing. You need to find someone more substantial. Someone who isn't afraid to be a man and give his word. You don't want to end up like this poor girl we're going to bury."

"You don't look too shook up about it," said Sunny irritably.

"I'm like you. I don't show my emotions. They attack me later when I least expect it. Over coffee on a nice new morning when I'm not thinking of anything remotely sad. They wait until I let my guard down and then they clobber me like a robber in a dark alley."

On the subject of Andre Morales, Sunny's mind went blank. No feelings, no words, nothing. Her mind was as simple and white as a boiled egg when it came to her boyfriend of six months standing in a bedroom with a scantily clad Guamanian princess. Andre, for his part, was nonchalant. Earlier he had pulled up a chair next to her and sat overlooking the vineyard and peeling an orange as though nothing had changed. He offered Sunny half.

"Don't you want to save some for Marissa?" she said. "Maybe you should divide it into thirds."

"You're angry."

"I don't think there is a word for what I am, but anger is certainly part of it. Does that surprise you?"

"Look, Sunny, I'm sorry this happened. I certainly didn't plan for this to happen."

Sunny held up her hand. "Not now. Don't do this right now while Anna is stretched out somewhere on a gurney thanks to exactly this sort of thinking."

"What do you mean by that? I didn't have anything to do with what happened to Anna. I've never even met her."

"I'm talking about rules, or the lack thereof. There are no rules in this house and now Anna is dead. I don't want to hear your excuses. You broke the most basic rule of being together and you know it." She sounded slightly hysterical even to her own ears.

"What, are you going to tell the teacher on me? Sunny, please grow up. I'm not going to apologize for unwinding with friends after a long night. If you want to make more of it than that at a time when we all have more important things to think about, be my guest."

"And I'm not going to listen to you pretend to be honest. I want to be with a man who isn't afraid to give me his word and stand behind it."

In the late afternoon, Sergeant Harvey called them into the living room, where the crimson Rothko and the nudes presided. Cynthia had been the last to give her statement and her eyes were bloodshot. She blew her nose and pressed a wadded-up Kleenex to her eyes. Molly Seth and Jared Bollinger sat next to her on the couch. Jared's boyish face looked sad and sweet, as if he was eager to help but didn't know how. Molly had pulled her blond hair back in a tight bun. She had her arm around Cynthia, rocking her like a child. Marissa, Andre, and Troy sat off to the side in chairs around a coffee table. Sunny chose a place as far away from Andre as possible, slumped in the same armchair as last night, still in her bikini and cover-up and flimsy skirt. Franco and Jordan sat on the oversized ottoman in front of her, holding hands. There were several police officers Sunny didn't know, and a man she assumed was Mike

Sayudo, the gardener who'd found Anna. Oliver Seth stood in back by the fireplace with his arms crossed. He seemed to have grown thinner and paler in the night. His eyes were rimmed in red and a purplish shadow lay beneath them. He looked extremely tired.

"Before we let you go today, I wanted to take a moment to reiterate that this is an open investigation," said Sergeant Harvey, pacing in front of them like the principal of a school for derelict students. "While we won't know exactly what we're dealing with until the autopsy report and preliminary investigation are complete, I would like to ask your cooperation in not speaking about this matter any more than absolutely necessary, whether to each other or to people outside this room. Some facts will become public knowledge soon, such as the fact that a death occurred and the cause of death is being investigated. I would appreciate you keeping more detail than that to yourselves until further notice. Meanwhile, rest assured we will pursue every aspect of the case in order to establish exactly what transpired last night and this morning, and how those events may have contributed to the death of Ms. Wilson. We have more than fifteen officers dedicated to investigating the matter, and there may be more as leads come in, evidence is analyzed, and theories are developed."

"Does that mean you think she was killed?" asked Molly.

"It's too soon to determine anything right now. For the moment, we're just gathering information, trying to establish exactly what might have occurred."

"But you know how she died," she persisted.

"We'll have a better idea once the autopsy comes back in a day or two." He looked around the room at each of them. "Before you leave, you will be given a card with an officer's name and contact information on it. You should feel free, and depending on the situation, obligated, to contact this officer immediately should you learn of or recall any new piece of information you think might prove useful to the investigation."

Sunny's mind was awash with emotion. Anna's death and Andre's betrayal folded into each other and it was impossible to know where her response to one left off and the other began. She only wanted to go home to her own kitchen. She'd had enough of the cloying softness of the chair she was sitting in and the carpet underfoot and all the other soft and shiny and luxuriously unmarred and unused surfaces of Oliver Seth's home. She wanted to go to work. She did not arrive at the restaurant each day hoping lunch would appear. She made it happen. If there were impediments, she overcame them. At Wildside, she reigned supreme, god of a small kitchen. Here she could do nothing but wait, wonder, regret. *Anna, what happened to you?*

"I ask you for your patience and cooperation in the coming days and weeks," said Sergeant Harvey. "Several of you may be asked to come into the station to respond to further questions. For those of you who live out of town, I request that you make whatever reasonable changes you can to your travel plans in order to stay in the vicinity for the next week at least. If you do plan to leave, the St. Helena Police Department would appreciate your notifying us of where you will be and how we can reach you."

The last time Sunny had seen Anna was in the hot tub, kissing Oliver. How long was she alive after that? What time was it when she overheard them fighting? Sunny had gone over it several times with the police. There was no way to know the exact time. Her watch had said one-fifteen when she went to bed and four o'clock when she heard the sobbing from upstairs. Certainly at four Anna was still alive, since Sunny had heard her crying. With a sickening feeling, she thought of the last time she jolted awake, early that morning. What was it that had woken her? Could it have been the sound of

Anna's body striking the pavement just a few feet from the French doors? Sunny looked around the room. In all probability, someone here knew exactly what had happened. The only one missing was Keith Lachlan.

Sergeant Harvey had stopped to confer with another officer. The room was silent. No one made eye contact or moved, as if doing so would be an admission of guilt. Sunny imagined Anna getting out of the hot tub and going to the master bedroom. What was she wearing when she had the fight with Oliver? A towel? Had she put the white dress back on? Or did she have some kind of negligee she slept in? If they knew what Anna was wearing when the gardener found her, it might suggest something about the minutes leading up to her death. Was she dressed, hair brushed, shoes on, as though ready to leave? Was she naked, torn suddenly from bed?

It was nearly six in the evening when they finally released everyone. Sunny climbed into her beat-up old pickup gratefully and headed down the hill. At a red light near town, her cell phone rang.

"Wade," she said, picking up with relief.

"What's up, sunshine? You've been off the radar all weekend."

"Long story."

"Care to tell it over dinner? Chavez is coming by in a minute and Lenstrom is on his way already."

"Thank God."

Wade cleared his throat. "He asked me if I thought it would be okay to ask you to cater the wedding."

"What did you tell him?"

"That I was pretty sure you'd be honored."

Silence. Their friend Monty Lenstrom had finally asked his longtime girlfriend, Annabelle, to marry him. Sunny had been dreading the inevitable catering request for weeks. Every time someone she knew got married, they assumed she'd prefer to work the wedding than to be a guest. It was a huge amount of work she always ended up doing at cost.

"Sun, I'm kidding," said Wade with a chuckle. "I told him to hire somebody and let you relax for a change."

"Not funny, Skord. Not tonight, anyway. I can't even think about dealing with Annabelle right now, of all the larger-than-life Bridezillas-to-be. It's bad enough I'm hosting the engagement dinner. What'd he say?"

"He said he was going to ask you the next chance he got. He was pretty sure you'd love the idea."

"Is the man blind, deaf, and dumb? Has he not been a witness to the week of sixteen-hour days the last friends' wedding cost me? All unpaid, I might add."

"So tell him no."

"Please. I've known him since he had hair."

"Then suck it up."

"I'll do the rehearsal dinner. And the snacks for the bridal party before. But I am not doing the dinner for two hundred people."

"Whatever. You two will have to sort that out. Get up here as soon as you can. We need to eat it, drink it, and clean it up by ten. It's a school night."

"Driving."

She hung up and accelerated past the string of gourmet-themed boutiques, antique shops, and restaurants, including her own, lined up along Main Street, otherwise known as Highway 29, the road to redemption in the form of Wade Skord and his mountain-top winery.

7

Sunny felt better already. From the moment she put her turn signal on and began the long chug up Howell Mountain, she felt that maybe the nightmare of the past twenty-four hours would finally end. What would she do without friends like Wade and Rivka and Monty? With a pang she thought of Anna. She'd asked for help and Sunny had failed her. Sunny had listened to her fight with Oliver, a man Anna had said frightened her, and had done nothing. Worse, she'd gone back to sleep as if nothing was wrong. Her instincts had failed her. She'd convinced herself Anna was being emotional and dramatic, when instead she needed help getting away from a dangerous situation. Now the unthinkable had happened and Sunny would have to live the rest of her life with the knowledge that she might have prevented it.

At the mailbox marked SKORD MOUNTAIN VINEYARD, she turned off the pavement and plunged down a steep ravine on a road rutted with potholes. Dust billowed up around the truck, chalking the air pale red in the failing light. At the bottom was Wake Skord's cabin. Judging by the collection of vehicles nosed around it, Rivka Chavez and Monty Lenstrom had already arrived. So much the better. Tonight Sunny wanted her friends close.

Wade's cat, Farber, leaped down from the railing with a thud and waited for her on the deck. Sunny scratched him between the ears and he bit her hand affectionately. Inside, they were already eating. Monty poured Sunny a glass of something ruby red. One of his pet Sonoma Coast Pinots. Rivka brought Sunny a plate and loaded it with salad, rice, and Chicken à la Wade.

Sunny had eaten dinner at Wade's plank table at least once a week for half a decade, more or less. During that time, he never cooked anything but the specialty of the house, which changed every year or so. In the beginning, it was a rib-sticking ground beef and potato concoction with raisins and green olives called Shepherd's Pie à la Wade, served with a jumbo bottle of green Tabasco. Later it was Tibetan Ginger Tofu Soup à la Wade. A few months ago, Chicken à la Wade started turning up. It involved a Dutch oven, stewed tomatoes, cubed prosciutto, fresh rosemary, and plenty of dry white wine. Comfort food. Tonight it had its work cut out for it.

"The specialty of the house," said Sunny. "My favorite."

"What'd you expect?" said Wade.

"Toast, fried eggs, and sardines?" said Sunny.

"Only for breakfast and lunch."

"I don't know how you keep from getting scurvy," said Monty.

"Chicken à la Wade has rosemary," said Wade. "That's green."

"I just realized something," said Rivka. "Shouldn't it be *Chicken au Wade*? Or *Chicken al Wade*. You being, for what it's worth, male."

"Cooking brings out my feminine side. Besides, no one calls me Al, and *au Wade* doesn't roll off the tongue the way *à la Wade* does."

"I'm ready for it to roll off my tongue for good," said Monty. "We've eaten this three times in as many weeks."

"That sounds like an invitation," said Wade. "Dinner at Monty's next Sunday."

Monty acquiesced. "Fine, I'll cook next time. We can do a roast chicken or pork loin with fennel pollen. I staked out a great new patch of wild fennel over the weekend. Easy access. No fence, no rabid dogs, no exhaust fumes. It's a good hundred yards from the road. Tall as my head."

"We should go big this year and package up a bunch to sell at the farmers' market," said Rivka.

"How big can you go with fennel pollen?" said Monty. "It takes a grocery bag full of flowers to make a spoonful of the stuff."

"So we do small packages. Everyone was asking me for more last year." Rivka looked at Sunny for support and her eyes lingered on her friend's face. "You got some color. Did you go biking?"

"I went to a pool party yesterday."

"And you're still wearing your swimsuit? That must have been some party."

Sunny looked down at the bikini and gauzy cover-up she was wearing. She'd forgotten. "Long story."

Rivka's eyes lit up. "I'll bet! Come on, dish. I want details. I need to live vicariously. I slept and pulled weeds most of the weekend."

"A pool party," said Monty. "That's so L.A. Were there cabana boys?"

"It wasn't a party exactly," said Sunny. "Just people over for a swim and lunch. No cabana boys, but they had just about everything else, including a full-time private chef and a kitchen that looked like something out of a design magazine and a huge Rothko in the living room. The real thing. Not to mention some pretty crazy wines. They must have pulled the cork on about three thousand dollars' worth of wine by the time the night was over, which was the least of what happened. I'm wiped out." For a moment she was tempted to leave it at that. A pool party at some rich friend's luxurious wine country getaway. Simple.

"And?" said Rivka. "There's more, I can tell."

"Not until after dinner," said Sunny. "I'm afraid it has a very unhappy ending."

"The old McCoskey knack for unhappy endings," said Monty. "Remind me not to invite you to my wedding. People have an uncanny tendency to drop dead when you're around."

"I've noticed," she said.

The conversation went on without her. When they'd finished eating, Wade said, "Now I want to hear why Sunny is all sunburned and silent, if she'll tell us."

Sunny nodded.

"If we're in for a long one, we have to clear the dishes first," said Rivka. "I can't concentrate with a plate of chicken bones staring at me."

When the table was cleared and their wineglasses filled, they settled into the living room, where Sunny told the basics of what had happened, starting with Anna Wilson's phone call Saturday morning inviting her over and ending with the gathering in the living room she'd just come from, in which Sergeant Harvey had suggested that none of them leave town or discuss details of the case until the initial investigation was complete. She left Andre Morales out of it, and skipped Sergeant Harvey's theory that Anna had been dead before the fall. A stunned silence followed.

"I thought I was joking," said Monty, removing his spectacles to polish them on a little cloth he took from his wallet. "You are definitely off the guest list."

Rivka gave Monty a look. "It has nothing to do with Sunny."

"Au contraire," said Wade. "It has everything to do with Sunny. This girl knew she was in danger. She said as much, right, Sun?"

"I guess so. It depends. She said she didn't know who her boyfriend was anymore, it was over, and she just wanted to get out of there. But a few hours later she was kissing him like everything was fine, and a couple hours after that they were fighting up a storm. At the time, it seemed like the usual 'he loves me, he loves me not' stuff to me. But none of that may have anything to do with her death, anyway. They don't even know how she died yet."

"They say they don't," said Monty. "I'll bet they know exactly how she died. They want the killer to slip up and reveal something only he would know."

"If she wanted a shoulder to cry on, she had this girl Jordan on the premises already," said Wade. "You guys hadn't talked in years. She's up there at the country house sweating bullets for whatever reason. She reads in the paper that her old pal McCoskey recently kicked the stuffing out of the most dangerous killer to come through town in decades. That's just the sort of friend a girl likes to have around when she's in the soup." Wade picked up a cookie from a plate Rivka put in front of him and aimed it at Sunny. "I say you were called in as reinforcements. This girl was scared. And for good reason, it turns out."

"And I let her down. Not only did I fail to help, I did absolutely nothing but drink her wine, eat her food, and go to sleep when she needed me. I heard enough to know there was some major domestic strife taking place upstairs and I did absolutely nothing."

"If you really think the boyfriend killed her, I'm glad you didn't go up there and get in the middle of it," said Rivka, getting up and going into the kitchen. She put water on to boil and came back. "In fact, if she weren't dead, rest her soul, I'd be cussing her out right now. She knew the guy. She knew he was dangerous. And she pulled you into it without so much as a warning. A good friend goes to the movie you want to see instead of the one she wants to see. A good friend does not ask you to stand between her and her homicidal boyfriend. Please. Who is this person?"

"You're assuming he killed her," said Sunny. "We don't know that. I assumed she OD'd, but the police are not treating it like an accidental death."

"Like I said," said Monty, "they know exactly what happened, but they don't want to show their hand."

"I still say it's not your job to straighten out somebody's life just because you knew them years ago," said Rivka, "and it was crummy of her to pull you into it in the first place. I don't get why you hung around."

"I kept asking myself that. It was just like the old days. I felt responsible for her. Like, as the sensible one, I should try to make sure everything was okay. Besides, she creates this aura of exclusivity—you feel privileged to be there. And it was hot and the pool was beautiful and they were serving good food and wine. Then after a while I was too sloppy to drive and I figured I might as well relax. I just wish I'd done something. Even just call the police before it was too late."

"It sounds like she made it her business to take risks," said Rivka. "Are you supposed to bodily prevent her from smoking and drinking and doing drugs? She's a grown-up. She had a noisy fight with her boyfriend that ended in tears. Happens every day. Who died and made you her guardian angel? Oh, sorry. Strike that. I just mean you shouldn't feel guilty for not saving her from herself."

"Yes, but everyone needs help sometimes. If I'd gone up there to see what was going on, she might be alive."

"And if a butterfly in the Amazon had flapped its wings a little harder, maybe it wouldn't have happened at all," said Rivka. "You can't hold yourself responsible for this. No matter what happened to her, there is no guarantee you could have saved her even if you'd broken down the door like freakin' Batgirl. You might even have gotten yourself killed. Who knows."

"You're getting off track," said Monty. "Batgirl wouldn't break down a door and McCoskey herself said the cops are not treating this like an accident. Ergo, suspicious death, as in murder. This is not about what McCoskey might have done. It's not that cute. This is murder. Somebody at the nice little pool party decided to off the hostess. Who? Sun, run through the guest list again."

"I bet it takes weeks for them to figure out what happened," said Wade. "It will take days just to figure out what drugs she was on, if any, right, Sun?"

"I suppose so. I don't know why this stuff keeps happening to me."

"Competence," said Wade. "That's one of the ironies of life. The more competent you are, the more trouble you attract because people come to you for help."

"The guest list," said Monty.

"Me. Anna Wilson. Oliver Seth," said Sunny. "That's Anna's boyfriend."

"He's the guy who owned the house."

"Right."

"Person of interest number one," said Monty. "What's he like? Fat, old, and hairy in all the wrong places, no doubt."

"Hardly. Young, thin, good looking. But not nice. Cold. And I'd say he has a temper."

"Like I said, person of interest numero uno. Next."

The kettle whistled and Rivka went to make tea. Wade interrupted to continue his line of thinking. "I've been noticing lately that irony explains some of the more puzzling truths in life. Only the good die young. Ironic. The wealthy are notoriously cheap. Ironic. The gentlest guys are the great big dudes with biceps like tree trunks. Ironic. Revolutionaries eventually start to act like dictators. Ironic. It goes on and on." He searched their faces for encouragement, got none, and continued anyway. "What if the core nature of the universe isn't love, as the movies would have it, but irony? It is the one sure way to keep things balanced. If one side gets too dominant, it flips over and becomes its opposite. If God has a sense of humor—and you don't have to look very far to see that must be the case—then irony is the ideal way to jerk the rug out from under the bullies. It's a great way to mess with people. You can search and strive and fight and scratch your way along for thirty years looking for a treasure, and you'll only find it when you give up and decide treasure is worthless, anyway. Irony. The great cosmic equalizer."

"Skord, you are making my head hurt," said Monty.

Rivka returned with a teapot and honey and went back for cups and spoons. Monty followed her and returned carrying a white pastry box tied with a pink silk ribbon. "Ironically, considering I don't even like dessert," he said, "I was down at the Ferry Building in the city today and brought back one of those chocolate cakes with the marshmallow puddle on top. No frosting, no pain. Anyone have room?"

"Always," said Rivka.

"We can circle back to the irony angle," said Sunny, looking at Wade dubiously. "I like Monty's approach. I need to think this through."

"Exactly," said Monty, heading back to the kitchen. He returned with a knife, plates, and forks. "Who's next?"

"Franco Bertinotti, the winemaker at Oliver Seth's winery. He and Seth seemed to be friends as well as employer and employee. He's about a century older than Anna's friend Jordan, but he kept holding her hand. He was holding her hand when we were all together in the living room this afternoon."

"Stranger things have happened," said Wade.

"Here's one of them," said Sunny. "She was also snuggled up in the hot tub with Keith Lachlan and the Guamanian princess."

"Ménage à trois?" said Rivka, gasping.

"At least," said Sunny. "Things were definitely getting interesting when I got out."

"Good thing you left," said Wade, looking askance.

"You lost me with the Guamanian princess," said Monty.

"Oliver's lawyer, Keith Lachlan, has a girlfriend, Marissa, who comes from Guam. She arrived at Oliver's house late last night. Not a real princess, or at least she wasn't wearing her tiara, and she certainly didn't kill anybody. She couldn't overpower a turnip. Tiny little thing with wrists like celery sticks. Next. Molly Seth, Oliver's sister, was there with her boyfriend, a guy named Jared. Bollinger, I think. Who turned out to be some kind of ex-boyfriend of Anna's, but she didn't know it."

"Anna?" said Monty.

"No, Molly," said Sunny. "Hello, pay attention. How could Anna not know her own ex-boyfriend?"

"Right. Back up a second. What about this Lachlan guy? How's he look?"

"Big guy. Huge, actually. Like six-four or -five. Caribbean originally but seemed pretty Americanized. He and Seth are always together, apparently. He went back to San Francisco late last night, before Anna died."

"How do you know?" asked Rivka.

"I heard Marissa tell Franco he left right after they got out of the hot tub. I heard Anna and Oliver fighting long after that, so he couldn't have killed her. And there was another guy staying at the house, a British artist named Troy Stevens. A friend, or rather ex-boyfriend, of Anna's."

"He's famous," said Monty. "I've heard of him."

"I think he's still in love with her."

"She's got her boyfriend and two exes in the same house," said Rivka. "Sounds messy. Anyone else?"

"Just the people who work there. A woman named Cynthia Meyers who is Oliver's private chef—good cook—and the gardener who found Anna. His name is Mike Sayudo. He was in the living room today before the police let us go, but I didn't meet him." Sunny poured herself a cup of tea and stirred in a spoonful of honey. "I'm sure there are other people who work there, probably plenty of them. It must take a dozen people to maintain that place. But it was the weekend and those were the only two around."

"As far as you know," said Monty. "Who knows who may have been in that house after dark. I'm sure there are plenty of places to hide."

And bedrooms, thought Sunny. She had decided to leave Andre Morales off the list of suspects. It was just too embarrassing to go into right now.

"Don't talk like that," said Rivka. "You'll give her nightmares. And me."

"I guess we can't entirely discount the idea of some random or even not-so-random person showing up," said Sunny. "But it seems doubtful to me. That place would be hard to break into. There's a security gate and surveillance cameras everywhere. Besides, it would be a very odd coincidence, since Anna already felt she was in danger. No, I would assume the obvious—that Seth killed her—except he's too smart. He wouldn't push his girlfriend out a window after a big fight and then hang around while the police try to decide what happened. The guy has more brains than that."

"Anybody can lose his temper," said Rivka. "Maybe he snapped."

"Maybe. In any case, the police will get the security tapes and the lab reports and track down what happened and who's responsible.

I'm inclined to think it was one of the guys at the party. Seth. Franco. The artist. Jared Bollinger. Like you said, it was a messy situation. Drugs, alcohol, and who knows what kind of grudges or jealousies were brewing. Knowing what happened won't bring Anna back, but at least they won't get away with it."

"Sounds like you're planning to stay out of it," said Wade. "I'm glad to hear that."

"Why wouldn't she?" said Monty. "Sun doesn't know anything more about what happened than anyone else, she's not in any danger, and nobody she knows stands to be accused. For once, it's not her problem." He handed Sunny a slice of cake.

"I have no desire to get any more involved than I already am," said Sunny. "I'm going home after I finish this piece of cake and I'm going to have a good cry and a bath and try to forget this weekend ever happened."

Rivka frowned and looked around. "I hate to be the one to break the bad news, but you guys are overlooking one small detail. Sunny is not only involved in this girl's death; if she turns out to have been murdered, Sunny could be a suspect. From the way you tell it, it sounds like you were in exactly the wrong place at precisely the wrong time without anyone to corroborate your story."

"You're right," said Monty, eyes wide behind his glasses. "No alibi. I never thought of that."

Sunny looked at Rivka and reached for her cup of tea. Monty's marshmallow chocolate cake had suddenly become too sticky to swallow.

8

Home by ten, asleep by ten-thirty, up at five, at work by five-thirty, just like a normal day. Sunny McCoskey sat in her office at the back of the restaurant, reviewing the new menu before printing it out on the restaurant's special stationery with the letterpress logo. Someone knocked at the back door.

"It's open!"

The screen door banged and an instant later Ted the fish guy stuck his bushy mustache into the office. He was pulling a dolly behind him with a cooler bungeed to it.

"Usual place?"

"Usual place."

He came back and handed her a clipboard with an invoice on it. She read. "Forty filets of fresh salmon?"

"Beautiful stuff."

"But forty filets? As in sides? That's, like, eighty pounds? That's, like, a week's supply, if it lasted that long."

"I wondered what you were doing with it. Can't take it back now. You're my last stop." He flipped through the clipboard papers and pointed to the order for forty filets of salmon.

"It's a mistake. We never order that much. Can't you call around and see if somebody will take half of it off my hands?"

"No time. But if anybody calls looking for more, I'll send them your way."

She sighed. "How did this happen?"

"You got me. I just catch it, clean it, ice it, serenade it, and deliver it before the coffee gets cold. Ordering is up to you all."

"Right. Okay. Well, we'll be serving salmon today, I guess."

"Not a bad idea."

Sunny shook her head. Eighty pounds of fresh salmon. They'd have today and tomorrow to sell it. By tomorrow night it would be over, at least as far as the restaurant was concerned. They could divide what was left among the staff. She looked at the menu in front of her. It was going to need some changes. Salmon carpaccio followed by filet of salmon followed by planked salmon, poached salmon, salmon ravioli, salmon mousse, and salmon soufflé.

Rivka arrived an hour later. She came into the office pushing her old beach cruiser and leaned it against Sunny's. On warm days like this, they both rode their bikes to the restaurant. Rivka was wearing what she always wore to work, rain or shine. Today the jeans were black and the tank top was red, presumably chosen to match the swooping blue and red swallows she had tattooed on the back of each arm.

"Absolutely perfect morning out there," said Rivka, catching her breath and checking herself in the mirror behind the door. Her long black hair was braided and wound into tight little mounds behind each ear. She smoothed down the baby hairs in front and turned back to Sunny.

"Did you check the Web site's e-mail account?"

"Not yet," said Sunny. "Did you order forty filets of fresh salmon?"

"We need to check it every morning from now on," said Rivka. "Over the weekend I installed a button that lets people request reservations online."

"Salmon?"

"Yes, I ordered the salmon. Forty pounds. I ordered a little more than usual because there are so many reservations on the book this week. And that last batch was so pretty."

"You ordered forty *filets*. There's eighty pounds of sockeye in the walk-in looking for a home."

"Oh. I must have gotten it mixed up. Eighty pounds is a lot of fish."

"That's right, Pocahontas. Tell Bertrand to tell everybody to sell salmon. Nobody gets out of here without ordering the salmon today. And anybody who gets *un amuse-bouche* compliments of the chef is going to be amused by salmon."

"Got it."

Rivka retreated to the kitchen and Sunny went back to the morning's paperwork. The Wildside Web site still made her a little uneasy. More than anything else about the business she was in, she liked the tangibility of cooking. There was nothing virtual about Wildside. Nothing artificial, faux, or simulated. No tromp l'oeil, no mock anything, no substitutions, no compromise. Her explicit intention had always been to make Wildside a tiny refuge of authenticity in an age of illusion, a time when food that smells like strawberry and tastes like strawberry is more likely to be guar gum and corn syrup. Having a Web site seemed to encroach, however slightly, on that authenticity. If she could cut the phone lines and insist that people show up in person and wait for a table without going out of business, she would do it.

Rivka, on the other hand, was determined to bring Wildside into the twenty-first century. Sunny opened the e-mail account Rivka had set up for inquiries coming through the Web site. A dialogue box said it was "downloading one of one messages." One reservation. Not exactly a crowd, but it was a start. The return address caught her eye. The e-mail had been sent by Oliver Seth at two-twenty in the morning. Sunday morning. The same morning Anna Wilson died. The subject line read "FW: Roma!" There was a brief message.

> *Sunny, this is why I'm leaving. It's all in the picture. I'll explain later. Suffice to say, my world has come apart. Please keep this safe for me. Call it an insurance policy. I must control my fate!!! Mum for now. Will call soon.*
> *Wils*

Wils was what Sunny had called Anna years ago. She scrolled down. There was a series of e-mails between Oliver and someone named Astrid. Sunny jumped to the bottom and skimmed up chronologically. They'd been sent over the past month, some quite recently, and talked about an upcoming business meeting with executives from a bank in Moscow that was interested in funding one of Oliver's new technology ventures. Then there was this from Astrid:

> *Darling, I've had the strangest dream this morning. We were in a ferry somewhere in the Greek Isles. The weather was glorious—that Mediterranean blue sky you love so much—but I was terribly afraid the boat would sink. You told me I was a fool to worry over nothing, that I would make the other passengers nervous. I knew if we could just get within sight of land, everything would be okay. Then we could swim if we had to. Without warning, an enormous wave swamped the boat and it sank quickly and completely. We treaded water. I was terrified the waves would separate us. You were angry with me and pushed me away. You said, "I told you not to be afraid. Now look what you've done!"*

Oliver wrote back, "Do not worry. Let them make waves. This boat is not going to sink, I promise you." There was an attachment, a photograph of Oliver in his gold aviators and a trim suit with his arm around a dark-haired woman in a white minidress. Not Anna, presumably Astrid. Rome. They stood in front of a tiny canary-yellow sports car at dusk. The Coliseum was in the background. It was summer, judging by their clothes and Astrid's tanned shoulders, and they looked extremely happy. Probably this summer, since Oliver was still wearing those same sunglasses. Guys like him lost or updated the accoutrements around their person frequently. Never the same sunglasses, cuff links, or phones for long.

Sunny examined the photograph more closely. Something about it reminded her of the old photographs of Frank Sinatra and Mia Farrow getting married in Las Vegas. Maybe it was the white trapeze dress or the modish suit Oliver was wearing. Maybe it was the aura of glamour they exuded. Life looked very good. Sunny pushed her chair back and stared up at Rusty, the wire rooster who presided over the room from the top of the bookcase. What was she to make of this? The e-mail had been sent from Oliver Seth's account, but it was from Anna, she was sure of that. The note was Anna's voice, and anyway, she'd never heard anyone else call her Wils. So that was the genesis of Saturday night's fight. After finding the surveillance system the night before, on Saturday night Anna had somehow gotten into Oliver's e-mail and found out about his relationship with Astrid. The brief exchange and the photograph made it clear he had another love, another life. And there must have been other e-mails, probably dozens of them. Anna would have been left with no hope that Oliver was anything but a deeply deceitful and dishonest person.

Sunny scrolled back through the exchange. At one point Oliver wrote, presumably referring to the photograph, "See attached.

Remember to control your fate. She's bullish on the new vintage." That must have been what Anna was referring to in her note when she said she must control her fate. But what did Oliver mean by "She's bullish on the new vintage"? Europa, certainly. Europa was pictured riding a bull on the label of Oliver's new wine, Taurus Rising. Sunny had seen it when Oliver himself showed it to her at lunch on Saturday. But what did that mean? Was it some kind of code or riddle? Whatever it was, Astrid had understood. She replied, "Got it," and went on to another topic.

Sunny printed out two sets of the e-mail, including the photograph. She sealed one set in an envelope for Sergeant Harvey and put it in her bag. The police would get the e-mails, but they would have to wait until the lunch rush was over. The other set she tucked into a tattered old copy of Richard Olney's *Simple French Food* for safekeeping, returning it to its place on the shelf under Rusty's watchful eye. Anna's insurance policy had failed as utterly as her attempt to control her fate, but Sunny would keep them all the same—at least until the police figured out exactly who was responsible for her death, and why.

Why had Anna sent the e-mails, anyway? Did she hope to use them against Oliver somehow? For money, even? Or did she only want to keep some tangible proof that he was unfaithful to her, to show she was not imagining his lies and infidelities? She reread Anna's message. *Call it an insurance policy.* She must have suspected she was in danger, but why? When you find out your boyfriend is a cheat and a liar, you're upset, not frightened. Anna had a reckless nonchalance about life and love, not to mention fidelity. Another woman would make her laugh or leave, not take out the only insurance available to her. There had to be something else in those e-mails. *It's all in the picture.* There must be something there she wasn't seeing. She needed to read them more carefully and try to see what Anna had seen. Sunny checked her watch. With eighty reservations on the books plus walk-ins, she had already burned more time than she could spare. It would have to wait until she got home in the afternoon.

"Anything?" said Rivka from the threshold.

"What?"

"Reservations from the site."

"Reservations? Oh, no, nothing so far."

"Well, it's only been up a few days. Build it and they will come."

Rivka went back to work and Sunny put on one of the white canvas smocks she wore when she cooked. What on earth had Anna found, snooping through Oliver's e-mail? Sunny tied her apron strings and looked in the mirror.

"Mum for now," she said, and headed into the kitchen.

9

Rivka changed the wooden sign to CLOSED and locked the door. She went over to the zinc bar that separated the tiny dining room from the kitchen and lay her cheek down on the cool surface. "That has to be a record," she said. "I've never cooked so much or so fast in my life."

Sunny stood on the other side, eating a plate of poached salmon. "I should testify in murder trials more often."

"Careful what you wish for. Do you think it's going to keep up like this?"

"I thought you wanted more business. You're the one who wants to open on nights and weekends," said Sunny.

"Doesn't more help usually go along with more business?" said Rivka.

"You have to make the money to pay for it first. If everything goes well and you survive long enough, then you hire more people. They call it sweat equity."

Bertrand, the slender, white-shirted maître d', sommelier, and gardener at Wildside, walked by Rivka and swatted her arm with a damp rag. "Up, slave girl. You haven't finished your chores."

"I can't move. I need a glass of white wine with two ice cubes in it. Please."

He went behind the bar and poured a glass. "I'll serve, but I'm not putting ice cubes in it. It's chilled, for God's sake."

"Cubes, please, I beg you."

"*Pauvre petite fille riche*," crooned Bertrand. "Here are your damn cubes. You want a scoop of ice cream in there to go with it?"

Sunny turned up the music. It had been a grueling day and the end was the hardest, when there was so much cleaning to do. She hefted a tub of ice out of the oyster bar, dumped it in the back sink, and came back for the next one. When that was done, she started wiping down the workstations. Rivka tackled the grill, scraping the hot surface with water and a metal spatula. Greasy steam billowed up around her. When the grit was gone, she sliced lemons in half and rubbed down the hot stainless steel until it was silver and shiny.

"You want to get a drink after this?" said Sunny. She'd been quiet all day about the e-mails and Andre and everything else on her mind. It was easy while the restaurant was busy. Between the two of them, they could just keep up if there were no distractions. Now the restaurant was empty and she needed to talk.

"As long as it's not alcohol," said Rivka. "I'm on the one-drink-a-day plan all week and I just finished it."

"Taylor's?"

"Perfect."

It took another hour to finish up and get out of there. The dishwashers were still hosing down the floor mats and mopping the tile when they left. They rode their bikes single file past stalled rush-hour traffic for a mile on Highway 29, provoking the occasional appreciative hoot from guys stuck in their pickup trucks. At Taylor's, Rivka staked out a picnic table on the grass while Sunny ordered green-tea milkshakes and garlic fries. They ate and brushed away flies, soaking up the last of the late-afternoon sun.

"How you holding up?" said Rivka.

"Okay," said Sunny.

"And? You look like you have something on your mind."

"I do. Something happened over the weekend. I left it out last night. So much happened all at once."

Rivka ate fries and waited.

Sunny looked around at the trampled grass and picnic tables under the big trees. The loudspeaker squawked someone's order number.

"Well, are you going to tell me?"

Sunny nodded.

Rivka ate a few more fries. Finally she dug in her knapsack and handed Sunny a folded-up newspaper. "I wasn't going to show you this, but maybe it will help. There's no need to keep things secret now."

The headline across the valley's daily paper read DRUG-FUELED SEX PARTY ENDS IN SUSPICIOUS DEATH. It described how Anna Wilson was found and listed the names of those involved, including "acclaimed local chefs and restaurateurs Andre Morales of Yountville's Vinifera and Sonya 'Sunny' McCoskey of Wildside in St. Helena."

"That's it. I'm going to have to move. Wildside has been weird enough since the last incident."

"You mean the Liberty Dock murder?"

"You've seen what's been going on. People used to ask to see me so they could give their compliments to the chef, say a lot of nice things about how they've been looking forward to having lunch at Wildside for their anniversary for the last three years, all that. Now they want to talk about Ronald Fetcher's trial."

"It'll pass. Nobody remembers that stuff for very long."

Sunny put her hand over her eyes. "It's going to be a freak show where the nymphomaniac drug addict chef performs daily."

"Hmm . . . That could be a problem. Not terribly appetizing. You'll have to make a big show of washing your hands."

Sunny folded the paper and pushed it away.

"I can't remember the last time I went to a drug-fueled sex party," said Rivka. "I never get invited to the good stuff."

"Don't believe everything you read."

"So there weren't drugs?"

"I don't know. Probably there were. I didn't see any. But Keith Lachlan, Oliver's lawyer, offered me coke. And I'm pretty sure Anna and a few others were on something. Coke, maybe Ecstasy, who knows. Anna was acting very strangely. No one seemed interested in sleeping even though it was really late. And they got very, uh, affectionate at a certain point. That's Ecstasy, right?"

"Could be. But it seems unlikely if they were drinking. You don't mix vitamin E with alcohol or you're in for a very unpleasant ride. If they do drugs, they would know that."

"They were definitely drinking wine and cognac earlier in the evening, not so much later on. The chemistry changed. Nobody seemed drunk. Just, you know, festive."

"Festive."

"Around midnight they were all in the hot tub, like I told you about last night. It was crazy. There were tongues everywhere."

"They?" Rivka raised her eyebrows.

"Okay, we."

"I'm sure that went over well with the patented McCoskey fear of intimacy."

"I got out of there pretty quickly."

"I'll bet." Rivka tapped the newspaper with her finger. "You didn't say Andre was there."

"That's what I wanted to talk to you about. After all the hot-tub business, the next morning I go hunting for my clothes—"

"Uh, sounds like you left something out."

"I went to bed. My clothes got hijacked by Seth's sister and her boyfriend."

"Explain."

"That part doesn't matter. Just listen. It's hard enough to talk about it."

"Go on. I'm listening."

"So the next morning I go looking for my clothes. I knock on the door of the room where I left them, and guess who opens the door."

"Don't say it," said Rivka.

Sunny nodded.

"Alone?"

Sunny shook her head. "He was with the Guamanian princess."

"Wait, which one is she?"

"The one who came late. The lawyer's girlfriend."

"The coke dealer's girl?"

Sunny nodded.

"You're sure."

"He answered the door in a towel. Though, in all fairness, I knocked on the door in a sheet." Sunny gave a weak laugh.

Rivka dragged another garlic fry through ketchup and put it in her mouth, chewing thoughtfully. "Well, damn. That was some party."

"I don't know where I am anymore. It's like I'm living in some sleazy parallel universe where everything is completely messed up."

"Don't worry, you're still right here in wineland, Auntie Em. Even if things have gotten a little weird." She shook her head sympathetically. "And you can't even get upset about it because your friend upstaged your breakup by going off and getting herself killed."

Sunny looked away.

"Was he there all day yesterday?"

"In the same room."

"And you didn't say anything to him or kick him in the shins or anything?"

"How could I? Anna is dead. There were cops there trying to figure out who killed her. It was not the best time for relationship drama."

"I would have lost it."

"We Vulcans cannot relate to you illogical humans," said Sunny.

Rivka sighed. "And just when we were beginning to pry little Sonya from her shell. It's a shame."

"I'm almost glad I'm too exhausted and traumatized to think about it," said Sunny. "Maybe it was all a misunderstanding, anyway. Maybe she's his long-lost sister."

"Maybe you can work it out."

"You think so?"

"Do you?"

They finished their milkshakes. After a while Rivka said, "I know you're not feeling very good about this right now, but Andre Morales isn't exactly the Prince Charming we want for our Sunny. The guy is a player. He may be hot, but he's been an inconsiderate ass all along, if you want my opinion. When all this blows over, you're going to be better off without him. You know that, right?"

Sunny made a face and took a napkin. She pressed it into her eyes and blew her nose, telling herself she was not, not going to fall apart at Taylor's like a jerk.

"You okay?"

"Close enough."

Rivka looked at her watch. "I have to get going. The Jamaican herbalist is going to be waiting for me." Recently Rivka had been dating a guy with big curls and a stall at the farmers' market.

"Now he's an herbalist?"

"He wants to start selling healing herbs from the mountains down there. He's got some growing in his backyard. I've been trying them out. Pretty good stuff."

"Not the usual herb, I hope."

"That market is pretty well saturated. These are teas you drink if you get a cold or a stomachache."

"The coke dealer—I mean Oliver's lawyer, Keith—is Caribbean, too. From Barbados."

"Let's not get them together," said Rivka, turning her bike around. "That guy sounds like trouble. Speaking of Jason, he's cooking Ital food at Wade's tomorrow night. You in?"

"I wouldn't miss it. What's an Ital?"

"In this case, oxtail and plantains. Or maybe curry chicken."

"On it."

She watched Rivka bump across the lawn to a side street and disappear down the road. She'd forgotten to tell her about the e-mail from Anna.

The traffic was still in a snarl on Main. Between people in parked cars opening doors and people pulling out of parking spots and frustrated drivers deciding at the last second to shoot down a side street, it was too dangerous to try on a bike. Sunny took the side streets toward home and kept going to the police station just outside of town. The woman behind the bulletproof glass had a swimmer's physique and greenish-blond hair. She told Sunny to take a seat while she tried to find Sergeant Harvey. Sunny heard her radio his car and Sergeant Harvey respond that he was a couple of blocks away and to ask Sunny to sit tight. The woman looked up. "Got it," said Sunny. She stared at the door, waiting for Sergeant

Harvey to come through it. He came from the offices behind her instead and made her jump.

"McCoskey! What can I do for you?" He had a manila folder in one hand and was working his pager with the other.

"Sorry to drop in on you," said Sunny. "I know you're busy with the new case. Do you have a few minutes to talk in private?"

"Come on back into the office. How you doing? You get any sleep yet?"

"Not much."

"Me neither."

They walked down a hall and into a tiny office, where he offered her a pinkish-gray metal folding chair. The filing cabinets were a pinkish, fleshy brown, too, like certain kinds of intestines and the underbellies of a couple of inedible mushrooms she could think of. The room's only window looked back on the murky hallway and the offices opposite. Spending more than a few minutes in a room like this would drive anyone to suicide, thought Sunny, or a life of crime. Most of the furniture was the color of some sort of offal. Even the telephone was a muddy beige. It was like being inside a giant gut. It was tragedy so maudlin it was almost funny. One more chip out of the dirty coffee mug on the faux-walnut desk with its laminate buckling, one more stack of yellowing paperwork on top of the scratched-up filing cabinets, and the room would achieve comedy through farce. She shifted in the miserable chair and it gave a metallic groan. Was St. Helena really so bad off that they couldn't afford a real chair for Sergeant Harvey's visitors to sit in? Couldn't the department pool their funds, rent a van one Saturday, and go requisitioning at the nearest Ikea? Sergeant Harvey grabbed a stack of pink phone messages left on his desk and shuffled through them. Probably he never gave the surroundings a second thought.

Or he might even like making his visitors suffer. Certainly no one would be tempted to linger.

"Chop-chop, McCoskey. I'm up to my ears," he said without looking up.

"Right. So, as you might imagine, it's about Anna Wilson."

"She have a drug problem as far as you know? Addict?"

"Recreational. Nothing serious, at least back when I hung out with her enough to say for sure."

"How long ago was that?"

"About four years."

"What happened? Why'd you lose contact?"

"We both lived in San Francisco. Then she went to Europe and I came up here. We talked and e-mailed a couple of times since then, but Saturday was the first time I'd seen her."

"What made her call you up all of a sudden after so long?"

"Like I said yesterday, I'm not exactly sure. Maybe just a friendly visit, maybe something more."

"Such as?"

"She seemed to be having some difficulties with her boyfriend and she needed moral support from her friends."

"Is that what she said, 'moral support'?"

"She didn't use those exact words."

"So she might have been interested in actual support, as in a buffer between her and someone else who had become abusive or who she considered potentially violent. A witness, at least."

"It's possible, but there were plenty of people around, if that's what she was after. The guy she shares a place with in Barcelona, Troy Stevens, was staying there at the house. And Franco, the winemaker for Taurus Rising, Seth's winery. He wasn't particularly a friend of hers, more of Oliver's, but he was staying with them, too. And her friend Jordan was there when I arrived, though I think she'd just driven up for the day from the city. Even without inviting me up, she knew she wasn't going to be alone in the house with Oliver anytime soon." Sunny waited until he looked up from the papers on his desk. "We went over all this yesterday, didn't we?"

"It doesn't hurt to go over it again. I was going to ask you to come down here for that purpose tomorrow or the next day, anyway. I know yesterday was a shocker. No offense, but you looked pretty ragged when we talked up there. I figured I'd give you a couple of days to get your head together."

"Thanks."

Sergeant Harvey penciled some notes on a piece of paper and went on talking without looking up. "I knew that fancy-pants boyfriend of yours was going to be trouble."

"The fancy pants usually are."

"Speaking of fancy pants, I think I have something of yours." He opened a drawer in his desk and tossed a Ziploc bag across the desk. "I believe these belong to you."

Her bra and underwear were inside. Sunny stuffed them in the messenger bag she used as a purse. "Thanks. Where'd you find them?"

"Laundry room. Rolled up in a towel."

"How'd you know they were mine?"

"I'm a cop. Besides, who else would wear that stuff?"

"What's wrong with it?"

"Come on, McCoskey. Dingy cotton knickers and a training bra with a hole in it? Technically, they're evidence, but seeing as they're not of much consequence to the investigation, I figure I might as well return them."

"I appreciate that."

"Not that it's any of my business, McCoskey, but you need a real man in your life, not a pretty boy just passing through."

Sunny rolled her eyes. "Thank you for your concern, but I think you happen to be wrong in this case. I diagnose too much testosterone in the current model, not a shortage of. If I ever go shopping for a man again, I will be looking for a wilty little thing I can keep in line with a stern glance."

"Don't confuse the trimming for the tree is all I'm saying."

"Point taken. Choose a simple, manly tree. To get back to the more pertinent issue I came to see you about?"

"Go ahead."

Sunny took the envelope out of her bag and handed it to him. "This morning when I got to work I found these messages in my e-mail. The photograph was attached. Anna forwarded them early Sunday morning. She sent them to the generic contact address on Wildside's Web site from Oliver Seth's e-mail account."

He frowned, flipping through the pages. "How do you know it was her who sent it?"

"I thought of that. I guess there's no way to know for sure, but it sounds like her. And she signed it Wils. That's what I used to call her. Maybe other people call her that, too, but I've never heard them. I think it's from her."

Sergeant Harvey nodded. "She send anything else?"

"Just that."

"Nothing else attached?"

"Nope. You guys get any word back on the autopsy?"

"Nothing definite yet."

"Anything indefinite?"

He stood up and went over to where the window to the outside world should have been. Instead, there was a poster reproduction of an oil painting of a bald eagle in flight over a rocky chasm and several framed certificates. "It's too soon to know much for sure. No cause of death as yet. I disclosed the main issue to you already, which is that, in my opinion, she was dead before the fall. Nothing from the coroner on that yet, either. They're still checking what kind of drugs, if any, were in her system, but that's going to take some time."

"So, in theory, it could still be an overdose."

"In theory."

"Not your theory."

"No."

Sunny raised her eyebrows. "Because . . . "

He went back to his chair behind the desk. "For now this goes nowhere beyond this room."

"You have my word."

"We'll do a press conference once everything is confirmed. Until you read it in the paper, you know nothing."

"Right."

"You say nothing."

"Right."

"Because I will know the source immediately."

"Got it. *No digo nada.*"

He locked eyes with her. "I expect the coroner to come back with suffocation. There were no big marks or injuries or signs of any major blows as far as I could tell. The only trauma looked to have been sustained in the fall from the window. However, the skin around her mouth looked slightly abraded, and there was an area on her upper lip that showed some superficial damage. She also had a bruise on one of her wrists. She was slight in build, not particularly muscular, and according to you and others, under the influence of some combination of drugs and alcohol. It stands to reason that anybody reasonably strong could have overpowered her."

"Overpowered her, thus the bruise, and stuffed something in her mouth, thus the abrasions?"

"That's what I'm thinking. They might have put some kind of tape over her mouth to keep her quiet. Something strong, like duct tape. It was late. She might have been asleep when the attack occurred, which of course would make everything easier."

"Or passed out." Sunny shuddered.

Sergeant Harvey nodded. His mobile phone rang. "Excuse me."

Sunny stared at the eagle poster while he took the call, listened, and said, "I'll be right there."

"Sunny, we're going to have to finish this another time. I'll contact you tomorrow. Meanwhile, the information I've shared with you is to remain strictly confidential."

"You can trust me."

"I know. That's why I do."

———————————

Weeds poked through the fence in front of Sunny's house and the rosebushes reached spiny arms over the sidewalk. She could smell them even before she reached the gate. It was good to be home. She pushed her bike through and was startled to see Oliver Seth. He stood up from the stoop.

"Sorry, I didn't mean to scare you. I tried the restaurant but you'd already left. I was hoping we could talk about an issue that's come up."

He looked tense but rested. There were no shadows under his eyes, nothing disheveled about his fresh-looking shirt and trousers, but his mouth was a straight line and he was frowning against the sunset.

"I'd ask you in, but it's so nice out," said Sunny.

"That's fine. We can talk here."

Sunny put the kickstand down on the bike and sat opposite him on the stoop. The gold sunglasses from the photograph were hanging from his shirt. He put his hands together the way she'd often seen businesspeople do, like they were about to bow in Japanese style. Maybe that's where the gesture had come from. Seth's hands were extremely clean. It appeared that he'd just had a manicure. His cuticles were neat, the nails buffed and shiny.

"The last couple of days must have been pretty rough for you," said Sunny.

"This is not a pleasant business," said Oliver. "Not for me, not for you. Not for anyone. But there are some aspects of what's happening that we can still control. Keep from getting worse."

"Such as?"

"Sunny, I'm going to put my cards on the table. I know about the e-mails Anna sent you. That's what I've come to talk with you about. I want to explain what was going on between us so that you'll understand what those e-mails mean, and what they don't mean. Anna and I had a big blowup the night she died. She had gotten into my e-mail and read through a lot of my personal correspondence and I was very angry about it. I thought, and I still think, she had no right to do that. No one does. The last thing I said to her was that I thought she should go back to Barcelona as soon as possible. Then I stormed off. I didn't see her again until . . . "

He closed his eyes and pinched the bridge of his nose as though fighting tears. Sunny wondered if the display of emotion was genuine or contrived for her benefit. It seemed too sudden to be real. But grief was like that sometimes. He looked up at her and went on. "Until the next morning, when I had to identify her body for the police.

"You can't imagine how terrible that was. I always thought we could work things out. Even after the fight, I assumed we would right ourselves. We always have. I was angry that night, but by morning, I had decided to try to make things work. We'd been partying too much lately. Life was getting out of hand. Anna was never someone to do anything halfway. We had that in common, I guess. I figured we'd take things slower, try to get grounded, maybe get some help, and everything would be okay."

"You're telling me you think Anna had a drug problem?"

"We had several problems. That was one of them."

"And the others? Oliver, I've read the e-mails. I know you were seeing someone else. Anna guessed it and she was right."

"Like I said, some of the problems were mine. This isn't about blame. I came here tonight to make sure you understand that the e-mails Anna forwarded to you represent extremely personal conversations between me and a woman who works for me with whom I am very close. For Anna, coming out of context, and in the state of mind she was in when she read them, they were understandably upsetting. But you have to put everything in context. I've always been fond of Anna, but we've never been seriously involved. We'd meet for a week here or there, whenever it was convenient for both of us. There was no pretense of exclusivity or anything permanent, it was just fun. That arrangement was mutual. The decision to try to be together in a more serious way was also mutual, and very recent. We'd just started talking about trying to have a real relationship a month or so ago. In the last couple of weeks, she started getting more and more obsessed with my supposed infidelity, conveniently overlooking her own, incidentally.

"We weren't perfect. Anna had vices, and so do I. But we had complementary vices, you might say. We fit each other. We understood each other, or I thought we did. I loved that I could take her anywhere and we would have a great time. She could walk into the dullest dinner party known to humanity and get everyone to open up. Art snobs, money snobs, technogeeks, you name it, she could disarm them all. Even the wives and the female CEOs liked her."

"She was always like that," said Sunny. "But there was a certain amount of trouble that went with it. If you met her for a drink after work, you might end up on a plane across the country before it was over."

"There we were too much alike," said Seth. "I don't stay anywhere very long, and she never had more than a toe on the ground. It may have been too much. With both of us up in the air all the time, there was nothing to stand on, nothing solid. Even if I'm not in my houses very much, they're at least mine. I know they're there. All she had was an apartment in Barcelona, and even that was really just an address. It's Troy's place. There was nowhere for her to go home to that was really hers."

"What about her mother? Doesn't she still live around here?"

"Up near the coast north of here. Over by Petaluma. They'd hardly spoken in the last few years, apparently. I had to call her to tell her what happened. She didn't even know Anna was in the country."

For the first time, Seth looked genuinely sad. Death was such an obscene invasion of privacy, thought Sunny. A person could lead a perfectly good life and when they died strangers at the morgue would undress them and open up their insides. Friends and family would go through every drawer, every possession, pore over their finances, decide who they were close with and who was peripheral. Anna, at least, had left very few effects to dispose of or affairs to manage. Sunny felt a pang for her mother. On the few occasions when she'd met her, she seemed like any other mother, loving and proud, and she and Anna had been close, at least then.

"That must have been a terrible conversation," said Sunny.

Seth put a hand over his eyes and took a few loud breaths. When he took his hand away, his face showed no emotion. Not sad, not happy. Just the tension she'd noticed when she first saw him.

"It was terrible because it was so mundane. I told her what happened and she hardly said anything. She was very quiet, very calm. She just thanked me for calling and said she would be in touch. But it was a terrible thing to have to say."

The air was cooling off and the twilight deepening. Sunny watched Oliver Seth, unable to read his face. Was he heartbroken? If so, he was remarkably composed.

"You also had a fight before Saturday, didn't you?" said Sunny. "Anna told me she had discovered hidden cameras around the house."

"Not that again. Another blowup over nothing. I'm not as big a pervert as Anna liked to think. I like mixed company. People from all walks of life. Artists, performers. And I have a lot of people coming through the house when I'm not there. Painters, installers, plumbers, cleaners. When people do things they don't want anyone to see—like shoot up or put away things they're planning to steal or make phone calls they don't want anyone to hear—they do it in the bathroom and in bedrooms where they can lock the door. I don't like hard drugs and I don't like thieves. The cameras are a simple security precaution, nothing more. I have better things to do than watch the housekeeper clean toilets and make beds."

"Does someone monitor them?"

"No, it's just for reference. We can go back and look if some problem or question arises."

"Like now."

"Yes, like now."

"And did you?"

"Watch the footage from Saturday? Not yet."

"Why not?" exclaimed Sunny.

"There are certain . . . complications."

"What complications?"

"Just complications. I'll tell you about it someday when the police have sorted everything out and we're all back to normal."

"What about the police?" insisted Sunny. "They must have the footage from Saturday."

"I doubt it."

"Why not? Oliver, you have to give it to them. Those cameras could tell us what happened."

"They might help fill in some of the blanks, but they won't show everything. There's no camera on that window."

"But they could show something important that occurred before she died, or in another part of the house."

"Possibly, but I doubt it. How much preamble is there to getting high and falling out a window? Listen, Sunny, I didn't come here to talk about security cameras. I know you've had a long day after a very painful weekend and I don't want to keep you. I came here tonight to ask you not to share those e-mails that Anna sent you with anyone else. Anna and I were trying to figure out our relationship. She did some not-nice things and so did I. Exposing the details of my private life won't bring her back, but it could cause a scandal I'm sure everyone would love to read about. I don't see what good that would do."

"You have my word," said Sunny. "No one sees them except the police."

Oliver frowned. "That's exactly what I'm talking about. If you give them to the police, they'll be public knowledge before long."

Sunny stared. "Oliver, I have to give them to the police."

"No, I wouldn't do that if I were you. If they ask for them specifically, sure. But you don't have to go to them on your own. I can have one of my lawyers call you if you like and explain it."

"Explain how withholding evidence from a murder investigation could be a good idea? They throw you in jail for that kind of thing."

"Who said anything about murder? Anna had too much to drink and fell out our bedroom window. It's a stupid way to die, but it's not murder."

"The police are calling it a suspicious death. It said so in the paper."

"That doesn't mean anything," said Oliver angrily. "They have to call it that until the autopsy comes back. It was an accident. A stupid, preventable, tragic accident that ended Anna's life and changed mine forever. End of story. You and I both know there is absolutely no reason the police need to see those e-mails. She had no right to send them to you in the first place. My personal affairs certainly had nothing to do with her death."

"You honestly believe she fell out the window."

"What else could have happened? She was very out of it, very emotional that night. I never should have left her like that. She opened the window to smoke one of her stupid cigarettes and fell out."

"Is that true? Did they find a cigarette?"

"I assume so. She sat there to smoke all the time. I assume that was what she was doing when she fell. She would sit there in the dark and smoke when she couldn't sleep."

Sunny studied his face. He'd shaved recently, but it didn't look as if he grew much of a beard, anyway. "That night, after your fight, or maybe before, did you kiss her?"

Oliver gave her a blank look.

"Did you kiss Anna the night she died? I mean a very passionate kiss, the way people do sometimes after a big fight."

"Why do you ask?"

"I just wonder about the last few hours of her life. What state of mind she might have been in."

He looked down. "I'm afraid they were probably pretty lonely. They were for me. I didn't kiss her. I wish I had. If I had, none of this might ever have happened. I let her push me away and I left."

"Where did you go?"

"Outside. I walked around. I ended up sitting in my car the rest of the night working."

"Working?"

He smiled cynically. "It's always business hours somewhere."

Sunny nodded. "I should tell you I already gave those e-mails to the police. I had to."

Oliver stood up. "Well, then I guess it's your problem now."

"What do you mean by that?"

"You're on their radar now. The police will have to check it all out. They'll wonder why she sent all that stuff to you just before she died, why she decided to reconnect with you on this particular weekend, out of all the weekends in the past four years. Whether she ever sent you anything else." He stopped and shook his head, smiling coldly. "Don't forget where you were that night. You're the one who said it was a suspicious death."

He gave her an odd smirk and left. Sunny got out her keys, but the front door was already open.

10

The house was stuffy and hot. Sunny walked through the living room and kitchen opening windows, stashed the leftovers she'd brought home in the refrigerator, and changed into shorts and flip-flops. In the back garden, a jungle of summer vegetables fought for room in two raised planters, giving off the tangy, fuzzy green smell of tomato plants. She turned the water on and inspected the garden while it ran. She harvested a dozen perfect tomatoes, but the basil had gone to seed. The last of the salad greens were struggling in the heat, thin and wilted and ready to call it off for the season. The neighbor's cat zipped across the yard, spooked at her presence. She sprinkled ground pepper all over the garden once a week to keep him from using the loose dirt as a toilet, but he still did now and then. There are some things you can't do much about, thought Sunny.

She pulled weeds and checked for pests until the watering was finished and it was dark. Three bright green tomato worms as long and fat as her thumb came off the tomato plants. She squashed them into a lime-green smudge in the dirt with a swipe of her flip-flop and headed inside. The talk with Seth had shaken her, but the garden had done its work. She was ready to have a closer look at whatever it was that had him concerned enough to show up at her house. She didn't believe for a moment that he thought Anna's death was an accident. Seth knew as well as Sergeant Harvey and everyone else that she had been killed. If he was out doing damage control, the stakes had to be high.

She made herself a plate of cold poached salmon and dill and poured a glass of wine from an open bottle in the refrigerator. It was the same wine she'd been drinking for more than a week, though not the same bottle. With each glass she noticed some new detail she'd missed or underappreciated. It was a locally grown Syrah blended Côtes du Rhône–style with a bit of Grenache and Muvedre. Smooth, mild, drinkable. The message light on the phone was blinking. She'd been too tired to listen to her messages last night after dinner at Wade's house. The first was from Wade himself, left early in the morning on Sunday. He sounded excited.

"Sun, we need to talk," he said. "I've been thinking and I think I'm onto something extremely important. You know how from the time I was a kid, I've been trying to work out how peace, love, and harmony, et cetera et cetera, could be the core nature of the universe when the planet is so goddamned messed up? I mean, no matter how many flowers and strawberries and songbirds are in the world, you can't call a creator benevolent who also happens to have cranked out a bunch of guys with claws and fangs who can only survive by ripping apart other creatures, not to mention this virus that goes around eating the faces off Tasmanian devils for a living. I mean, whoever came up with that is just sick, right? Well, I stumbled onto an idea the other day walking up on top of that ridge over above the Beroni place and I think I've finally got it figured out. You ready? I hate to tell you something this important on the phone, let alone your machine, but it's so exciting that I can't—"

The line cut off and the next message cued up.

"Typical," said Wade, sounding disgusted. "Anyway, here it is. *Peace and love and goodness are not the core nature of the universe.* It's nice to think they are, but they're just not. It's wishful thinking. Peace might be the goal, but, and here's the breakthrough part, *the core nature of the universe is actually irony.* Irony, Sun. Trust me, this is pure genius stuff. Give me a holler when you get home and I'll walk you through it."

That one's a keeper, thought Sunny. His third call was more on-topic.

"I guess you've seen the paper by now. They've got it on the front page online, too. Now, if that's not a clear-cut case of irony stepping up to the plate and knocking a home run right into the bay, I don't know what is. The only woman I know who is—" He stopped to laugh, which turned into a coughing fit. "The only woman . . . Ha!" More laughter, more coughing. "The only woman I know who is more repressed than my ex-wife gets busted at a sex party. Now, that is ironic. Anyway, don't let all this get to you, McCoskey. This, too, shall blow over. Well, except for what happened to your friend. Uh, well, anyway, gimme a call."

Sunny dialed Skord Mountain. Wade picked up on the first ring. "McCoskey."

"What's with the hacking cough on your message? Are you dying up there or what?"

"You mean this morning? I was eating peanuts. Sucked one down the wrong way."

"And I am not repressed. What do you know about my sex life, anyway? As far as you know, I could be a nymphomaniac."

"If you were, it would fit my theory perfectly. The prudish types are always the naughty ones deep down. They don't call them sexy librarians for nothing."

"I'm not prudish."

"Reticent."

"No."

"Excessively cautious."

"Whatever."

"Seriously now, what are you going to do about this mess?"

"What can I do? Anna is dead. Nothing's going to change that. Like you said, everything else will blow over in time. Hopefully the police will figure out what happened quickly. Then I go on with my life."

"You coming to dinner tomorrow? Riv and the hunter gatherer are coming over to cook."

"I'll be there."

They said good-bye and Sunny set up her laptop on a little wooden table tucked into the corner next to the fireplace. While it was booting up, she finished the last of the poached salmon, put the plate in the sink, and poured another glass of wine. Then she pulled up a chair and reread Anna's e-mail and the exchange between Oliver and the woman named Astrid. They were to meet with investors in Moscow. Astrid had had a dream a boat was sinking. Oliver told her not to worry. He told her to control her fate. There didn't seem to be anything terribly important in any of it. Yes, they seemed intimate. But she couldn't see why Oliver should be so protective of that information. By his own admission, he and Anna were not together exclusively, or hadn't been for long. None of it made sense. Anna called it an insurance policy but she died, anyway. Oliver wanted it hushed up, but nothing in it was terribly damaging. And what did he mean by, "She's bullish on the new vintage"?

Sunny stared at the glass of wine on her desk, the distillation of a year in the life of a few patches of rocky soil and the vines that grew on them. The memoirs of a short, happy life on a sunny slope. It was the consumable record of the rainy spring days and the hot summer ones, the chilly nights and the breeze through the big eucalyptus the next field over, the roots forcing their way down, the nibble of jackrabbits, the buzz of insects, the tread of workers' boots, the tractor with its metallic diesel smell, all of it compressed down to a sequence of flavors in the mouth, a melody, each aspect a note, each note finding its place relative to the others to record the life of a grape. It was entirely ephemeral and yet utterly tangible.

Franco Bertinotti said he would "commune with the grapes and see what they have to tell us." In the end there were two kinds of winemakers, thought Sunny, the Falstaffs and the intellectuals. The Falstaffs like to drink wine, so they make wine. The intellectuals are interested in the idea of wine and what it represents. Despite his trim physique and fastidious nature, Oliver Seth was a Falstaff and Franco Bertinotti was an intellectual. She considered it slightly odd that Oliver had chosen to establish a winery before getting married or having children. Usually it was the other way around. People generally had their careers and families and then tried their hand at winemaking with the proceeds in retirement. Oliver's success so early in life had made it possible for him to sidestep the distinction between work and play, and to simply do as he liked. It was easy to forget, given his situation, that he could hardly be more than thirty years old. He had called his estate his citadel. It must be the self-sufficiency he liked. He had his hilltop vineyard, his garden, his olive trees, his chickens, and even his pig, like any good Roman citadel.

The Seth citadel was probably still under siege, thought Sunny, occupied by the St. Helena police. They would have his computer by now. After the body, that was the first thing they took back to the lab these days. If so, they had the e-mails already and he knew it, unless he had deleted them early Sunday morning before the police arrived. He took a risk coming here, thought Sunny. Guilty or innocent, he was a hunted man now. The police would have someone watching him day and night. They were probably monitoring his cell phone and credit cards, following his car, making sure he didn't fly off anywhere. She wondered if he was suspect number one in Sergeant Harvey's eyes.

A sound outside made her glance up instinctively. Something inside her knew what it was before she could even think about it. A cool, sweet breeze came through the open window. Footsteps, a gentle knock at the door.

She went over and stood in front of it. "Who is it?"

"It's me."

She opened the door. Andre Morales had his motorcycle helmet under his arm and his gloves in his hand. "Can I come in?"

Just like that, six months together was reduced to one question he hadn't had to ask since their first date. The nights he came over, late after work or early for dinner, he would walk in without knocking and stand in her kitchen and take off his helmet and gloves, then his jacket, and finally the leather riding pants he wore over his jeans. It was her favorite bit of performance art. Then there was the sound of his voice, and the warm, honey smell of him. His hair was soft and heavy and always smelled of the chamomile shampoo he used. She stood aside to let him in.

"Sun, it was not what you think. You know that. I wanted to call you earlier, but I didn't want to talk about it while you were at work."

"I wasn't at work last night. Neither were you."

"I know. I should have called. I just . . . I didn't know what to say. So much had happened. I needed some time to think."

He took her hand and tried to lead her to the couch.

"Don't. Let's just get on with it. Why were you there? I mean, you said you didn't know Anna."

"I know Oliver," said Andre. "He comes into the restaurant when he's in town. He called and said he had some interesting people over and I should come by after work. You know how I am after we close. I can't just go to bed."

"It looked like you did."

"Come on, that's not fair. You were there, too."

"But I went to bed alone."

"I didn't go to bed with her."

"Is there another bed in that room?"

"Okay, maybe we slept in the same bed but we didn't sleep together. We just slept. You know what I mean."

"And you think that's the point."

He rubbed at his forehead and groaned as if the conversation gave him physical pain. "Okay, you're right. You're right. I know you're right."

If he had come to feel and understand, thought Sunny, that there was genuinely something wrong with sleeping with the Guamanian princess even if he didn't bother to actually sleep with her, it would be something. A small something, but still something. A streak of light seeping out from under a closed door.

"The thing is, Sunny, I'm not used to having a girlfriend. I guess I've never really had what you would call a real girlfriend. I admit I made a mistake, but I don't want to make any more. I don't want this to end. I want to rewrite everything, the way I do things, with you in it, with you first."

11

"**And you fell for that line?**" Rivka Chavez was standing at her workstation making strategic cuts in a raw chicken so it would lay flat to be cooked under a brick. "*¡Híjole!* That guy ought to sell real estate."

"You weren't there. It was very romantic," said Sunny, tying her apron strings and smiling to herself.

"I'm sure it was. Snow jobs make everything look pretty. And how exactly did he talk his way out of what happened?"

"He said it wasn't what it seemed. You know, they were just there, like I was."

"And did that explanation sound good to you before or after he showed you what's under the biking leathers?"

Sunny held up her hand. "No interrogation, please. We had a beautiful night and I want to enjoy it. It was like waking up from a bad dream. I was so sure it was over, then suddenly there was this reprieve. I can't tell you how good that felt, especially after everything that's happened."

"I'm just trying to shed a little light on how this whole reconciliation went down," said Rivka. "Did he call you and you said, 'Come on over, let's talk'?"

"No, he didn't call."

"So he doesn't call for, what, two days. Then he shows up and says, 'Baby, it's all good,' and that's it, everything's hunky-dory again."

"It was only one day."

"Two days after the incident," said Rivka, eyebrows raised and holding up two fingers incredulously.

"He said he needed some time to think. He seemed sincere." Sunny rubbed her hands over her face. "I need an aspirin or a Coke or, like, a transfusion. I'm seeing spots."

"Up all night?"

"Most of it." Sunny retreated to the walk-in so she wouldn't have to look at Rivka. She came out with a tub full of greens and went to work.

"What if he was the one who opened the door on you and some guy?" said Rivka. "Would you let him wonder what he'd seen for a day or two before you showed up unannounced at his house and assumed you could turn on the charm, take him to bed, and all would be forgiven? Come on, Sunny."

"He admitted he was wrong."

"And that's enough for you?"

Sunny picked up a bunch of red mustard and gently pried apart the leaves, rinsing away streaks of fine black soil between them. "If it's sincere, yes. I'm willing to give this one more shot. He says he's going to make some changes and I believe him."

"Time will tell," said Rivka, sounding skeptical. "At least you had a fun night."

A knock at the back door interrupted them. Sunny saw Sergeant Harvey through the screen door and dried her hands. "You're up early."

"I was in the neighborhood. You have a minute to talk?"

"Let's go in my office."

Sergeant Harvey made the cluttered little room look especially puny, as if he'd drunk the wrong potion and his head might hit the ceiling any minute.

"Sorry about the mess."

"The McCoskey roost never changes."

He sat on the couch between a stack of cookbooks and an old wooden Bandol wine box filled with pieces of driftwood. Sunny moved it to the floor to give him some room and put a pile of vintage cooking magazines on top of it so she could sit in the chair opposite him. In the kitchen, order reigned. This room was for daydreaming. She had the impression that Sergeant Harvey did not approve. He was staring at her desk. Under a river rock was a rumpled heap of notes written on yellowed and stained scraps of paper.

"What's all that?"

"My inspiration. Whenever I have an idea for a new variation on a dish or a new combination of flavors or something, I write it down and stick it in the pile."

Sergeant Harvey leaned forward and extracted a few from under the rock. "Some of these must be three or four years old. 'Basil is as good sweet as it is savory. Basil and candied lemon. Basil panna cotta. Basil and strawberry. Basil and watermelon. Basil and linden-berry? Basil and aniseed?'"

"When it's time to do a new menu, if I need ideas, I look through there."

"'Simple tomato and cucumber salad, whole fish grilled with olive oil and lemon, mash of split peas on crusty bread, grilled eggplant, grilled calamari with capers and lemon, crackling dry white.'"

"Greece. The wrong side of Paros, to be precise. Best vacation food I've ever eaten."

That was what this office was for, thought Sunny, sense memories and inspiration. It was a place for layers of experience to settle over one another, mix, meld, and become something new. And for periodically attempting to keep the federal, state, county, and city bureaucracies at bay and, every other week, for calculating and dispensing the modest wages paid to the Wildside staff, now less one server who had given notice recently in order to spend three months doing yoga and having colonics in Thailand.

Sergeant Harvey grunted and put the slips back. He shifted around, trying to get comfortable on the Victorian relic of a couch, its velvet cushions sagging under the Harvey strain. Behind him was a still life of radiant yellow lemons in a dark bowl on a dark table. There was something almost more human about the lemons. It was that crew cut he wore. And the plateau of eyebrow pinched together in the middle. And the igneous chin. The man was like a squared-off and chiseled statue of himself.

"I'm glad you stopped by," said Sunny. "I was going to give you a call. Something odd happened last night after we talked."

"What was that?"

"Oliver Seth was at my house waiting for me when I got home. He was there to ask me not to show you the e-mails I gave you."

"Interesting. He say why?"

"He said it was just personal stuff that would make a scandal and wouldn't help with the investigation. What puzzles me is why he would bother. I mean, you have his computer by now, I assume. He knows that. You therefore have the e-mails, and he knows that, too."

"Will have."

"Meaning?"

"The system is encrypted. We collected three laptops and some servers from his place. The lab can't get anything off them but gibberish. They're working on decoding it now."

"Is that legal?"

"Encryption? It's a bit of a gray area, but yeah. He has a right to store his personal documents however he chooses, just like the rest of us. He can write them backward in pig Latin if he wants to. We're working on a way to persuade him to help us out voluntarily with translating them. We'll get it ironed out, but for now it's definitely slowing us down."

"So in fact you didn't have the information I gave you."

"That's right."

"And he knew it. I wonder what's in those e-mails that is so important. He's involved with some woman halfway around the world named Astrid. So what. That's not exactly earth-shattering news. What?"

Sergeant Harvey looked irritated. "Sunny, I'd tread lightly on this one if I were you. You're in this thing up to your eyeballs and the heat is on. I've got half of St. Helena from the mayor on down to the guy bagging groceries at the Safeway breathing down my neck, checking up to see if I'm doing everything I should be doing to figure out what happened to your girlfriend. I do not need the McCoskey touch to complicate matters. If you get the impulse to start asking your own questions, I'd advise you to think twice this time."

"Duly noted."

"That doesn't mean you can't call me with stuff like you brought in last night. If you come into possession of a piece of evidence, or if you remember something that might be important, by all means get in touch. But do not go looking for trouble on this one or you just might find it. You cook, I'll investigate. *¿Comprende?*"

"*Capisco.*"

He checked his watch. "I gotta get going, so I'll be quick. The reason I came by is we need you to come down to the station sometime in the next day or so to be swabbed. We need to get a sample."

"A sample of what?"

"DNA. They swab the inside of your cheek. Takes about ten seconds, no big deal. Routine stuff, don't worry. You were at the scene at the time of death. We gotta collect and compare with whatever physical evidence we find elsewhere. Process of elimination."

"What physical evidence? I thought there wasn't any."

"There's always physical evidence. It's only a matter of what kind and how much. Just drop by the station. It'll take five minutes." He looked around the room. "You're not going to be happy about this next bit, but I can't get around it."

"Something worse than taking a swab of my DNA for police records? I find that hard to imagine."

"I need to take your computer for evidence. That e-mail Anna sent you. We're going to need it."

"I already gave it to you."

"Yeah, that's a start, but we'd like to take a closer look."

"At my computer."

"Yes."

"Steve, this is my only computer. This is it. This is what I use to run the restaurant. I have all my records on there. The payroll. I can't even write a check without it."

Sergeant Harvey nodded but his look was uncompromising. "I realize it's an inconvenience, but it may be important to our investigation."

"All my recipes. My archives. All my e-mails. Everything."

"You must back everything up somewhere."

"Yes. Well, not lately. Some stuff is backed up, some isn't. I'm not, uh, the best with computers." She sighed and shook her head. "How long will you need it?"

"It would be considered evidence in the investigation into Anna Wilson's death."

"Meaning you're going to keep it for months. Years. I might never get it back." She rubbed her eyes, trying to remember what her rights were, if she ever knew them. "Steve, you know how much I hate to do this, but if you want my computer, you're going to have to come back with a search warrant."

Sergeant Harvey's cheeks flushed red. "We can do it that way if you prefer."

"I do."

"Okay."

Sunny's heart was beating fast and she could tell her cheeks were as red as his. "I can't just let you take it right now. I have my business to think of."

"I'd think you'd want to find out what happened to your friend."

"I do, but there's nothing on my computer that will help you. I gave you the e-mail she sent already."

"Well, then, if you change your mind, let me know."

"I will."

Sergeant Harvey left and she heard him stomp down the back steps. Her hands were shaking when she went back to work, and she shaved a chunk of her fingernail off with the lemon zester. "Dammit!"

"Breathe, McCoskey," said Rivka over the sizzle of the grill.

12

The game was to hold all the little bits of information in her head long enough to execute whatever was supposed to be on the rows of plates in front of her, then forget everything and start over with the next batch. Four salads, one without cheese, one with dressing on the side, a request she despised but was willing to indulge, one vanilla bean crème brûlée, one slice of Mama McCoskey's pineapple cake, one nectarine tartlet. Two peach-and-prosciutto plates. After that one salmon tartar, thank God; if Bertrand and the waitstaff could only try to move a little more of that, please, thought Sunny. A loud jangle from the back of the room broke her concentration.

The black phone on the back wall of the kitchen was so old it looked as if it was made of Bakelite and probably was. It had two real bells with a tiny metal hammer between them and a rotary dial. Only a handful of people had the number, among them Sunny's parents, Monty, and Wade. None of them used it unless it was some kind of emergency. She looked at the bowl of salad she had just started dressing. A couple extra minutes in the oil before it hit the table would make the greens too soft, their architecture beginning to sag. But there wasn't time to finish the plates the way she liked.

Just twenty more seconds, that's all she needed. Again the jangle from the back of the room. She looked around. Rivka was busy with a full grill; besides, it wouldn't be for her. Bertrand was occupied on the floor. Sunny abandoned the greens.

"Wildside."

"Is this Ms. Sunny McCoskey?"

"Speaking. Who's this?"

"Franco Bertinotti."

"Excuse me?"

"Franco Bertinotti. Don't tell me you have forgotten already! It's been only three days since we met."

Sunny stared past the kitchen at the zinc bar and dining room beyond it. Waiters, both of them, glided between the bar and the tables, depositing a fork here, an espresso there, pausing to hear a request. One of them breezed by the bar, checking to see if his order was up. Bertrand, maître d' and de facto sommelier, was presenting a bottle to a client with his usual matter-of-fact authority. She wondered why Franco Bertinotti would be calling, and on the bat phone in the middle of lunch rush. "How did you get this number?"

"That is a funny story. I ran into a friend of yours at a business luncheon. A wine tasting for some Italian wines with whom I have a sort of relationship. This guy was called Monterey Lenstrom. You know him? We discovered we had you in common and I suggested to him that it was very important that I reach you urgently. He gave me this number. I hope you don't mind the intrusion."

"We're in the middle of the lunch rush. Can this wait until after three?"

"I will be brief. I was hoping we could get together. To talk a little about this terrible business."

"I finish at five."

"I am staying at the new hotel with the little bungalows in the Carneros. You know it? You will find me having my evening cocktail by the pool between five and seven."

One of the waiters cruised the zinc bar a second time looking for his salads. These people certainly loved their pools, thought Sunny. "See you then."

She went back to her station and scraped the bowl of greens into the garbage.

At five o'clock, Sunny left the restaurant's closing chores undone and rode her bike home to collect the truck. She headed back down Highway 29 toward the Carneros in the slow and steady evening rush. Half an hour later, she drove up a dusty slope past a ramshackle house and a horse trailer to the incongruously chic hotel entrance. She parked facing a couple of Appaloosas grazing on the other side of a barbed-wire fence. Both horses and hotel had a wide-open view of the Vaca Mountains to the east.

Sunny walked through the lobby with its high ceilings and fireplace sitting room and headed down to the pool, a blue rectangle laid bare to the sun and view. A handful of bathers soaked up the last of the day's heat. A lone swimmer moved quietly through the water. Sunny scanned the umbrellas and chairs for the Sicilian's black trunks. A strikingly beautiful woman walked past her in heels and sunglasses, her black hair shining. She sat down next to a handsome-looking older gentleman with a European tan and white hair styled short. Sunny looked again. It was Franco Bertinotti. The girl stepping out of her sundress to reveal a black bikini was Jordan Crowley. Sunny went over and Franco half stood to kiss her on both cheeks. "You remember Miss Crowley?"

"Of course."

"Sit down, join us." He waved to the waiter and asked for another chair, then held up the bottle of Etude Rosé he was drinking. "Another of these. And two more glasses, thank you."

"You drink the pink," said Sunny. Back before everyone had suddenly become frenzied Californios with no time, plenty of long, do-nothing afternoons had been spent with friends at a makeshift table in her backyard eating funky cheeses, grilled sausages, and raw oysters and drinking lots and lots of pink wine. Not the sweet stuff, but the crisp mineral kind, chilled cool but not cold. Once in a while, in the middle of the pale days of winter, with the table loaded with risotto and Parmesan and chanterelle salad, someone would open an incongruous Bandol pink and for a few sips it would be summer again.

"Always," said Franco, raising his glass.

"We're just starting to appreciate rosés here. Californians were traumatized by Cold Duck in the seventies. People are still getting over it."

"The Germans! Always finding ways to save money."

A couple of Napa high-school boys in waiters' uniforms carried another chaise up next to Franco's and adjusted the back. Sunny sat down in her jeans and put her feet up, displaying a pair of well-worn cowboy boots.

"Miss Crowley was good enough to join me here," said Franco, "before I got too bored. The police officers asked me to stay in place through the end of the week so they can be sure I didn't murder our friend Anna."

"Don't say that," said Jordan. "She wasn't murdered."

"Do you think she strangled herself?"

"I just don't like hearing those words. I don't want to think about how she died."

"Well, we'd all better think about it unless you want to see our friend Oliver spend the rest of his days in jail."

"I don't care where they put him. I wouldn't be surprised if he's the one who killed her, anyway."

"Don't be ridiculous," said Franco. "He didn't kill her. On the contrary. He did everything in his power to improve her life."

The waiter returned with the wine. They were quiet while he finished pouring out the first bottle and opened the second. Franco raised his glass. "Long life."

"Long life," said Jordan.

"Long life," Sunny echoed, and drank. "Why do you say she was strangled?"

"It is a fact. There were marks here, and here." He touched his throat and lips. "Probably someone put a gag in her mouth to keep her quiet while they did it."

Jordan stared straight ahead in her sunglasses. She must have heard this bit of news already, thought Sunny. "How do you know there were marks?"

"The police revealed as much during one of our more colorful interviews, when the guy in charge was trying to shame me into a confession. He's lucky I didn't do it. Your California police would have absolutely no chance against a Sicilian. They kidnap people and keep them in caves in the mountains for years where I come from just to make a few bucks. In Sicily we know how to keep quiet. It is a matter of survival. It is in the genes."

The waning sun was surprisingly warm. Sunny started to sweat in her boots and jeans. A woman across from them got up and stepped down the stairs into the pale, sparkling water. Sunny envied her. "What do you think happened to Anna?"

"You mean who killed her?" said Franco.

"I guess so, yes."

"Even if I knew, or thought I did, I certainly wouldn't say. Murder is a dangerous business."

"Oliver killed her," said Jordan, "directly or indirectly."

"You must stop saying that," said Franco, holding up a finger. "They may have had a quarrel, but Oliver didn't kill her. Why would he? The man is not a monster. Besides, if he wanted her gone, there were much easier ways of accomplishing it than to make himself a murder suspect with all the danger and inconvenience that presents. He's more intelligent than that, if nothing else."

"Maybe he didn't plan it. Maybe it just happened," said Jordan.

"Oliver Seth did not murder his girlfriend. The idea is ridiculous."

"Stop saying that word," said Jordan. "I really can't think of her dying that way."

"He did not put an end to his girlfriend," said Franco. "Is that better?"

"It would be better if it hadn't happened at all."

"With that I agree."

"If you're so sure about what didn't happen, you must have some idea what did," said Sunny.

"I honestly don't know," said Franco. "I wish I did. I was hoping you might share your insights on the matter."

"I don't have any," said Sunny. "I was asleep until the police woke me in the morning."

"You heard nothing in the night?"

"I heard Oliver and Anna fighting."

"We all heard that."

"The next thing I knew, it was morning and we were being asked to talk to the police."

"And there was your boyfriend, appeared out of thin air," said Franco.

"Yes."

"He didn't tell you he would be there that night."

"No."

"That must have been unpleasant." He put a hand on her knee as though in commiseration and stood up. He went over to the pool and dove in, swimming with the easy, confident stroke of a practiced swimmer.

Sunny glanced toward the pool. "Have you known him long?"

"I just met him on Saturday, like you."

"Oh, really? I thought you must have known each other longer. You seem very relaxed together."

"He called me out of the blue. I didn't have anything else to do, so I came up for the day. I think this business with Anna has made us all feel a little lonely. Whatever happened with you and your boyfriend? Did you patch things up?"

"We're working on it."

"I'm sure it was just a big misunderstanding."

"That's what Andre said." Sunny hesitated a moment. "Did you see yesterday's paper?"

"Who didn't? I feel sorry for Anna's mother. It's not bad enough her daughter is dead, they have to run that kind of story to make it sound sensational."

"You mean the whole sex and drugs business."

"It's ridiculous. So we were having a good time. I don't care what people think, but I feel bad for Sylvia."

"Some sex party, anyway," said Sunny. "If I believe Andre's story, nobody actually had illicit sex that night except Molly and Jared, and how illicit is sex between two single, consenting adults?"

Jordan blushed and put her sunglasses back on. Sunny wondered what had embarrassed her. She knows something I don't, thought Sunny. I'm being naive to think nothing happened between

Marissa and Andre that night. Of course something happened, and Jordan knows it.

The sun dipped into the haze along the horizon and the light turned a richer shade of gold. One of the horses held up its head and nickered, and she could just hear the far-off soft sound of it. Franco pulled himself out of the pool and stood dripping in front of them. A pool attendant handed him a towel, which he used to scrub his hair and wrap around his waist. He resumed his forty-five-degree incline and glass of Pinot Rosé.

"What did I miss?"

"Did you see yesterday's paper?" said Sunny. "We were just saying how ironic it was that nobody actually had sex at the big sex party."

"Well, some of us didn't." He gave Jordan a look and she ignored him but looked uncomfortable. Maybe they got together that night, thought Sunny. But Franco went to bed long before the others. In the hot tub, Jordan had been warming up for à ménage a trois with Keith and Marissa, but Keith went home soon after Sunny left and Marissa ended up with Andre. Unless . . . Sunny felt sick. What if they had simply transferred their affection from Keith to Andre? Voilà, a real sex party.

"What about Marissa?" said Sunny. "What does she do? For a living, I mean."

"She's a party planner," said Jordan.

"What a charming euphemism for what she does!" said Franco. "I suppose that makes me Bacchus."

"What do you mean?"

"Ms. Lin is a purveyor of exotic people and the exotic substances that make them go," said Franco.

"You mean she's a drug dealer."

"She is not a drug dealer," said Jordan. "She hosts dance parties in the city. She's been doing it for years."

"But if you need some assistance enjoying one of her dance parties, she can help you," said Franco.

Sunny turned to Jordan. "Why do you think Oliver killed her?"

"He's a control freak. Anna was the one thing he couldn't control. They'd been fighting. She was going to leave him. I'm not saying he planned anything. I think he lost his temper and that was it."

"Did he have a violent temper?"

"Every man that powerful does."

"As tragic and important as all this business with Oliver is," said Franco, "it is not why I wanted to see you. I have another motive, in addition to enjoying your company, of course. In most places in Italy, particularly the south, and everywhere in Sicily, a little restaurant like yours would be required to pay a substantial retainer to the local business organization. It could never grow without it, or even survive." He looked at her with blue eyes made bluer by the surrounding tan skin. "I knew a little fish restaurant in a cove next to the famous point called Scylla. You know it from the story? It is an ancient myth. On one side is the Scylla monster on the cliff, on the other the Charybdis whirlpool that eats up the ships. It is a real place in Sicily. This little restaurant did not want to pay the membership fee that was requested of them. It was shortsighted thinking. In the end, they could not keep their staff, they never had a good relationship with the suppliers, customers didn't come. The owner was forced to close up shop and move away to escape his debts. They found him some weeks later in the trunk of a rented car. The next owner made a partnership with the local powers and, *boom*, huge success. He retires, comes back to see the operation whenever he likes, life is good. I was thinking of this story in relation to your situation."

"Why is that?"

"Because I can see that you are tired, and that your business is not growing, but I have the impression that you are talented and you work hard. Fortunately and also unfortunately, there is no higher power here so far."

"You mean Mafia."

"Those that run things. But in any case you could still take the lesson from Scylla and Charybdis. You could make a powerful partnership in order to expand, so that someday you might not have to work every day. Your employees would be happy then. There would be more business, more opportunity to move up, more money for everyone. You would be happy."

"My employees are happy now."

"Don't be defensive. I'm only trying to help you by suggesting that if an opportunity should come your way, you might be wise to consider it."

"If one should, I will."

"Good. Now, why don't you go into the spa over there and buy yourself a swimsuit so I don't have to look at denim and a man's work boots on such a beautiful woman. This is how a woman's foot should look."

He leaned over and lifted Jordan's leg by the ankle, holding it to display the freshly painted nails and high sandal. She laughed and lifted it away.

Sunny shook her head and pulled herself up from the lounge chair. "Thanks, but I need to get going. You're staying here at the hotel?"

"For the moment," said Franco. "Why don't you join me tomorrow for lunch?"

"I'll be at the restaurant all day."

"Then we will come to you. I would like to try this restaurant everyone is talking about."

"Is everyone talking about it?"

"Some people, my dear. And after that, I will attend to the last of my wine business at Taurus Rising and then, with the authorities' and Oliver's blessing, I go back to Roma at the end of the week to resume my affairs there."

13

Wade Skord sat on his back porch in his work clothes. His face and arms were covered in a powdery film of dust, the same that tinged his jeans and white T-shirt rusty red. Terra-cotta stripes marked creases around the armpits and wherever he'd leaned against a piece of machinery.

"Half man, half mud," said Sunny.

"Tractor duty," said Wade, unlacing his boots. Sunny went inside and came back with two glasses of ice water. They sat on the deck and watched the sky turn pink. Rivka's yellow blip of a car appeared at the top of the hill and inched its way down the slope toward the house, red dust billowing up behind. Rivka and her new boyfriend got out.

"I can't believe she got all that boy in that little car," said Wade. "He must have been bent in half." He excused himself to take a shower. Rivka and Jason, her new crush, joined Sunny on the deck. He was a Jamaican transplant with wide shoulders, narrow hips, and hair like a dandelion who could sell just about anything he dragged to the farmers' market on Friday mornings. Last year it was wildcrafted blackberries and watercress. This year his stand was mostly selling Bob Marley T-shirts and Jamaican jerk spices and curry powders. Sunny watched Rivka. She was clearly under his spell. Who could blame her? He was charming, handsome, and had a body that "rocked the house," as Rivka said.

It was nearly dark when Monty arrived a few minutes later. "Forty bucks to have a car detailed," he said, slamming the car door, "and look at it. That dust works its way into every crevice and nothing can get it out." He stomped up the porch stairs, brushing his sleeves and trousers. "What kind of lunatic would live all the way out here with the raccoons?"

"Our dear friend Wade?" said Rivka.

"I rest my case," said Monty.

They carried groceries inside and Jason got started cooking. Wade came out of the bedroom smelling like soap, wearing clean jeans and a plaid shirt. His gray head of cowlicks was still wet and had been combed neat but was already beginning to break free.

"Sun," he said.

"Skord."

"Taste of the evil brew?"

"How evil?"

He sauntered over to the cardboard box that served as the wine cabinet. Wade's house was randomly but more or less evenly divided between rural spartan and wine country luxury. Half rustic cabin, with splintering wood and an ancient potbellied stove, it also had plank floors any New York loft dweller would die for, million-dollar views, and the occasional piece of Italian modernism just when you least expected it. The house, like the man, was a jumble of non sequiturs and juxtaposed opposites. From her spot near the butcher block where Rivka was cubing potatoes, Sunny could see the entire house except the office and the bathroom. Wade raised his nose and glanced toward the kitchen. The air was already filled with the spicy aroma of garlic, onions, and curry sizzling in olive oil. He held up a bottle.

"Fresh Pinot Noir. Central Otago, New Zealand. Mailman brought it."

"New World exotic. I'm in."

"You see the paper tonight?" said Rivka.

Sunny shook her head.

"Apparently Oliver Seth had his computer encrypted. They just cracked the code and there were a bunch of e-mails to some woman he was seeing."

"It said that in the newspaper?"

"Yep."

"They find anything else?"

"It said it would take a while to go through everything."

Wade poured and handed glasses around. "To the newest cook at Skord Mountain."

Jason picked up a glass to acknowledge the toast, then turned back to a spitting skillet. Rivka went over and peeked around his elbow. "Isn't your heat a little high?"

"You got to fry curry hot so it sits right in the belly. We're under control out here. Go relax."

Sunny took a drink of the pomegranate-red wine. It had a pleasantly astringent taste that woke her up after the long day. "I found out something else today, too," she said. "I went to see Franco Bertinotti, the guy who—"

"That's the guy I met," interrupted Monty. "So he got ahold of you. Good. I gave him your number. Interesting guy. Turns out he had a hand in a couple of my favorite Barolos going way back."

"Why didn't you give him my cell number?"

"He said he needed to reach you right away, before he left town. You don't answer your cell at work, and nobody picks up the office phone when you're open."

"So call the main restaurant number. It's in the phone book. The bat phone is for family."

"I'll make a note, Frau Diva. Since when is it so hard to escape your fans? He wanted a quick way to reach you and I gave it to him."

"Who is this guy?" said Rivka.

"He called today during lunch rush. The winemaker who works for Oliver Seth. Sicilian, lives in Rome. I went to see him tonight and he told me that Anna had marks on her throat and mouth. Or at least that's what the police told him. I think there's a chance they could have been lying, trying to trip him up if he was guilty, but I think she must have had some kind of marks on her somewhere."

"What kind of marks?"

"I'm not sure. Bruises, I assume. On her mouth it was an abrasion. She was suffocated or strangled."

"And we still have no idea who did it," said Rivka.

"No, but something will turn up. I've been thinking about something Steve said. 'There's always physical evidence, it's just a matter of how much.' Anna was intoxicated, tired, maybe even asleep when it happened. It would have been relatively easy to come into her room and smother her without much noise or struggle. But she didn't just slip lightly into the great beyond. She was murdered. It was a violent act. If you were planning to do such a thing, wouldn't you take a few precautions?"

"Such as?" said Monty.

"Let's say it was me. I know I'm stronger than she is, and I have the advantage because I'm the aggressor. But she still might scream before I could cover her mouth. And I don't want her to scratch me and get my DNA under her fingernails. If you smother someone, even if she's asleep or drugged, there could still be a fight." Sunny looked around the group. "If you were planning to overpower and suffocate someone in a houseful of people without anyone knowing, what would you bring with you?"

"A gag," said Rivka.

"Gloves," said Wade.

"Wouldn't you just knock them out?" said Monty. "Otherwise they might overpower you and get away."

"Too risky, too messy," said Sunny. "And in this case, not necessary. That's where the opportunity comes in. With all the wine and God knows what else that was in Anna's system, I think just about anyone could have overpowered her, especially if they got to her when she was asleep and prevented her from breathing. It would have been a fairly easy job. If you smash someone over the head, you're bound to do it too hard, in which case you're going to get blood everywhere, or not hard enough, in which case you're in even bigger trouble."

"The whole thing is so disgusting if you really think about it," said Rivka. "Can you imagine holding someone down and not letting them breathe until they died? It turns my stomach."

"It's called burking," said Wade. "Very tidy. You get somebody drunk, wait for them to pass out, and then hold your hand over their mouth and nose. Fast, simple, clean."

"So our guy wasn't so clever," said Sunny. "He put something over or in her mouth that did some damage and he left some bruises."

Jason came at them brandishing a spatula. "Hey, hey, hey. Enough of this talk or you are going to ruin my supper. We're a happy occasion here. We've got good food, good wine. Enough of this murder business. You're going to spoil my curry with all this bad talk."

"Duct tape!" said Monty. "They always use duct tape to cover the person's mouth."

"Exactly," said Sunny. "And duct tape could leave an abrasion on her mouth when you take it off."

"Jason is right," said Wade. "All this talk about suffocating help-less victims is depressing. Can't it wait until after dinner?"

"Just one more minute," said Sunny. "I'm getting to the point. Let's go through it from the beginning. You get what you need from somewhere on the estate. Garage, kitchen, whatever. Maybe you even brought it with you, who knows. So let's say you get some-thing to use as a gag or to cover her mouth—maybe Monty's duct tape—and you wear gloves so you don't leave any fingerprints or get scratched. You suffocate Anna in her sleep and push her body out the window, where you hope her death may be construed as an acci-dent. Maybe you do it so it will take longer to find her, presuming, as the murderer might, that she will be found sooner in bed than she would outside. Whatever the reason, now you just have to dis-pose of the evidence. It's four in the morning, maybe five. You don't have much time. You've got a ball of used duct tape, a pair of rubber gloves, and who knows what else to get rid of. You can't leave that stuff around because it could have your DNA on it. What do you do with it? You can't risk leaving the property—you might be seen or caught by the security camera at the gate. The police will check all the obvious places like trash cans and under the bed. You can't flush rubber gloves and duct tape—what if they get stuck? You have to find a safe hiding place without making any noise. Somewhere so safe the cops can tear the house apart and not find it."

"Where?" said Rikva.

"That's the question. And more important, is it still there?"

"Of course not," said Monty.

"Why 'of course'?" said Sunny. "If you hide it well enough to keep it from the cops during their big scavenger hunt, why risk moving it later and being seen?"

"If you put a curse on my curry with all your death talk, I'm not cooking for you people ever again," said Jason loudly from the kitchen. "That's it. No more curry. No jerk chicken. No plantains, no ackee and saltfish."

"You could bury it," said Monty.

"And leave a fresh pile of dirt?" said Sunny. "The police know to look for that kind of thing. I thought of the compost heap down at the garden, but I'm sure they went through there as well."

"You could eat it, like they do with drugs," said Monty.

"Who could eat a rubber glove?" said Rivka.

"You could put it, uh, where the sun don't shine," said Monty.

"You're lucky the police didn't pursue this line of thinking over the weekend," said Rivka. "Could have made for some interesting searches."

"In theory, I guess that could work," said Sunny. "If a person was in a desperate frame of mind."

"Or feeling adventuresome," said Monty.

Wade shook his head. "Nobody in his right mind would keep that kind of evidence on his person where it might be found, especially in a place it would be pretty damn hard to explain. He'd burn it. Or bury it. Or stick it somewhere in the house where it would take a while to find. The cops can't look everywhere."

"They had a pig. Maybe you could rub it with peanut butter and feed it to the pig," said Sunny.

"A pig won't eat duct tape no matter what you rub on it," said Wade. "If they had a goat, I'd say maybe. A goat'll eat the siding right off your house. Pigs are finicky. I had a pig that wouldn't eat a cookie if it had a bite out of it. He liked 'em round."

"So if there is any evidence, it could be anywhere," said Sunny. She walked over to the sliding glass doors and looked out at darkness, across the dry grass, light as milk in the moonlight, at the sagging barn where Wade made some of the best Zinfandel the Howell Mountain appellation had to offer. Farber, Wade's cat, was stalking toward the overgrown patch of rhubarb and asparagus that grew on the other side of the winery. Off to hunt mice and wood rats.

They gathered at the plank table. Jason set a steaming bowl of rice and a Dutch oven full of curry chicken on the table. Sunny brought out an heirloom tomato, basil, and fava bean salad. Monty added baguettes from the bakery in Yountville and several bottles of wine. There was a Mayacamas Chardonnay to start, then a couple of local Pinots to compare. Everyone was hungry. Wade put João Gilberto on the dust-encrusted boom box he carried out to work every day, and they ate listening to the music and saying little until plates began to go around for seconds. The days since Anna's death had been stressful. It felt good to eat, drink, and relax.

Wade held the bowl of rice and Sunny passed her plate. He dished up seconds, ladling the rich yellow curry chicken with onions and potatoes over it. She inhaled deeply. "Spicy. Is that Habanero?"

"Scotch bonnet. Same thing, more or less," said Jason.

"Where did you learn to cook?"

"At home growing up. We cooked every day. I never ate in a restaurant until I worked in one."

"I think this might be what's been missing from my life," said Sunny, looking at Rivka. "Spice. We need more spice. Is there anything spicy on the menu at Wildside?"

"Loads of flavor, not much spicy."

"That's right. No spice. Nothing hot. We need more hot. Or at least a little bit of hot."

Truth be known, she was a sip or two over the top. It felt great to unwind, even if she had to use the sledgehammer approach of alcohol to do it.

"Anything but more salmon and I'm happy," said Rivka.

"So this guy Smith," said Monty, pausing to take a drink of wine as though he'd just noticed the glass in his hand, "is mega-rich."

"Seth. More money than anybody I've ever known. Billions, apparently," said Sunny. "He had real art in his house. Like art you see in museums. It was like staying at the Bellagio."

"When did you ever stay at the Bellagio?" said Rivka.

"You know what I mean. Art. Decadence."

"Millions and billions sound alike, but a billion dollars is a serious pile of cash," said Jason. "I heard this thing one time. You think about all the time that's passed since Jesus Christ was born. Sixty minutes in an hour, so—what's that?—six hundred twice plus a hundred and twenty twice, that's a thousand four hundred and forty-four minutes in a day. That makes about ten thousand in a week and about forty thousand in a month, so let's say roughly four hundred eighty thousand in a year. You with me? Multiply that by a couple thousand years and you get pretty close to a billion minutes since the time of Christ." He pointed to each of the faces around the table with his fork in turn. "If somebody gave you one dollar for every minute that has passed since Jesus was over there in Bethlehem sawing wood and hammering nails, you'd have about a billion dollars."

"All that money and his big dream is to do what you do every day," said Sunny, looking at Wade. "His big passion is making wine."

"Ironic, isn't it?" said Wade. "These days, if you want to live like a peasant and make wine and have chickens and a pig and dig up your own vegetables, you have to be part of the wealthy elite. Farming is the new status symbol. I remember when store-bought food was how you snubbed your neighbors. Only the schlumpy households had to get their hands dirty. Now it's the reverse."

"Like in Europe," said Monty. "The gentleman farmer."

"I guess we're all grown up," said Wade. "Land is going to keep getting more expensive. Pretty soon the weeds won't be able to afford a place to live."

Monty held the bottle over Sunny's glass. *"¿Mas vino?"*

"I shouldn't."

Monty poured.

"That guy Franco you think is so great, I think he threatened me when I saw him," said Sunny. She told him what Franco said about the Sicilian Mafia and the little fish restaurant in Scylla.

"Are you sure he wasn't just being colorful?" said Monty. "And I don't think he's so great, but if he was really in charge of what he claimed to be in charge of, he's a hell of a winemaker."

"Of course he was threatening you," said Rivka.

"Why would he threaten me?" said Sunny.

"Sounds like he's trying to protect his meal ticket. He's probably worried you're going to help send Oliver Seth to jail. What does he look like?" asked Rivka.

"Bertinotti? Decent looking, for a guy older than Wade. Short white hair, lounge-singer tan, reasonably fit. Well-groomed, by American standards."

Wade ran his hand over two days of stubble. "Some of us have better things to do than sit around by the pool. I'd say you're reading too much into it. Sounds to me like he's laying the groundwork for a business proposition."

"You don't want to mess with Sicilians," said Jason. "I knew some of those guys back east. They're as tough as Jamaicans."

"Maybe he's the one who killed Anna," said Rivka. "He's covering his tracks. He wanted to see you to test the waters, see what you might know."

"Maybe he did it, or maybe it was Oliver, or the gardener, or one of the ex-boyfriends hanging around. It could have been anyone," said Sunny. "I still don't see any reason why Franco or anyone else would want Anna dead. When we know why she was killed, we'll know who did it."

"My money's on the lawyer," said Monty.

"Keith Lachlan? Why?" said Sunny.

"He's the only person who left the party, he's close enough to Oliver to be involved in whatever personal business may have been going down, and you yourself said he was huge. Overpowering a little drunk girl would be all in a day's work."

"Keith is the guy from Barbados, right? Run away," said Jason. "Dem Bajans always cookin' up some trouble. They're ruthless like the Brits but cunning like Jamaicans." Sunny noticed he used his accent only to emphasize certain phrases. Otherwise he sounded like any other California kid.

"He a black guy?" asked Jason.

"More or less."

"How's he look?"

"Handsome in an un-cola sort of way."

"Meaning?"

"You know, the 7-Up guy in the white suit and the wicker chair? Never mind, you're too young. Tall, shaved head, nice skin, nice smile. Drinks too much, or something of that order. Didn't look too healthy. His eyes were dull and kind of jaundiced."

"Yellow eyes notwithstanding, I don't think this is your guy."

"What makes you say that?"

"Racial profiling. A rich, good-looking Bajan wouldn't kill his best friend's girl and run away. For one thing, islanders are super-stitious. A Jamaican *bad mon* will take *him cutlass* to a *mon troat*, but he's not going to sneak up on his best friend's girl like a coward.

That's inviting some kind of retribution. You don't want to get a curse put on you by the local shaman. In Barbados and Haiti and all over the West Indies it's the same. And honor is a big deal, especially among the rude boys. He wouldn't betray the friendship. But maybe they weren't friends anymore. Maybe they had become enemies all of a sudden. So we leave that to the side. He still wouldn't kill her. Which leads to problem number two. We run hot down in the Caribbean. If this guy goes into this girl's bedroom in the middle of the night, he's going for one reason and one reason only, beg pardon to the ladies."

"That's just talk," said Monty, blushing and sounding flustered. "Maybe he's the one islander who doesn't mind being a coward. Maybe he's the only Caribbean guy out there who's not much with the ladies."

"I know one thing for sure," said Jason. "If he really is straight out of the islands, he could be as ruthless as they come. To survive down there well enough to make it out to California, you've got to be a killer. I just worry that when they go looking for this particular killer, they're going to find the nearest black man, like always."

Rivka stared mush-eyed at Jason. Monty Lenstrom took his spectacles off and cleaned them on a square of fabric he took from his wallet. Sunny sat deep in the couch, fighting sleep.

"Another example," said Wade, continuing a ramble about his new theory. "That Beach Boys song that goes, 'She'll have fun-fun-fun till her daddy takes her T-Bird away-ayyy'." He sang in a scratchy falsetto. "Dad gets wind his daughter has been racing around in her new car instead of studying, so he takes it away. Little does he know, he has just delivered his precious little girl into the arms of the pursuing male. Ironically, by trying to shield her from one danger, he makes her vulnerable to an even worse threat."

"That's not irony, that's a parable of modern paternalistic society," said Rivka, sitting up. "It's the signal that it's time for the girl-chattel to be shifted from the property of the father to the property of the suitor. The father, who initially gives his daughter the spoils of his wealth, must disenfranchise her in order to prevent her from disrupting the male power structure by gaining independence."

Wade looked stunned. "Okay, maybe that one's too complicated. Let's look at another example. You only hurt the ones you love. Irony. Another one. The surest way to lose something is to find a special place for it so you won't lose it. Irony. I'm serious! What if the universe achieves stasis—balance—not through compassion, as I was once foolish enough to believe, but through irony? The irony theory solves the greatest riddle of existence: If God is all powerful, why does he allow pain and suffering? Because, ironically, God is not all powerful. Irony is how a benevolent but not-all-powerful god makes sure the smarty pants don't overrun the place. Irony is the ultimate check on power. It underpins everything."

"I think I know what you mean," said Monty. "Like, I've always wondered why crackers and chips go soft when you leave them out, but bread gets hard. Why shouldn't bread get soft?"

"Ah, that's a different principle at work," said Wade, his eyebrows rising to the challenge. "Whatever your strengths are, you degrade toward their opposite. Crispy gets soft, soft gets crispy."

"But obsessed nutcases just get nuttier and nuttier," said Rivka. She looked at Wade and Monty. "Hello! Crackers get stale because they absorb moisture from the air. Bread dries out because it releases moisture into the air. It's about relative water content, not metaphysics."

"Ironically, the girl who looks like the high-school dropout is actually the brains of the group," said Wade.

"You might be right about crackers," said Sunny, "but bread is more complicated. It doesn't dry out. If it did, warming it in the oven wouldn't make it soft again, it would make it harder. It's soft because heat makes the starch soften up. As it cools down, the starch recrystalizes and it gets harder."

Monty looked over his glasses at her. "How do you know these things?"

"Cooking is chemistry," said Sunny.

"Ironically, putting dry, hard bread in a dry, hot place makes it more moist," said Wade, staring at his friends with a ridiculous look of triumph. "Another one. When do you find your true love? When you're not looking. Ironically, the desire for love is the most effective repellent against it."

"That is regrettably and painfully true," said Monty.

"So irony explains everything," said Sunny.

"Not everything," said Wade. "Only things that are, say, out of balance. Irony is the great corrector."

"Would you say murder is evidence of something out of balance?"

"Definitely."

"Then by that logic, we should be able to apply your theory to Anna's death and figure out what happened."

Wade's eyes sparkled. "Yes, we should." He thought for a moment. "The trouble is, you have to know who the joke is on. I'll give you an example. I have a friend from way back who always wanted to be a great artist. Was one, really. Worked so hard before one big show, he gave himself spinal meningitis and nearly died. Nothing much happened in his career. He did a bunch of great work, a few critics recognized it, a few pieces went to good collections, but nothing really took off. Finally, after years of struggling to get by, he gives up. Decides it's not worth it, he's not going to paint anymore. To hell with it. He moves back to Montana, where his family has some property, reverts to his old carpentry hobby, and starts building furniture in the barn to make ends meet. Whereupon he is immediately hailed as a modern master of furniture design and his chairs end up in the MoMA and the Smithsonian. The list of people waiting to pay forty grand for a chair is as long as my arm. Now, that, my friends, is irony. Not the work of a cruel god, but the best gesture of a compassionate creator in over his head. 'You can't always get what you want, but you can get what you need.' 'Careful what you wish for.' 'Every cloud has a silver lining.' Irony is at the heart of all our wisdom sayings."

"Since when have the Rolling Stones been indoctrinated into the canon of cultural wisdom?" said Rivka.

"Nineteen sixty-eight," said Wade.

Jason yawned and Rivka stood up. "Ironically, since I'm very tired and have to get up early, I'm going home," she said.

"That's not ironic," said Wade.

"You're right," said Rivka, and gave him a sock in the arm.

She and Jason said their good-byes and headed out the sliding door. Monty followed close behind.

"So you're saying there are two kinds of irony," said Sunny when they'd gone. "Punitive and benevolent."

"That's my current thinking," said Wade. "You get what you deserve, for better or worse. If something bad happens that can't be helped, it at least comes with a silver lining. On the other hand, every blessing is a little mixed."

"I can't think of any way Anna deserved to die. This is all very cute rhetorically, but reality has plenty of unmitigated tragedy in it."

"Ironically, a benevolent universe can only retain its goodness by allowing genuine evil to exist," said Wade. "Ironically, just when the girl no one could catch was finally ready to settle down, it was too late."

Too late, thought Sunny. She put down the glass of port she'd been sipping and decided to put her shoes on and go home to bed. Ironically, it was at precisely that moment that she fell into a deep, sound sleep on Wade Skord's couch and didn't wake up until long after the sun warmed her cheeks the next morning.

14

The shriek of the coffee grinder woke her.

"Sorry, I thought you were awake," said Wade.

"With my eyes closed?" said Sunny.

"Okay, I lied. I couldn't wait any longer for coffee."

She sat up, feeling exactly like someone who has slept in her clothes on a friend's couch without washing her face or brushing her teeth. "Ugh. What happened?"

"You drank half of New Zealand and passed out. I wasn't going to let you drive and I figured you'd punch me if I took you to bed, so that seemed like the best place to leave you."

The percolator started perking and the smell of an extremely potent brew wafted her way. Synapses sputtered.

"Tell that thing to hurry up. I might snap in half like a dry twig if I don't get some coffee in the next thirty seconds or so. What time is it?"

"You should always drink a few glasses of water after you down a bottle of wine. A good mountaineer always pees clear."

"I'll remember that next time I pass out. The time?"

Wade consulted the clock on the wall directly in front of them. "Six fifty-seven."

Sunny hauled herself up and took a seat at the kitchen table. Farber the cat rubbed against her ankles. Wade made toast with butter and honey and joined her. There was a bowl of blueberries and a plate of strawberries.

"Just like a B and B." Sunny picked up a strawberry and smelled it. "From the garden?"

"Dirt to table in under ten minutes."

"Impressive."

"We aim to please."

Wade got up and came back with coffee. They sipped, watching the new day outside the glass doors. Sunny spoke first.

"If irony is the core nature of the universe, then the person who loved Anna most, who most wanted her to stay alive, must have killed her. That's Oliver Seth."

"Only if the joke is on him," said Wade, waggling a weathered finger at her. "You have to figure out who is the butt of the joke, cosmically speaking. Who was behaving like the biggest jackass?"

"You mean other than me?"

"As far as I can tell, you behaved with the usual McCoskey restraint."

"That's what I mean. If I'd been more impulsive, I would have gone up there to their room when my intuition told me to and Anna would still be alive."

"If, if, if. You must stop torturing yourself about it, Sun. There's no way to know what might have happened. Think of *Lawrence of Arabia*. Maybe it was written. You just never know what might have happened. If I'd married my high-school sweetheart, I'd have ten kids and a dog by now. Do you want to look back and create a bunch of feelings of regret, or shall we try to figure this out?"

Sunny smiled into her cup. She felt an annoying rush of tears for no specific reason. Her head hurt. The whole lunch-for-sixty-to-eighty-visitors juggling act was about to start all over again. Sometimes she wished she had a regular job and a boss and could just cop a husky voice and call in sick. She met his eyes. "Right. Onward."

"Let's try it like this," said Wade. "Who was trying to defy their fate? Think about the Taoist idea of *wu wei*. You float along like a cork at sea. You don't fight the current, you work with it. You go up the waves and down the waves. The irony kicks in when you try to fight the inevitable. How do you drown in a riptide? You swim as hard as you can toward shore until you exhaust yourself. How do you get out? You relax and swim with the current, at an angle toward the beach, until you're out of the rip or close to shore. *Wu wei*. You use the forces greater than yourself to achieve your goals. Then there's Oedipus. Everyone thinks that's a story about how you can't escape your fate. Yes and no. The Hellenic Greeks knew their stuff. In my opinion, it's a mystical teaching story written to illustrate, among other points, that irony is the core nature of the universe. Try too hard to control things beyond your reach—by violence, for example—and you create the opposite effect. Oedipus's parents thought they were getting over on the gods by hiding their son, but it all came back to bite them in the ass. If they'd just accepted the prophecy, he probably wouldn't have fulfilled it."

Sunny frowned. "What, you mean by talking open and honestly with their son about how he was destined to kill his father and marry his mom? You think that would have worked?"

"I'm still sorting out the nuances of the theory."

"I can see that," said Sunny. "Besides, if I knew who was resorting to violence to change their fate, I would know who killed Anna even without your theory."

"Let's take another angle," said Wade thoughtfully. "Ironically, if you want to know a man's weakness, you have to look at his strength."

He watched her with eyes sparking under an overhang of snarled eyebrow. His uncombed hair was a savage mass of gray cowlicks. He gave Sunny a sage look that came across somewhere between pompous and deranged. She couldn't help laughing and shook her head. "I don't get it."

"Stick with me, you'll catch on. What is Monty's strongest attribute?"

"Savviest nose and most incisive palette in a valley stuffed to the gills with wine experts."

"Exactly. And what is his biggest weakness?"

"We're talking about a man who wears glasses electively. Where should I start?"

"Think Achilles' heel. Achilles probably had bad breath, a nasty temper, and back hair, but his only real weakness, like all the weaknesses that matter, was innately tied to his greatest strength. In Monty's case that would be . . ."

"Wine. As in drinking too much of and spending too much on."

"I rest my case. Greatest strength and greatest weakness ironically and innately linked."

"Brilliant, but how is that relevant to my situation? And bear in mind I have to leave for work in seven minutes or less."

"We have to work backward. What weakness, or shall we say vice, led to Anna's murder?"

"That would be nice to know."

"Well, it wasn't greed. She didn't have money, right?"

"None of her own as far as I know. But if she had wanted money, she could have married it whenever she wanted. Or earned her own. She was very clever."

"Isn't that the kind of woman other women resent?"

"Some. I'd say Molly Seth, Oliver's sister, falls into that camp. And Anna thought Oliver's cook, Cynthia, resented her."

"Did she have any reason to want Anna gone?"

"Molly? No, none that I can see. I'd say she was irritated to have her around, that's about it. The cook might have been resentful of having to wait on Anna, but it's her job, after all." Sunny studied the contents of her coffee cup, considering the many passions Anna Wilson had inspired over the years. "It was mostly men who reacted to Anna. They adored her."

"And those she rejected? What about a spurned lover?"

"Troy Stevens. Possibly even Molly's new boyfried, Jared. But neither of them seems to hold any current resentment."

"Okay, scratch resentment. What about fear?" said Wade.

"Oliver may have been afraid Anna would reveal his secrets. But afraid enough to kill her? I seriously doubt it."

"What about fear of commitment? When I heard the story, the first thing I thought was she must be pregnant. A guy like that doesn't want to be tied down to a wife and a baby."

"No, that's not it," said Sunny. "Anna was as skittish as he is. More so. If anything, she was the one who needed to be convinced to settle down. Besides, Oliver Seth can afford as many children and ex-girlfriends as he cares to acquire. He has enough money to pay his way out of any situation."

Wade sipped his coffee. "We are talking about an incredibly violent act with enormous consequences. The individual would need to be powerfully motivated. Who wanted something bad enough to kill an innocent girl?" He smacked his lips thoughtfully. "I don't see it. Either we're looking at it from the wrong angle, or there's a missing piece."

The missing piece was in those e-mails Anna had sent, Sunny was sure of that, but she just couldn't see it. Maybe Wade would be able to make sense of them. For now, she needed to get to work. Tonight they could look at them together. She finished a piece of toast and followed it up with a strawberry. What she really wanted was a plate of bacon and eggs with potatoes piled on the side, but there wasn't time. Wade picked up Farber and gave him a scrub around the ears. The morning sun lit up the storm of fur it produced. The cat threw himself against Wade's chest, purring loudly. Sunny looked at the clock. Half past seven. Time to roll.

Outside the truck's open window, the roadside vineyards flourished and the cool morning air was full of summer smells. Sunny took the winding turns slowly, letting the truck coast down the hill. In a couple of months it would be harvest time and the crush would begin. The sight of lush leaves and tight green clusters of nascent grapes was a balm to her tattered nerves and throbbing head.

On Highway 29, as she accelerated into a straightaway, the truck hiccupped. She gave it more gas. It chugged and lurched. The pedal touched the floor to no effect. She switched to the reserve tank. A moment later, the engine died. Instead of admiring grapevines, she should have been watching the dashboard, which clearly showed a now complete lack of fuel. There was a turnout ahead. The truck coasted, winding down to a crawl. In the rearview mirror, a semi approached at full speed. The valley's narrow, two-lane artery with its tractors and tourists on bicycles didn't slow anyone down. Cars and trucks of every size barreled through the countryside as if they were on the interstate. She hit the hazards and prayed. The pickup's tires tipped over the edge of the pavement onto the dirt turnout just as the semi loaded with two trailers of gravel blew past, inches away.

Several more cars zipped by, rocking the cab of the truck. Sunny flipped the lever back and forth between the main and reserve tanks, turning the key pointlessly. The truck chugged and failed. There was a gas can in the back, but it would be a long, not to mention humiliating, walk in either direction to the nearest gas station. She got out her cell and dialed AAA. She was on hold when a black Jaguar driven by a blond woman in big sunglasses braked and pulled over just ahead. Molly Seth got out and walked back to the truck, picking her way through the gravel in high heels. *Double merde!* thought Sunny, hanging up. Molly was dressed like a matador in black capris and a black bustier over a white blouse. Sunny got out.

"That thing die on you?" said Molly.

"I forgot to fuel up. Preoccupied, I guess."

"Aren't we all. Come on, I'll give you a lift. I'm headed up to Oliver's. We can send one of the guys back with gas."

"I can call three A."

"I insist," said Molly, her eyes meeting Sunny's behind the dark glasses.

Sunny shivered. It was cold enough in Molly's car to chill Chardonnay and the air-conditioning was going full blast. She groped under the seat for the lever to move her seat back. A hammer and work gloves lay at her feet on the floorboards. Under the seat was a roll of something. She picked it up. Duct tape. Sunny glanced at Molly, whose fingertips rested lightly on the wheel. The road was flying by.

"I have a couple of houses to show this morning," said Molly, "but I wanted to stop by and see how Oliver is holding up. The last few days have been terrible. The police just let him back into the house last night."

"You're a real-estate agent?"

Molly took a card from a center compartment and handed it to Sunny. "Second homes, mostly, if you know anyone who needs one."

At the security gate leading to Oliver's property, everything appeared normal enough. There were no police cars and the gate swung open when Molly announced herself. The Jaguar cruised up the hill and they parked in front of Oliver's garage. Mike Sayudo, the gardener who'd found Anna's body, headed around the corner of the house carrying a garden hose.

"Give me your keys. I'll ask Mike to take one of the other guys and go get your truck."

"Are you sure? I could go with them."

"It's no trouble. Go ahead inside. Cynthia is there. I'll be right in."

The front door was open. In the kitchen, Cynthia was wiping down the counters in a low-slung tank top, skinny jeans, and heels. She had her hair in a ponytail and her eyes made up. She gave Sunny a big smile and seemed happy to see her.

"Car trouble is the worst. But I'm almost glad. It's so good to see people here other than the police," she said, drying her hands. "Oliver should be back soon. He went down to the winery for a moment. We're just trying to get back to normal around here, or as close to it as we're likely to get. It won't ever feel quite the same here again." She sighed. "What can I get you? I just made a pot of coffee, but I can make an espresso, cappuccino, anything you like."

"Regular coffee sounds great," said Sunny.

"Are you sure? A cappuccino is no trouble."

"Honestly, regular coffee is fine."

"I'll have a cappuccino," said Molly, walking in. "Could you bring it to us outside? It's such a beautiful morning." She looked around the kitchen. "Where is Oliver?"

"He'll be back in a few minutes."

They went down to the table under the arbor where everyone had had dinner the night Anna died. A twinkling glare glinted off the pool's surface. The pool guy was skimming leaves and another gardener was working on the lawn, as though nothing had happened and guests would be arriving soon for the next dinner party. Molly sent them away and lit a cigarette.

"That was lucky you coming along when you did," Sunny said. "I'd probably still be sitting by the road waiting for help."

Molly nodded and gave a half smile. "My pleasure."

"Have you heard any news from the police?"

Molly shook her head. "They're not exactly going out of their way to keep us informed."

Cynthia arrived with their coffees, strawberries and melon, and a plate of biscotti. "There's cream and sugar. Do you need anything else?"

"Just let me know when Mike gets back with Ms. McCoskey's vehicle."

"I'll do that."

Cynthia went back up to the house. In the distance a chainsaw chugged to life and dug into its work with a steady whine. Molly stirred sugar into her cappuccino but didn't drink it. She went back to smoking her cigarette and watching Sunny. They listened to the drone of the distant chainsaw, a light breeze pushing back strands of Molly's blonde hair.

"And you?" said Molly. "Have you heard anything?"

"Nothing much. The paper said the police cracked the encryption on Oliver's computer."

"I saw that," said Molly.

"And they discovered the business about the other woman."

"What a ridiculous idea. How can there be another woman when you're not married? And they still don't know what killed her."

"I don't think the autopsy is back yet."

"Autopsy! Such a grim word. Autopsies and police reports and funerals. I can't wait until all of this business is over. At least Oliver has Cynthia here to help him get through it."

"Are they close?"

"Close enough. Cynthia adores him. And it's someone to cook for him and be here when he gets home so the place isn't empty. I hate to see him alone in this big house, especially at a time like this."

"I'm not alone," said Oliver, coming down the stairs. "Keith is coming up later today, and Franco is going to stay on for a few more days until he heads back to Europe." He kissed his sister and acknowledged Sunny. "I hear you ran out of gas. Both tanks? That takes talent."

"Or something. It's not quite as hard as it sounds. There's a problem with the switch. It's supposed to draw down one tank at a time. Lately it's been drawing both, I don't know how. Still, my fault for cutting it too close. I'm sorry to take your guys away from their work."

"Don't worry about it. There's not enough work to keep them busy all day around here, anyway."

Cynthia came down and Oliver asked her for a cold washcloth and a cup of hot tea. She smiled sympathetically and went to fetch them.

"Are you sick?" asked Molly.

"No, no, I'm fine. Just trying to wake up. I couldn't get to sleep last night."

"You're working too much," said Molly.

"The opposite," said Oliver. "Not enough. I've got too much time on my hands. I can't really do anything until all this terrible business about Anna is under control."

"Sunny was just saying something about the police unlocking the encryption on your computers."

"I saw that. It's a bogus story, of course. But who knows, it might work. I assume they planted it to try to flush out the bad guy, since they insist there is one."

"Why do you think it's bogus?" said Sunny.

"Because the best cryptographers in the world couldn't crack that encryption. I warned them before they took everything. You have to bring the system back up the right way, with the right passwords, or the data goes into emergency mode and encrypts using the most powerful encryption ever invented. Once that happens, that's it. It's gibberish. That's the whole point. You steal my computer, you steal junk. Even I can't decrypt it. No one can. For all intents and purposes, the data self-destructs."

"All of it?" said Sunny.

"All of it."

"Even the surveillance footage."

"Everything."

"So if somebody breaks into your house and takes your computer," said Sunny, "you lose everything? Including the surveillance footage that could tell you who stole your computer? What good is that?"

Oliver chuckled. "*I* don't lose everything. The guy who stole it does. The system gets backed up every night at two A.M. PST. We only lost the material from two A.M. onward. Unfortunately, in this case, that is precisely the material that would be most useful to have."

Sunny thought for a moment. "So the data on the hardware is locked up, but all your files are still accessible somewhere. Can't the police just look there?"

"They could."

"But you won't let them."

"The servers are operated by our offices in Rio de Janeiro. They are more than welcome to seek whatever material they like through that country's official channels."

Sunny glared at him. "Aren't you at all curious what happened to Anna? There could be something on the surveillance tapes that helps the police figure out who killed her."

· "I know who killed Anna. Anna killed Anna. I don't have to look at surveillance tapes to know that. I was with her until two in the morning. She was drunk and high and alive. It's what comes after that that might be valuable, and that's gone forever, thanks to the police. They're on their own as far as I'm concerned."

Cynthia came down with the washcloth and tea for Oliver. He wiped his face and neck. Cynthia stood behind him and massaged his shoulders. Oliver closed his eyes.

"Everyone okay? Sunny? More coffee?" she said.

"Nothing for me, thanks, Cynthia."

She left and Oliver sipped his tea. Sunny waited a few minutes for him to speak, then broke the silence. "You said you left Anna at two o'clock in the morning. What did you do after that?"

Molly took her sunglasses off. "Oliver, don't answer that. She has no right to ask you questions."

Oliver waved his hand as if to brush her away. "It's okay. It's not as though I haven't been through this a dozen times with the police. I was upset from our fight. I didn't want to go to bed. There's a path behind the house up to a bench where you can sit and watch the stars. You can see the lights down the entire valley. It's a good place to sit and think, and that's what I did. I sat there for a long time, and then I went into the garage and got in my car. I was going to take a drive, but I changed my mind. I sent a few text messages, then I must have fallen asleep. When I woke up, Mike had already found Anna and called the police."

Sunny finished her coffee, watching him. Oliver shifted in his chair and looked around, shaking his head as though overcome by a sudden wave of irritation. "Is that everything you want to know?"

he said. "Or would you like me to describe how it felt to wake up in my car with the hangover of a lifetime in order to go stand over a beautiful girl with her head cracked open from hitting the cement. Right over there, as a matter of fact," he said, pointing. "I'm sure I could re-create the scene for you. The grotesque way only the whites of her eyes showed through half-closed lids, and how the smell of blood mixed with the smell of freshly cut grass in a way I'm sure I will never be able to forget. And would you like to know what I did after that? I went into the bathroom where her hairbrush and her toothbrush and her mascara were still out on the counter like she would walk into the room at any second and ask me what I wanted for breakfast and I cried like a baby. That is, until the police began to interrogate me, which they have hardly stopped doing since then."

Cynthia came out of the kitchen and walked down the steps to where they were sitting. She frowned when she saw Oliver rubbing his temples. "Mike asked me to tell you he's back with the truck," she said, picking up their dishes.

Sunny stood up. "Thank you for being honest."

Oliver jerked his head up. "How would you know if I'm being honest?"

Sunny studied his face for a moment. Inscrutable. Was he making some kind of joke? She decided not, thanked Molly for her help, and walked back up past the lawn and the little creek cascading down and into the chill of the air-conditioned house. Out front, Mike Sayudo was talking to the pool guy.

Sunny walked over. "I can't thank you enough."

"No problem."

She looked at the pool guy. "Where does all the water come from around here? I mean for the pool and the lawns. The hills look so dry."

"From a well they put in last year."

"And it comes out of the ground crystal clear like that?"

"It comes out looking like lemonade and smelling like rotten eggs. To get it just right, you have to work with it," he said with obvious pride. "We've got five filtration systems running here twenty-four-seven. You could bottle the water in that pool. It's as close to perfect as money can buy."

"Sounds expensive."

"We're running upwards of a quarter of a million dollars' worth of equipment, and that doesn't include maintenance and operating costs. But it sure is pretty." He gave her a grin.

Sunny looked up at the rocky hillside behind the house. A rough path led up through chaparral. She glanced back at the house and the double garage doors and got in the truck. She drove down the strip of cement that wound down the hillside like a pale gray ribbon running past Cynthia's garden, the pig's enclosure and the little cabin where the chickens roosted, the tennis court, Cynthia's house, and finally the winery. Almost nine o'clock. Rivka would be wondering what happened to her. She picked up the phone and dialed the restaurant.

"Steve called," said Rivka when she answered. "He said to remind you to drop by the station today to comply with his request. Those were his exact words. He said you'd know what he meant."

Sunny hung up and dialed Wade Skord. "I think I need a lawyer. The police want a DNA sample. Who was that guy who helped you out with the Beroni business?"

"Harry? I'll have to look up his number," said Wade. "Don't do anything until you talk with him."

If giving a DNA sample was really no big deal, Sergeant Harvey wouldn't mind if she didn't comply right away.

15

Rivka straightened the candles in a tarnished silver candelabrum and lit them. The flames stood upright in the stillness of the warm evening. They'd opened the French doors off the dining room, and now the air inside the restaurant was as heavy and hot as it was outside. Sunny had finally finished the last of the cleaning, prepping, ordering, accounting, and other chores she'd let slide recently. Now she came out to the patio with two glasses of white wine. She handed one to Rivka.

"You call Skord?"

"He's on his way," said Sunny.

They heard a grunt and Monty Lenstrom peeked over the fieldstone wall that hemmed in the patio. "Hey! Is someone going to let me in or do I have to climb the tree? I've been knocking for half an hour."

"Come round the back," said Rivka.

She returned with Monty trailing behind. "Didn't you hear me knocking? My knuckles are raw," he said.

"Who uses the front door after closing time?" said Rivka.

Between the three of them they had the table set, the salads plated, and the salmon steaks off the grill in under ten. Wade Skord banged on the back door just as they were sitting down.

"I can't believe I'm eating salmon again," said Sunny. "I feel like a grizzly bear."

"Makes your coat shiny," said Wade, taking his seat.

"Riv, please tell me this is the last of it."

"It is. I divided what was left between the dishwashers."

"Good. At least they'll get their omega-three fats." Sunny looked around the table at her friends. She settled on Wade. "You'll never guess what happened after I left your house this morning."

Wade looked up with his mouth full and a gloss of olive oil on his chin. He shook his head. "No idea."

"The Ranger let me down. Ran out of gas right after I got on 29."

"So that's why you were late!" said Rivka.

"Serves you right for driving that heap," said Monty.

"I'll forget you said that," said Sunny. "That's just the beginning." She told the story of how Molly Seth had pulled over in her black Jag and everything that had happened at Oliver's house. "As incredible as that house is, it still gives me the creeps," she said. "All that water makes me nervous. You look around and you see a landscape that's just a couple of rainstorms ahead of the Gobi Desert, and meanwhile his place is nothing but lawns and waterfalls. It's like Las Vegas. You get the feeling everything is being used all at once and one day the taps are going to dry up and it'll be like *Road Warrior.*"

"That's the bootstrapper talking," said Rivka. "Always conserving resources. You'd make a terrible rich person."

"He's lying for sure," said Wade.

Sunny followed his glance and handed him the plate of grilled salmon. "About what?"

"Everything," said Wade, taking a slab from the plate and squeezing a lemon over it. "As someone with extensive experience sitting on hills contemplating stars, I can tell you this guy is no stargazer. I buy the part about him sitting in his car firing off text messages. That makes sense. There are only a few different ways to cope with life. You can work, you can drink, you can go to the gym, or you can wander around the countryside looking at stars. This guy's a worker."

"Hard to know for sure."

"I'm sure. You said he evaded your question, right? You asked him if he was telling the truth and he made a joke."

"More or less. I thanked him for being honest and he asked me how I would know he was."

"It's human nature. Even the worst of us are still programmed to avoid outright lies. You tried to force him to say whether or not he was telling the truth. He avoided the question. He's lying. End of story as far as I'm concerned."

"Even if he was lying, that doesn't tell us much," said Sunny. "Lying about what? And why?"

"What about all this encryption business?" said Rivka. "He admitted the system gets backed up each night to his office in Brazil. That could only happen online. Obviously, he must be able to access everything online somehow. He could turn that access over to the police right now. But he won't. Ergo, he has something to hide."

They sat around the table thinking. Sunny broke the silence. She took an envelope out of her bag and handed it across to Rivka. "I've been wanting to show you this for a couple of days. It's a printout of some e-mails Anna forwarded to me the night she died. I got it on Monday. The police made the gist of it public in yesterday's paper, so there's no reason not to share it now."

Wade took a final bite of salmon and pushed his plate away. "Explain."

"The night she died, Anna got into Oliver Seth's e-mail. She found some correspondence between him and one of his employees, a woman named Astrid. She forwarded it to me for safekeeping."

"They sound like lovers," said Rivka, skimming the e-mails. "That must have been what they were fighting about that night,"

"Presumably."

"Definitely lovers," said Rivka, holding up the photograph of Oliver Seth and Astrid with the little yellow convertible in front of the Coliseum.

"Nice gams," said Monty, taking it from her.

"Nice ride," said Wade, leaning over. "That's the new Smart Roadster, if I'm not mistaken."

"The question is, why did she think this e-mail would protect her?" Sunny held out her hand and Rivka handed her the papers. Sunny read from them. "'Please keep this safe for me. Call it an insurance policy. I must control my fate.'"

"That's what Oliver writes in one of his e-mails," said Rivka, taking the papers back. She flipped through them. "Here it is. 'See attached. Remember to control your fate. She's bullish on the new vintage.' What does he mean by that?"

"It has something to do with his winery, Taurus Rising," said Sunny. "Oliver showed me a bottle. There's a bull on the label with a girl on its back. 'She's bullish on the new vintage' is clearly a reference to the label. But what does it mean, if anything? Maybe it's just some silly in-joke between them."

"A girl on a bull," said Rivka. "Is it the rape of Europa?"

"Exactly," said Sunny. "What about 'Control your fate'?"

"It could be another threat," said Wade. "The rape of Europa is another Greek myth, like Scylla and Charybdis. Points to your Sicilian friend, if you ask me. Rape, abduction. Maybe you control your fate by keeping your mouth shut so you don't end up like Europa carried off on a bull."

"It's some kind of riddle," said Monty. "Having to do with the attachment. That's the photograph of them, right?"

"Maybe it's just some kind of romantic innuendo," said Sunny. "Oliver is a Taurus, the bull. He's the bull carrying off the girl."

"It still doesn't make any sense," said Rivka.

"I'm with Monty on this one. It sounds like a riddle to me," said Wade.

"I love riddles," said Monty. "We have to crack it or I'll be up all night. Bella won't let me near the *Times* crossword anymore."

"I thought you were obsessed with some My Little Pony video game," said Rivka. "Annabelle called me a few nights ago practically in tears because you wouldn't stop for ten minutes to help her with your wedding plans."

"While no one appreciates the diminutive horse more than I do, the activity to which you are referring is called The Legend of Zelda, and it's not a video game, it's an artificial universe where one can push the boundaries of the human experience."

"Do you actually stay up all night playing a kid's game?" asked Rivka.

"Occasionally a long period of focused time is necessary to truly experience the Zelda world."

"It's an illness. You do realize that, right? You're an addict. You need help."

"Why don't you mind your own beeswax and go get another tattoo, Jezebel."

"Would you two stop, please?" said Sunny.

"And you want to know what the big wedding-planning crisis was?" said Monty. "What font to use on the invitations. By the time this is over, the woman is going to need medication, or I will. Finally she gave up and let me pick."

"And?" said Rivka.

"Hello? Copperplate. Letterpress on acid-free heavy cream stock. Very tasteful."

"So I guess nobody has an answer to the riddle," said Sunny. Three blank faces stared back at her in the candlelight.

"This printout kind of sucks," said Wade, squinting hard at the picture of Oliver and Astrid. "It's all grainy. Maybe there's some detail we're missing."

"Like what?"

"I don't know. Like what's that on the seat of the car?"

Sunny stared at the image. "I can't tell. I'll bring out my laptop and we can have a closer look."

She came back with her laptop and put it in front of Wade, illuminating his face with a blue glow. He held up his glass. "It's bad enough to bring a computer to the table, but to leave your guest on empty?"

Sunny sighed and went inside. She found an open bottle of Flowers Pinot behind the bar. When she came back Rivka had opened the e-mail from Anna. She hesitated at the attachment.

"Eight megabytes? Isn't that kind of huge? Pictures are usually not more than a couple megs."

"Oliver probably has some crazy high-tech camera," said Sunny.

"Maybe they planned to make a poster," said Rivka. She zoomed in on the front seat. "It's nothing. Just her handbag."

They all stared at the picture, then at one another.

"We're barking up the wrong tree here, folks," said Wade. "And meanwhile, it's getting late and I gotta put the grapes to bed."

"Maybe the police will figure it out," said Rivka. "Anybody check the papers today?"

"Look online," said Sunny. "You can jump on Bismark's WiFi from here."

They all waited, staring at the screen. Nothing happened.

Monty looked at his watch, an expensive TAG Heuer Annabelle had given him that he was immodestly proud of. "I gotta get going."

"You don't want to keep Zelda waiting," said Rivka.

"Shoot, it's frozen," said Sunny.

"Control-Alt-Delete," said Monty, putting on his coat.

"Control your fate," said Rivka.

There was a pause just long enough to take a slow breath during which three bodies stopped, their expressions frozen, while three overworked brains labored, crunching data, sorting it into categories, making links and associations. The spark of discovery leaped from their eyes simultaneously as the same words formed on their lips at the same moment.

"Control-F8!" said Rivka, Monty, and Sunny in unison.

Wade, who had been holding his glass of Pinot up to the candlelight and studying it intently, lowered it to look at them in astonishment.

Sunny carried the laptop back into the office and hooked it up to the Internet. With Rivka at the controls and the others looking over her shoulders, they went to Taurian's Web site and tried typing Control-F8. They tried the Web site for Taurus Rising wines and looked for Taurian Web sites in Brazil, Italy, and Russia. They googled Oliver Seth and tried Control-F8 at every site that seemed officially connected to him. Nothing happened. Wade was the first to give in and go home. A few minutes later, Monty called it quits.

"Maybe we're wrong," he said, looking up from the marks he was making on a piece of notepaper. "Maybe it's an anagram. 'Control your fate' could be 'Fool not ate curry.'"

Rivka and Sunny looked at him.

"I'm just saying we could be wrong. Maybe Control-F8 has nothing to do with anything. Either way, I have to go home and get some sleep."

"He's right. Whatever it means, we're not going to figure it out tonight," said Sunny. She looked at Rikva. "I need some sleep and so do you. We have to be back here in six hours."

"I'm out of here," said Monty. "Thanks for the grub and the puzzle hour. Next time we can do the crossword. Oh, and don't forget we have to get our heads together on the menu for the engagement party. It's coming up fast. Annabelle said she wants peaches in the salad. You think that's possible?"

"Definitely," said Sunny. "A fine idea."

"I mean, do you think you can find some peaches that taste like peaches used to taste. Like maybe from those guys who gave us that box last year that was so amazing."

"Those guys sold out. Hasta la vista, peach trees; hello, multiplex theater and parking lot. But I have some other connections. I think I can score for you."

"Great. You're the best, you know that, McCoskey? See you guys."

They heard the back door bang shut and Monty stomp down the stairs.

"You said yes?" said Rivka. "I thought you were boycotting weddings forever."

Sunny shrugged. "How could I say no?"

"But Annabelle? She's going to make you crazy."

"It's just the engagement dinner. I'm the host. She can only micromanage so far."

They heard someone come back up the stairs and open the door. A second later Monty stood in the office doorway. "No utter fool racy!"

"Meaning?" said Sunny.

"I was hoping you would know. Nothing? Never mind, then."

He left and the door slammed again. "What a waste of time," said Sunny, giving a great yawn and stretch. "I desperately needed to go to bed." She rocked her head back and tipped it side to side, popping the vertebrae in her neck audibly. Her feet hurt, her skin felt like the sweaty inside of a leather sneaker, and she had a headache that was getting worse like the whirring of an engine getting louder and louder. She scrubbed her hands through her short hair, skimming out the clips that held a fringe of bangs off her forehead while she worked. "Let's go," she said. "I'm beat. We can try again tomorrow."

Rivka closed the last of the Web sites and stared at the image of Oliver and Astrid glowing on the screen in the gloomy room. "I'd like to control your fate, Mr. Seth, and your little hot-body girl-friend's, too," she said, and hit Control-F8 one last time. She stared at the computer. "Uh, Sun . . ."

"No more. I can't see. I'm going blind, I swear. I need to go to bed."

"Still, I think you're going to want to see this."

Sunny walked over. On top of the photograph was a pop-up box. *"Passwort eingeben."* She looked at Rivka. "Where'd that come from?"

"Control-F8. Are we agreed on *Europa?*"

Sunny nodded. Rivka typed in the letters and hit Enter. Nothing happened.

"Maybe it has to have a number in it," said Sunny. "The new vintage is also the only vintage. His first. I think it was 2001."

"Europa2001," said Rivka, typing. "Nothing. How many tries do we get before it locks?"

Sunny held her breath. "Try Europa01."

Rivka typed and hit Return. The screen blinked black and then, starting from the top, the photograph began to unravel, bit by bit. A moment later, the photograph was gone and they were staring at a letter on Taurian letterhead.

Sunny looked at Rivka, put her finger to her lips, and went to pull down the shade in the office window. Her mouth had gone dry and her heart thumped double time. She stared at the screen. "Holy crap."

"That's why the file was so big," said Rivka. "It wasn't a photograph. It's a message hidden inside a photograph."

Sunny reached over and hit Control-P. She picked up the printout as though handling an ancient scroll. It was dated May, just two months earlier.

Dear Astrid,

Per our discussion, Keith will help you set up the LLC through the office in the Caymans. I have given him power of attorney for any legal documents that need to be filed. You have access to funding via account #129635. It should be adequate for your needs, but if not, Chimon can assist you at tel. (+49) 030-90616-5002.

As for the POs, if we can't get them in time, we'll have to create them. Also the letters of intent and whatever else Keith says we need. Do all the correspondence in Russian. That will make the documents look more authentic and also slow things down if we happen to get into trouble. Translations are tedious and expensive! Keith can provide you with samples of what this kind of thing looks like. You can grab their logos off the Web. They don't have to be perfect, they're just placeholders, but we need them now. By the time anybody questions them, we'll have the real thing. Leave nothing to chance!

I look forward to seeing you in Rome, though I was sorry to hear your father would be away.

Sincerely,

Oliver

Sunny folded the letter and put it in her pocket. "Shut that thing down and let's get out of here."

"Do you really want to carry that around?" said Rivka, gesturing to the letter. "I think it's safe to assume Anna died because of what's in that letter."

Sunny looked around the office and shivered. "No one knows what happened here tonight. I'll give it to Steve first thing in the morning on my way in. Come on, I'll drive you home."

Rivka shut down the computer. "You want to take this home?" she said, tapping it.

Sunny frowned. "Let's leave it here. I won't need it tonight."

Rivka picked up her backpack to leave, then changed her mind. She disconnected the computer and shoved it in a desk drawer, then followed Sunny out, pushing her bike beside her.

It was late when Sunny finally pulled up in front of her house. She walked through the door and kept going straight to the shower. Clothes hit the floor. Hot water came down. Steam filled the bathroom like a sauna. Her skin turned pink in the heat. The night had drained her body of its warmth. When she felt warm again at last, she dried off and dropped the towel next to the bed, slipping between cool sheets. Her heart thumped in her ears, its percussive beat her last impression before she fell into a dreamless, timeless oblivion. She woke to full sun. Late, again. She pulled on a clean T-shirt and jeans, brushed her teeth, grabbed her bag, and walked out the front door. The morning was still fresh and cool. Seven-thirty, maybe eight o'clock. She breathed in the sweetness of the front yard with its tangle of herbs and flowers, everything climbing, reaching, straining toward the sun. Mammals, thought Sunny. We're such savages. Ripping and crushing everything around us.

Someone had stuck a flyer on the truck's windshield. Out canvassing early, thought Sunny, or late last night. Ambitious. The single sheet of paper was folded in thirds. She tossed it on the seat beside her, then changed her mind and picked it up. It was moist with condensation and the ink stuck together in places. She peeled it open. It wasn't the flyer she expected, nor another of the nasty notes she sometimes got from the guy next door complaining that her roses were climbing over his fence or her yard needed weeding or she'd left her truck parked in front of his house, not hers, thus preventing him from parking immediately in front of his house, which had the perverse effect of making her want to park in front of his house instead of hers. No, this was something odd. A printout of a dark, muddy photograph with three words written underneath. *Silence is golden.* She looked closer. Someone sleeping. An arm, a face in profile, a tiny fleck of gold. She put a hand to her ear, touching the gold stud. The hairs on her arms rose and a chill tickled the back of her neck. She locked both doors, made herself turn around and look behind her in the bed of the truck, saw with relief it was unoccupied, and started the engine. Her eyes took in the street, the front yard, her little house with its cedar shingles and brick stoop. A car passed, its driver oblivious to her scrutiny. A kid on a bike turned down the street and pedaled by. Whoever had left the photograph was long gone.

16

The news van from the local TV channel was parked out front of the police station. So much for that plan. Sunny made a U-turn and headed toward work. Traffic was moving slowly down Main. Two house painters in work whites came out of Bismark's carrying coffee and got in a truck loaded with ladders and buckets. Sunny pulled in after them. She sat in the truck and dialed Rivka's mobile number. It rang until voice mail picked up. She hung up and dialed again. The third time, Rivka answered.

"I was on the other phone."

"You're still at home?"

"I'm running late. I'm just out the door. I'll be there in ten minutes."

"Listen, Riv, do me a favor. Go outside and take a look around. On your doorstep, your car, your bike."

"Right now?"

"Yeah." Sunny waited.

Rivka came back on the line. "If you left me an Easter basket, somebody stole it."

"Nothing on your car?"

"Just dust. Why?"

"Somebody left a very creepy message on my windshield this morning. I'll tell you about it when I see you. Listen, instead of going to work, meet me at Bismark's as soon as you can, okay? I'm here now."

"What's going on?"

"Just get over here and I'll show you what I mean."

She spent the next twenty minutes listening to a backlog of messages on her home phone, the office phone, and the main number for the restaurant. Andre had called several times. Sunny checked the time. It was nearly eight o'clock. He would be busy at work. Most of the other calls were business. Reservations, sales reps hawking wine and restaurant supplies, one of the bussers asking to change his day off. Sergeant Harvey had called the restaurant and the house, sounding stern and official in both messages and reiterating his request for a DNA sample. Franco Bertinotti had called to say there would be a memorial service for Anna, but the connection faltered at precisely the wrong moment and she couldn't hear the details. She finished jotting down notes and went inside the café. The smell of fresh coffee almost made her forget how the day had begun. She took a cup and a newspaper and chose a seat with her back to the wall and kept her eyes on the door, like a gangster wary of assassins.

The front page had a follow-up story on the Wilson murder. The only new development was that the police were continuing the investigation, meaning there were no new developments. At the end was a notice saying the memorial service was being held at eleven o'clock at the Mission San Rafael. That, at least, was helpful.

Sunny put the paper down and watched the morning commuters come and go. She was thinking that she might just sit in this spot all day and not move or say anything when Rivka came in and flopped down across from her.

"So what's all this about a creepy note?"

"You want a coffee? I need a refill."

Sunny came back with two fresh cups. "Don't you think it's weird that we have gods associated with wine and fire, but none for coffee? Where is the espresso god? If Americans were going to worship anything, wouldn't it be coffee? Or what about chocolate? Where is the Prometheus of chocolate?"

Rivka put down the newspaper. "In Mexico City. He's called Quetzalcoatl. I don't know who's responsible for coffee. I think that was up to your people."

"The Italians started it," said Sunny. "Espresso, at least. Or was it the Turks? Wait, I remember. The Ethiopians started coffee. The Abyssinians. It was their job to come up with a god for it."

"Maybe it's not holy," said Rivka.

"Of course it's holy. It's as holy as wine."

"If Americans were going to worship anything, they'd worship TV," said Rivka. "Where's the television god? Or the god of guns. Are you going to tell me about the creepy note or not? You're freaking out, I can tell."

"I know." Sunny slid the folded paper across the table. "That was on my windshield this morning. Look at my ear. See that? Normally I take my earrings off when I go to bed. Observe the gold post. That photograph was taken last night."

"Somebody came into your house and got close enough to take a picture without waking you. How'd they get in? Was your door locked?"

"A camel train could have come through that place last night without waking me. I always lock the door, but, you know, I was pretty tired last night. Maybe I forgot. I don't know. And I was sleeping the sleep of the dead."

"Don't say that," said Rivka. "You think they knew about what we found? There's no way anybody could have known, right?"

"You mean the letter? No way. You think?"

"I don't see how. I didn't tell anyone anything last night. Not even Jason. I went straight to bed."

"Me, too. But somebody obviously knows we cracked the code." Sunny put her head in her hands and scrubbed at her hair, then rubbed her eyes and pinched the bridge of her nose before looking back at Rivka. "The only thing creepier than somebody in the house watching me sleep is somebody watching us at Wildside last night."

"It's definitely creepier that they were in your house."

"You know what I mean."

"And why does it have to be about last night? You know lots of information about this case. Maybe they just want to shut you up in general."

"Maybe."

They sat there for a while without talking. Pretty soon Sunny noticed Wade Skord stomping the dust off his boots outside the café door. She touched Rivka's hand and gave her a look. Rivka nodded, silently agreeing to wait before they revealed what they'd learned last night to anyone, even Wade. Wade got his coffee and was scanning the room for a table when he spotted them.

"Isn't it a bit late for you restaurateurs to be loafing around?" he said, taking a seat.

"Just fueling up," said Sunny. "And contemplating this." She handed him the paper and explained where she'd found it.

"I think it's safe to assume it's a threat, right?" said Sunny.

"Unless you're looking for a roommate."

"Could it have been taken through your bedroom window?" said Rivka.

"I doubt it. They were all closed except for the one right next to the bed, and they'd have had to push it open more and climb almost all the way through it to get the right angle. I'm sure I would have heard a window opening right there in the bedroom. They're all sticky and loud."

"You figure it was Seth?" said Wade. "He showed up at your place once already trying to keep you quiet."

"Or someone he hired," said Sunny.

The girl behind the counter called Wade's name. He got up and came back chewing a bagel. He tapped the paper with a fingernail as hard as flint. "I don't like this. This isn't just some nasty prank, you know. Seth or otherwise, whoever tiptoed through your tulips last night has done it before. This could be the same guy who killed your friend. You tell Steve about it?"

"Not yet."

"You need to. Right away."

"I'll call from the restaurant. Speaking of that, we'd better hit it."

Wade stood up. "I'm coming with you."

Three cars pulled into the back parking lot at Wildside and three puzzled drivers got out, collecting in front of the office window, which had been boarded up with wide planks.

"You been remodeling?" said Wade.

"What the funk?" said Sunny.

They went inside. The kitchen was as they'd left it, but Sunny's office had been ransacked. Carefully, but ransacked nonetheless. Files were out, drawers were open, books were off the shelves. Even the painting of lemons had been taken down and leaned against the wall. Sunny found the copy of *Simple French Food* on top of a heap on the floor. The copy of Anna's e-mail she'd left there was gone. Rivka crossed to the desk drawer. The laptop was gone, too.

"I think I need some air," Sunny said, and walked outside. Rivka and Wade followed her. They sat on the back stoop.

"You have the devil weed?" said Sunny.

"Smokes?" said Rivka. "Not anymore. Remember, we're reformed."

"Damn."

"That's Harvey's handiwork if I'm not mistaken," said Wade. "I recognize his style from when they did my place. Polite but thorough."

"At least they boarded up the window when they were done," said Rivka.

"Nice of them," said Sunny.

"Gives you a chance to do your spring cleaning," said Wade.

"I needed a new laptop, anyway," said Sunny.

"And I thought Steve had a crush on you," said Rivka.

"Maybe this is his way of showing it," said Wade. "Kind of sweet, really."

"Anything's possible," said Sunny.

"Why break a perfectly good window?" said Sunny, her voice rising into the telephone. "You could open the back door with a credit card. Or you could have called me! I would have come down and let you in. I'd give you a key. Do you know what that window will cost to replace?"

"You should have thought of that a few days ago. You should have helped me out, Sunny. This is a murder investigation, not a tea party. You told me to get a search warrant, so I got one. We came in the easiest way we could and left the place secure. You can't ask for more than that."

Sunny sighed. She'd been on hold so long waiting for Sergeant Harvey that the phone made her ear numb. She crossed the room and closed her office door. "All right. Fine. You win. You want help? I'm going to help you out right now. Last night Rivka and I were fiddling around with those e-mails Anna forwarded and we solved a little riddle for you. That photograph of Oliver and the other woman? It's not just a picture. It's a letter. That's what Seth meant by 'Control your fate.' You hit Control-F8 and it asks for a password, then unravels to show a letter. It's some pretty incriminating stuff having to do with his business practices—fraud, what I assume is a Swiss bank account number, everything. That's what Anna found, that's why she sent it to me for safekeeping. Presumably, that's why she died. You have my computer now, you can take a look yourself, but you'll need the password."

"What is it?"

"First tell me one thing. Is the autopsy back? Do you know how she died?"

"Are you trying to pressure me, Sunny?"

"Not at all," she said quickly. "I'm just trying to help you—help us—put the pieces together."

Sergeant Harvey hesitated. "Suffocation."

"What about the encryption? Any luck cracking it for real?"

"No comment."

"Any other real leads? I mean other than the obvious, which would be Oliver and Keith, right? It had to be one of the two of them, right?"

"Sunny . . ."

"I know, you can't talk about it. What about this woman Astrid? Have you contacted her? She knows everything that was going on with Oliver's business."

"We're trying. We haven't been able to track her down yet."

"And did Oliver tell you how his computer security worked? How the system backed up every night at two in the morning?"

"Yep. Sounds like he told you, too."

"We had a little conversation yesterday. I ran out of gas and Molly Seth picked me up. Long story. So have you found it? If it backs up online, it must be accessible online somewhere. I've googled it a bunch, but I haven't been able to find anything. Have you had any luck?"

"Nothing yet. Believe me, we're working on it. Listen, if you're going to keep asking questions, let's make it official and you can come on down to the station."

"No can do. I've got, like, eighty-six people coming by for a fancy lunch in a couple of hours."

"Then give me the password and we can both go back to work."

"Europa01. 'She's bullish on the new vintage.' He was referring to the artwork on his wine. Europa. The vintage is 2001."

"Got it. Thanks for that."

Sunny heard the dispatch in the background and Sergeant Harvey respond. "Sunny, I've gotta get going. We can talk later."

"Okay."

"Oh, and McCoskey?"

"Yeah."

"You've got until tomorrow noon to give us that DNA sample. Otherwise I haul you in and do it the hard way. Got it?"

"Got it."

"Good. Sorry about the window."

"No problem."

She hung up the phone and grabbed her car keys.

"I'll be back as soon as I can," she said to Rivka on her way out.

"Where are you going?"

"Anna's memorial. Do the best you can without me."

The memorial was held in the old pink Mission San Rafael, its plaster brilliant in the midday sun. Easels outside the entrance to the church held collages of photographs spanning an abbreviated life. Sunny stopped to look at one of a gangly adolescent Anna in a gymnastics leotard, hair pulled back in a tight bun, legs like stalks, with the same daring smile Sunny had seen on her face just five days ago.

The crowd filled the pews and lined the walls. Sunny stood at the back of the church straining to hear what was being said up front. A priest led the congregation in prayer and Sunny mumbled along with everyone else. The open doors behind her seemed to suck the last of the cool air out of the shadows instead of offering relief from the heat. It became stifling hot. Soon her armpits were slick with sweat and a trickle ran down her side. The black pumps she wore to solemn occasions pinched her toes. She studied what she could see of the pulpit, wondering if her flowers had arrived in time, and if so, which of the arrangements—all of them ugly and unnatural-looking—might be hers. She'd placed the order hastily this morning, right after she looked up Anna's mother's number and left her a message saying she would be at the service.

Up near the front, Keith Lachlan was standing against the wall, towering over those around him. Marissa wasn't with him. Sunny scanned the crowd. She could see Oliver Seth in the front row next to Anna's mother. The seat on the other side of him was empty, as though no one else dared to go near him. Anna's father, the grizzled old artist, was slumped at the end of the row. In between prayers and hymns, people stood and spoke about Anna's childhood and early days in California. Sunny caught a word here and there. She began to feel nauseous. The crowd at the back stirred restlessly and fanned themselves with their programs. Several people slipped out. The congregation was reciting "The Lord Is My Shepherd," when Troy Stevens inched past Sunny and out the door. She followed.

He walked down a path between palm trees in the dazzling light and sat on a bench with a view of Mount Tamalpais, standing like a sentry to the west. He put his head in his hands.

"Okay if I join you?" said Sunny.

He moved over. "I had to get out of there. What's the point of all that, anyway?"

"It gives people a chance to grieve," suggested Sunny.

"Is that what that's called?"

She shrugged. "It's not my thing, either, but what else are you supposed to do?"

"Anna would have hated it."

"Definitely."

Troy was wearing a black denim suit with pin stripes and his black Chuck Taylors. He took off the jacket. Underneath was a dark gray T-shirt that made his arms look the color of mayonnaise.

"How've you been?" he said.

"Okay. You?"

"All right. I'll be better when I can get the hell out of here."

"How long are you staying?"

"I'm not sure. The cops asked me to stick around until next week in case they need me. I've got the time."

"You didn't say anything up there," said Sunny, looking back at the church. "I thought you might."

"I wanted to, but her mom wouldn't let me."

"Why not?"

"She and Anna had a falling-out a couple years ago. You notice there was no mention of anything in her life since she moved to Europe? Sylvia thinks it's me who corrupted her. My decadent European lifestyle." He smiled ironically. "Mama's little girl can do no wrong."

"Well, I guess you can't expect her to be critical of her own daughter, considering the situation."

"No, but I thought she'd be able to see through Seth. She thinks he's a *gentleman*," he said, marking the word with air quotes. "That guy makes me want to puke. I can't believe he had the balls to show up."

He took a bottle of children's aspirin out of his pocket and chewed a handful of tablets the same shade of pinkish orange as the church.

"You want some?"

Sunny declined.

"I know that bastard killed her, or at least he knows who did," said Troy.

"You mean because of the fight they had?"

He shook his head. "I don't know. I don't know anything. I just want to get out of here."

"Where are you staying?"

"They gave me the pool house at a youth hostel just outside of Napa. Pretty nice digs, actually. View of the vineyard. All the pastoral accoutrements. Courtesy of the incorporated city of St. Helena."

People started coming out of the church, squinting in the sudden light. Sunny watched the exodus. Molly Seth walked out with her arm through Jared Bollinger's. She was wearing a cream-colored suit and a pale gray hat with a veil. Behind her was Marissa Lin in a tight black dress.

"Maybe it was that crazy bitch Molly," said Troy, watching them. "She hated Anna. Incest between those two if you ask me. Half the time she was sleeping over in the guest room."

"Why would she hate Anna?"

"She was jealous. Between her and Cynthia, Anna got nothing but dagger eyes around that joint."

"I need to talk to Marissa," said Sunny, standing. She dug in her pocketbook for a business card. "I'd like to stay in touch. Call me and let me know how I can reach you?"

He nodded and Sunny walked toward the crowd. She waited until Molly and Jared had moved off before approaching Marissa, who embraced her like a friend.

"Well, at least that's over," said Marissa, dabbing at her eyes with a balled-up tissue. "For a while I didn't think I'd be able to make it. Are you okay?"

Sunny nodded. Marissa looked at something and Sunny turned to see what it was. Keith and Franco had come out of the church and were standing off to the side, talking with Oliver. He turned to the next group of mourners and they continued down the stairs toward the street.

Sunny looked back at Marissa. "Andre explained to me about the other night, and how it wasn't what I'd first assumed. Did you and Keith have an argument about it?"

Marissa shook her head and smiled ruefully. "It wasn't that. Sometimes it's just time to part ways."

Sunny nodded. "I've been meaning to ask you about something Anna mentioned to me the day she died. I can't seem to get it out of my head. She told me Oliver has hidden cameras all over the house. She'd just found out about them the night before."

"Yeah, I know about the cameras."

"From Anna?"

"No, I've known for a while."

Sunny touched her elbow and led her away from the others. "You were friends with Anna. You must want to know what happened to her as much as I do."

"Maybe even more so."

"The data from those cameras may still be accessible online. Oliver told me the system gets backed up each night. The question is where."

"Probably an FTP site somewhere. If he wants to keep it hidden, I doubt you or anyone else is going to find it."

"Marissa, what are those cameras there for?"

"Security, I guess."

"Yes, but not exclusively. Some of them are there for entertainment purposes, aren't they?"

Marissa met her glance and held it. "Possibly."

"Did you ever see any of it? I mean, have you ever watched any of the video footage that was shot at his house?"

"Yes," said Marissa slowly. "I have. Keith showed me some footage from one of those cameras once after a party."

"So he must know how to access it."

"Probably. It was more than just a clip. We scrolled through a bunch of footage online. I have no idea what the URL was, though."

"I don't suppose he'd tell me," said Sunny.

"Probably not."

"He might tell you."

"I doubt it."

"You could ask him."

"If I did, I'd have to speak to him."

The bell on the mission tower began chiming loudly in an up-down peal. "I need to get going," said Sunny. "If you change your mind, you know where to reach me."

"Wildside."

Sunny nodded.

Marissa put her sunglasses on. "Good luck," she said, and turned away.

17

The cab of the truck was searing hot. Sunny took the fast lane north on Highway 101. In record time, she made the stair-step journey across the flats on 37, up 121, across the Carneros ridge on 12, and up 29 to St. Helena. At the restaurant, Rivka was doing her best to keep up with a lunch rush in full fury.

"It's about time," she said, without looking up.

"Pull that," said Sunny, pointing to a ribeye steak. She grabbed a set of tongs and put the steak on a plate. "Smell that? Use your nose to tell when it's done, not your eyes. Your eyes can't tell what's going on inside. Your nose is never wrong. I came back as quickly as I could."

"You should have gotten a ride with her friends."

"What do you mean?"

"Check out table nineteen. They were asking for you."

Sunny walked to the zinc bar, where she had a better view of the dining room. Franco Bertinotti and Keith Lachlan were seated at the second-best table in the house. Franco saw her and beckoned. Sunny smoothed her white jacket and was about to go over when Bertrand appeared at her side, gripping her elbow excitedly. "You see who's here?"

"Yep, I'm going out to talk with them right now."

"I sent over *une demi-bouteille de Vilmart* and some starters."

"Good. What are they drinking now?" asked Sunny.

"Une demi-bouteille de Vilmart."

"That doesn't look like a half-bottle in the bucket."

Bertrand squinted at the dining room. "They don't have a bucket. You're looking at the wrong table. I'm talking about table eight."

Sunny looked. "I don't know those guys."

"The guy on the left is Mike Helton."

"Who's Mike Helton?"

Bertrand goggled at her. "Hello? NASCAR. You know, race cars. Zoom zoom. He's the president. He's like Enzo Ferrari for Americans. I mean, I guess that would be more like Bill France and that crew, but he's still racetrack royalty. You're American. You should try to learn these things about your culture."

Sunny eyed the party at table eight. "Dude with the mustache? Wade will wish he was here."

"Magnificent, isn't it? No one else could wear a mustache like that. Let's go over and I can introduce you."

"Let's let them eat their lunch in peace for a while. We can polish their wingtips and steam their jackets later. Right now I have to interrupt somebody else's meal."

She detached herself from Bertrand and approached Franco and Keith's table wearing her most gracious proprietor's smile. Their first course had already arrived. Keith was working on baked goat cheese with frisée, his enormous hand dwarfing the salad fork. Franco had already finished his carpaccio. All that was left was a green smear of olive oil, a strip of pecorino, and two leaves of arugula. A bottle of sparkling wine cooled in a silver bucket at his elbow.

"You guys made good time," said Sunny.

"Always," said Keith, flashing a confident smile. "Nice place."

"Thanks."

"Funerals always make me hungry," said Franco. "That one in particular. This is such a sad, sad business. One must refresh the spirit. I see you have had to make a repair to your window. Did you have visitors? Perhaps Napa Valley is more like Sicily than I thought?"

"Just a broken window," said Sunny, looking him in the eye. She took the bottle—J. Schram pink—from the ice bucket and topped up their glasses.

Franco held up a leaf of arugula. "No one in the world has rocket better than this. No bitterness, soft texture, almost sweet. Perfect."

"That came out of the garden in back," said Sunny. "It's largely a matter of freshness. Most arugula you get at the market has been in a box longer than that leaf has been in existence."

"Still plump with the milk of mother earth," said Franco.

"You could say that." She glanced back at the kitchen. A flash of flame shot up. "I'd better get back there before we have to evacuate. Did you order already?"

"Just the starters."

"Why don't you let me take care of you. I'll send out a few different things for you to try."

"Even better," said Franco.

She sent out tiny pizzas with caramelized onions and anchovies first. After that came an *amuse-bouche* of soft-boiled duck eggs with *crème fraîche*, a dab of caviar, and a finger of toasted brioche. She adjusted the eggs in their little porcelain cups and aligned the brioche sticks. Bertrand carried them out. He came back a few minutes later and paused at the dessert station, watching Sunny plate a couple of fig tarts with honey-ginger ice cream.

"And?" she said, moving with swift precision, adding a spray of golden sugar and a pristine mint leaf to each. "How did they like the eggs?"

"The old guy knows how to eat. He sucked his down."

"What about the other one?"

"Caribbean *mec*? No go."

"He didn't eat it?"

"Didn't even touch it."

"Why not?"

"How should I know? He was probably too busy playing with his little BlackBerry."

"There goes half an ounce of the best caviar on the continent."

"I wouldn't say that."

She looked at him. "You ate it."

"Of course. Waste not, want not. Incidentally, the egg was very slightly underdone."

"It was three and a half minutes exactly."

"Do three minutes and forty-five seconds next time."

"The white is supposed to be soft."

"Soft, but not transparent. It should be just this side of opaque. This was soft and, in places, semi-opaque, even leaning slightly to the transparent."

"Fine, three minutes and forty-five seconds." She checked the dining room. "You're right. He's got his thumbs on his BlackBerry. That is so rude."

"His friend doesn't seem to mind."

"I mean to us. Can't he take an hour out of his day to pay attention to something other than a little glowing screen?"

Sunny walked over to the zinc bar for a better look at Keith Lachlan. He'd put his phone down on the edge of the table and was eating again. The waiter came by to pour from a new bottle of wine.

"What are they drinking out there?" she asked Bertrand.

"You know those last two bottles of Kongsgaard Chard? Now there's only one."

Sunny sucked in a long breath. "The Judge? Wow, they're not messing around." Her eyes ran up and down the kitchen restlessly. "Listen, Bert, let's show these hot shots what we can do. I want to make sure they have a really, really good time, you know what I mean? We've got to keep the ball rolling. Let's bring out a couple of things they won't be able to resist. Like maybe a Spottswoode Cab."

"Gone."

"All of it?"

"*Tout fini.*"

"Then a Kistler Pinot. Or a Joseph Phelps. One of the older Insignias."

"We have a half-bottle of a good Phelps. Not Insignia, but a very good one."

"Fine. And maybe that Shafer you've been sitting on like a mother hen. Keep their glasses full."

"The 'ninety-three? I must protest."

"But I insist."

Bertrand scowled. "And I refuse," he hissed, lowering his voice. "Their palates are shot already. They'll be drunk as skunks, and on our best hooch."

"That's how we like it. Besides, if they can't finish it, that means more for you."

"If anyone gets that bottle it should be our friends at table eight, not your table of who-knows-who-they-are." He paused, softening. "Why don't you let me find something that will please them extremely well without ruining my day."

"Fine. But make it snappy."

Bertrand rolled his eyes and went to pull the bottles. Sunny watched him present the first one to the table with just the right amount of reverence. He brought the second shortly afterward. Soon the table was filled with half-empty glasses. Sunny sent out plates of braised duck legs, followed by risotto, followed by salt cod ravioli. For nearly an hour, she sent out plate after plate until they came back half full.

"They're done. Wiped out," said Bertrand, stopping back with a demi-rack of lamb that had hardly been touched. "They are using my fifth-best Sonoma Pinot like mouthwash and cannot swallow another bite of fish, fowl, or mammal. Are you trying to kill these guys?"

"Okay, I guess this is it. Riv, I need your help," said Sunny. Rivka came over and Sunny pulled her close. "Listen, I'm going out to talk to these guys. You come out right after me and I'll introduce you. Engage them for a minute, then we'll both get out of there quickly. Don't linger."

"What's up?"

"I'll explain later. Just make sure they're looking at you the whole time."

"No problem."

Rivka took off her white jacket and left it on the counter. Underneath was the white tank top and lacy black bra that was her standard work uniform. She took a fresh apron and tied it tightly around her hips. "Distracting enough?"

"Definitely."

The dining room was thinning out. Just a few tables remained, most of them on the patio, most of those picking at dessert, sipping cappuccinos, or sitting back, finishing their conversations. Keith and Franco had been there for over two hours. Sunny took a deep breath and went out to their table, where Franco greeted her like a returning hero. A moment later, Rivka appeared at her side.

"This is my sous chef, Rivka Chavez. Rivka, this is Franco Bertinotti, the winemaker at Taurus Rising Vineyard I told you about, and Keith Lachlan, Oliver Seth's lawyer and, I think, business partner?"

"Sometime business partner," said Keith. "Delighted to meet you."

"I just wanted to express my most sincere condolences for your loss," said Rivka. "I can only imagine how difficult this time must be for you." She put both hands over her heart in a gesture of sincerity.

"My dear, did you have a hand in the meal we have just enjoyed?" said Franco, looking into her beautiful brown eyes with their Bambi lashes, just as Sunny had hoped he would.

"Just these two right here," said Rivka, holding out her hands coyly. He took them in his and gave them an earnest squeeze.

"Marvelous," said Franco. "Where did you learn to cook?"

"Right here," said Rivka. "I learned everything I know from Sunny." She turned slightly so that Franco might have the opportunity to notice the tattoo on her upper arm.

"What is this?" he said, taking the bait. "What have you put here?"

Rivka modeled the swooping red and blue swallows on either arm. Franco and Keith took turns admiring them.

"I've had them for years," said Rivka, "but I just started a new one. It's not finished yet." She leaned down and pulled aside her shirt to reveal the top half of a mermaid reclining across her shoulder blade. The two men examined it with interest. Sunny pulled two wineglasses from her jacket pockets and splashed a taste into each, wiped the neck of the bottle and a corner of the table with a fresh napkin, and slipped it back in her pocket together with Keith's BlackBerry. Rivka stood up and Sunny handed her a glass.

"To Anna," said Sunny, looking at each of them. They touched glasses and drank.

"I have a small dessert coming in just a moment," said Sunny, putting the glass down. "Would you like a port or an Armagnac to finish? Bertrand has a favorite port that tastes especially delicious with the fig tart."

"Whatever you recommend," said Franco. "We are in your hands."

Back in the kitchen, Sunny slid the BlackBerry into Rivka's back pocket.

"You speak crackberry, right? It's Keith's. Find the Web address for Oliver's data. You've got about four minutes. I'll try to put it back while they're occupied with the port and dessert."

"I wondered what you were up to," Rivka said, and ducked into the office. Sunny grabbed Bertrand on his way past.

"Dig up one of our best ports. Something old and expensive that will make them feel obligated to drink it. And trot out the bottle so they know. See if you can get them talking about wine or whatever seems to interest them. Turn on the Frenchy charm. I want these guys to fall in love with us."

"I'll do my best," said Bertrand dryly. "So, are these guys critics or family?"

"Something like that. I'll explain later. Just make sure they're not sitting around talking to each other."

He went back down the cellar stairs to find a good port and Sunny went to work preparing a dessert sampler with three of her favorites, including a honey cake with *fromage blanc*, a tiny flourless dark-chocolate bomb with a swipe of raspberry purée, and the promised fig tart with its buttery crust and showstopper ice cream. When it was ready, Rivka still hadn't emerged from the office. Sunny looked in.

"Did you find anything?"

"Maybe." She finished making a note on a sheet of paper and handed the device to Sunny. "Let's hope so."

Sunny put the dessert plate on the zinc bar and watched the waiter deliver it to the table. Soon after, Bertrand presented a bottle of Taylor's as if he were handling a sacred object and filled two small glasses with the deep purple wine. Keith and Franco seemed in no hurry. Sunny spoke to their waiter, a guy who spent winters in Baja surfing and living in his van and came back to work the extra shift Sunny added each summer.

"Did they order coffee?"

"Two espressos macchiato."

"Good. I'll take them over. Oh, and these guys don't get a check."

"You're going to comp them? You do realize they ordered a nickel's worth of wine before you got here."

"I know, I know. I don't really have a choice. We have to give these guys the serious VIP treatment."

"Who are they?"

"That's what I'm trying to find out." She watched him walk away. "Maybe I can bill Steve Harvey," Sunny muttered to herself.

She fired the two shots and put a fresh napkin in her pocket, willing calmness and her hands to stop trembling. At the table, Franco had just loaded a forkful of tart and ice cream in his mouth. Bertrand was holding forth on his best topic and Keith was listening intently. Sunny put the two espressos down and tidied the table, removing an empty glass, wiping a few crumbs, and replacing a dirty napkin with a clean one. At the same time, she deposited Keith's phone underneath it.

"People like the idea of old wines, but mostly they want instant gratification," said Bertrand. "They want to buy the wine and drink it now, so even your big, expensive Cabs are mostly built to drink sooner rather than ten or twenty or thirty years down the line. They'll age well for maybe five years and after that they start to come apart. Winemakers today need Robert Parker to be able to open the bottle on the day it's released and give it a ninety-five. That bottle of wine is not designed to improve with age. Conversely, the Cabernet that's going to age like a great Bordeaux is generally not at its drinking best when it's young. You can't have your Cab and drink it, too."

"But you can have your port and your tart and espresso," said Sunny, taking Bertrand's place. The sommelier gave them a nod and glided off toward his NASCAR president, the bottle of Taylor's clutched before him in offering.

"I can't wait to tell Oliver that the only thing smoother than his Andre Morales is Andre's Sunny McCoskey," said Franco, looking up at her. "He'll wonder why Morales kept such a secret from us. And I think I know. He doesn't like the competition. But the secret is out now, and I will make sure it is known. We must find a place for you in the new arrangement, or something else at least as good."

"The new arrangement?"

"The Vinifera expansion or the new restaurant or whatever they decide to do, assuming they actually come to an agreement."

"They will," said Keith. "Morales drives a hard bargain, but we've just about got him nailed down."

Sunny smiled wanly and said nothing.

"My dear, this has been a most decadent afternoon," said Franco. "I am completely sated and revived thanks to your remarkable abilities. But even the good things must end eventually, and I am beginning to feel guilty that we have left our friend Mr. Seth to return to an empty house after the day's ordeal. We need to go and entertain him. Show him that all life is not ended, even if it seems that way at the moment."

"I'd like you to be my guests today," said Sunny.

"Nonsense."

"I insist. It would be my pleasure."

"In that case," said Franco, "we have no choice but to accept your generosity." He reached inside the jacket hanging from the back of his chair and pulled out a wallet and a slender golden pen. He extracted a business card and wrote his mobile number on the back of it before handing it to her.

"But I warn you," said Franco. "I plan to make it up to you."

"Andre said Oliver was a friend," said Sunny, fuming in the back office. "He's not a friend. He's the VC he's been primping for all these months."

"I can't believe he never told you," said Rivka.

"I'm beginning to see a pattern," said Sunny. "I think if I confronted him about this, he would just say he didn't want to bother me about it or he was going to tell me but never got the chance or something like that. Just like his explanation of that morning I found him with Marissa, and not contacting me afterward. It's not about doing the right thing, it's about doing whatever he wants and wiggling out of it afterward."

"He's not true blue," said Rivka.

"No matter how much I want him to be," said Sunny.

"It's a shame."

"You're telling me." Sunny let out a sigh. "That much hotness is a terrible thing to waste."

"I hear you."

She sighed again. "Well, damn. I have to forget about it for now. I'll deal with it later. We have bigger fish to fry. Did you find anything?"

"Who knows? BlackBerrys don't cache much browser history. But there were a few interesting Web sites and FTP addresses on there. I wrote them down."

Sunny examined the list. "None of these include *Taurian* or Oliver's name, but I guess what we're looking for might not. What are these numbers?"

"IP addresses. It's a way to access a server without a domain name. All Web sites have an IP address. Not all of them have a domain name."

Sunny put the list in her jeans pocket. "My laptop is gone and I don't think we should do it at your place."

"They have computers at the library."

Sunny looked doubtful. "This could take a while."

"My house, then."

Sunny nodded. She went out to the kitchen. The dishwashers were hard at work, Bertrand was restocking supplies, and the last of the waitstaff was sitting at the bar finishing lunch. Between the portrait left on her truck, the smashed window, Anna's service, and the visit from Franco and Keith, it had been a long, nerve-jangling day.

"Bert, could you lock up tonight? Rivka and I have a little errand to run that can't wait."

"*Way*," said Bertrand, sounding half Parisian and half Valley Girl. "No problem. Bring me a macaroon."

Sunny turned to Rivka. "*Vamanos.*"

"Why does Bertrand want me to bring him a macaroon?" asked Sunny, starting the truck and pulling out of Wildside's parking lot.

"I told him I was going to Yountville tonight to the new bakery before it closes."

"Why?" asked Sunny suspiciously.

"Because that was my after-work plan before you started stealing BlackBerrys."

"Because . . . "

"Because I wanted a cookie."

Sunny looked at her. "We have a whole shelf of the best cookies in town at the restaurant."

Rivka raised her eyebrows. "But not those cookies. I'm doing recon. If you set up shop and start selling fancy cookie treats in my town, it's like calling me out. I have to respond."

"Yountville isn't your town."

"It's close enough. I just want to see what all the fuss is about. Besides, Jason likes their macaroons."

"Ah, now I get it."

They pulled up at Rivka's place and went in. Sunny locked the door behind them and Rivka closed the blinds. While the computer booted up, Sunny put the teakettle on to boil.

"We hit the numbered addresses first, right?" said Rivka. "If any of this is of interest, I think that's where it will be." She typed in the first set of numbers with Sunny looking over her shoulder. A gray box popped up asking for a user name and password.

"Here we go again. User name Oliver Seth. And we go with the usual password, right?"

"Right."

Rivka typed Europa01 and hit Enter.

"Denied. Any other ideas?"

"Too many. Let's try the other address before we start a guessing game."

Rivka typed the second set of numbers and another gray box popped up. She entered Oliver's name and password and hit Enter again. An instant later a directory appeared. Sunny looked around the room reflexively. No one could see in. They were alone, the windows covered, the door locked.

"Now what?" asked Rivka.

"We look for the camera footage from Saturday night."

Rivka rummaged through a sea of folders and files. Sunny made tea and waited.

"I think I've got something," said Rivka at last. "It's loading."

The something turned out to be grainy black-and-white footage of the master bedroom, shown on a screen the size of a sticky note.

"Look at the time. That's from the morning," said Sunny.

"Hang on, I think I get it now. They're in half-hour increments. What time do you want?"

"Just look at the very end of whatever got uploaded from that day. I went to bed around one or one-thirty. Oliver said it backs everything up at two each night. The police unplugged the system the next morning, so everything after that is lost for good."

Rivka chose another file. This one showed the master bedroom in darkness. Rivka scrolled forward. Anna walked across the screen and turned on a lamp beside the bed. Oliver came in after her.

"This is so strange," said Sunny. "This can't be more than a few hours before she died."

"They're fighting," said Rivka. "Look at her face. She's screaming at him."

"Isn't there any sound?"

"No sound."

Rivka scrolled forward again. They watched breathlessly as Oliver Seth walked over to Anna and pulled her to him, wrenching her arm as she struggled to pull away, her face defiant.

"I'll bet that's how she got the bruises on her wrists," said Sunny.

On the tiny screen, Oliver let her go and turned away. Anna walked out of the frame toward the window and Oliver followed. Rivka scrolled ahead until they saw Oliver walk back across the frame toward the door.

"That's it. That's the end of what the camera recorded in that room."

"Two o'clock."

"Yeah," said Rivka, looking at her with wide eyes. "That could be it. That could be the murder right here. Anna is still over by the window somewhere when Oliver leaves."

"Except I heard her crying much later. Like around four in the morning."

"How do you know it was her crying?"

"That is a very good point," said Sunny. "I can't believe I didn't think of that. I don't actually know it was her. It definitely sounded like a woman, so I assumed it was Anna. But it might have been someone else."

"Like someone who came in and found her dead," said Rivka.

"Let's watch it again." Sunny reached over and clicked on Play. She hit Pause as Oliver walked out of the room.

"Look at his face," said Sunny. "What is he feeling right there?"

Rivka looked more closely. "I can't tell. He looks serious."

"That's what I mean. He looks stern but otherwise totally composed. He's walking out after a disastrous blowup with the woman he loves and he looks like a guy with a toothpick leaving a business lunch."

"Let's keep going," said Rivka. "There are a bunch of other cameras to go through."

Most of the cameras showed dark, empty rooms. In one bedroom, Jared Bollinger pulled on his clothes and helped Molly get dressed, buttoning up her shirt between passionate embraces.

"What time is that?"

"One-thirty."

"Impressive. They were already in a lather an hour earlier."

Later, the same camera showed Marissa Lin applying some kind of cream to Andre Morales's face.

"Speaking of lather," said Rivka.

"At least he was telling the truth," said Sunny.

"He said a hot Guamanian princess gave him a facial in her underwear?"

"Well, not exactly."

They watched Andre pull Marissa to him and kiss her.

"Looks platonic to me," said Rivka. "I grab Monty like that all the time."

"Let's just get through this," said Sunny. "I'm beyond exhausted."

"There are only two cameras left."

One of them was aimed at the kitchen. Cynthia Meyers stood at the stove, stirring a pot.

"Is she really cooking at, what, one-thirty in the morning?" said Sunny.

"Yup. One forty-seven, to be exact."

"What could she be making at that hour?"

"A pie," said Rivka.

"How do you know?"

"Look at the counter. That's a pie dish."

They watched Andre Morales come into the kitchen with a towel around his waist.

"What a show-off," said Rivka. "He is so in love with himself. Put on a shirt!"

He spoke to Cynthia. She nodded and walked out of the frame. Andre stirred the pot on the stove, tasted the mixture, and added a few drops from a bottle on the counter.

"Vanilla?" asked Rivka.

"Looks like it. What's he doing now?"

Andre walked over to the sink and opened the cabinet underneath. He took out a box, pulled two rubber gloves out of the top, and put it back.

"I think I'm going to be sick," said Sunny.

"There is no way he killed her," said Rivka.

"No, definitely not. But what is he doing with rubber gloves at that hour?"

The footage ended and Rivka turned around to face Sunny.

"Maybe he's exfoliating her?"

The last camera showed the gate at the bottom of the hill. They watched a dark screen. Rivka scrolled to the end.

"Nothing."

Sunny thought for a moment. "Wait, let's go back and look earlier. Like starting around midnight."

Rivka loaded the earlier footage and they scrolled through it.

"Nothing in that one, either," said Rivka.

"Let's keep going," said Sunny. "I want to make sure we don't miss anything. What time is this?"

Rivka kept scrolling. "Quarter after one."

"Wait, something's happening," said Sunny.

A light appeared and Andre pulled up to the gate on his motorcycle. He buzzed the intercom, the gate opened, and he drove through. Rivka scrolled through the remaining footage.

"That's it," said Rivka. "Just Andre arriving at one seventeen. Is that what you were looking for?"

"No. Keith Lachlan left after I got out of the hot tub and went to bed. They said very soon after. That would be about one in the morning."

"We covered everything from midnight to two."

"Exactly. Why don't we see his car leave?"

Sunny took out her phone and dialed Sergeant Harvey's number. She got voice mail. "Steve, I need to talk to you right away. It's important. Give me a call tonight if you can. It doesn't matter what time."

Rivka looked at Sunny. "I have a very bad feeling about all this."

18

Rivka didn't want to sleep alone. Sunny dropped her at Jason's house, promised she would go straight to Wade's, and drove to her place, anyway. She sat in the truck outside, brooding. Two thoughts bothered her. One was the idea of someone—could it have been anyone *other than* Keith Lachlan?—creeping silently into her house—*how?*—and her bedroom, where she lay oblivious and entirely vulnerable. The other was Anna snuggled up to Oliver in the hot tub with Keith across from her, sandwiched between Marissa and Jordan. Not long afterward, Keith purported to leave, but he didn't drive down the hill and out the gate, at least not immediately. By morning, he was gone, so he must have left sometime after two. Why the delay?

Keith leaves, or at least says he is leaving, thought Sunny. Soon after, Andre arrives. Marissa and Andre take a bedroom and play spa. Oliver and Anna go off and eventually quarrel. What about Jordan? She wasn't with Marissa and Andre. The video showed that much. Sunny assumed she'd gone to bed alone or else with Franco, but what if she hadn't? What if she continued on the path she'd started down in the hot tub? What if she was with Keith?

"That's it!" said Sunny out loud, rapping her finger on the steering wheel. "That's why she blushed when I said no one had illicit sex at the supposed sex party. Because she had illicit sex that night—with her friend's boyfriend. And that's why Marissa and Keith broke up. Marissa must have found out and dumped him."

She felt in her back pocket for the card Franco Bertinotti had given her at lunch and called the number written on the back. He was only too glad to give her Jordan's number when she said she wanted to invite her and Marissa up to the restaurant for lunch. She punched it into her phone. Jordan picked up and Sunny explained why she was calling.

"I know it's kind of odd to call out of the blue like this, but I have a question I need to ask you. An important and somewhat personal question. Can you talk?"

"I have a few minutes, yeah."

"I mean are you alone."

"Alone? Not exactly, but go ahead."

"The night Anna was killed, everyone got out of the hot tub around one in the morning. I went to bed. Not long after, Andre arrived and he and Marissa went off together. What I want to know is, where did you go?"

"After the hot tub? I went to bed."

"Alone?"

"Of course."

"That's what you told the police," said Sunny. "And I can see why you would. But you weren't alone. You were with Keith."

"Don't let your imagination run away with you," said Jordan. "The truth is much less sensational. Keith went back to the city and I went to bed. The next thing I knew, it was morning and there were cops everywhere."

"Honestly, I really don't care who slept with whom," said Sunny. "It's none of my business. And I don't care what the police know or don't know. That's up to them. For my own reasons, I need to know when you and Keith got together and when he actually left the house. That's it. I have no intention of sharing what you tell me with anyone else. I just need to know."

Sunny waited for her to respond. Nothing.

"It's going to come out soon, anyway," said Sunny. "Marissa knows you were with him. I know. It's just a matter of time until the police know, and then you could be in big trouble for lying about it. I just need to nail down the timing. If you help me, I might be able to figure out what happened to Anna once and for all, and that would help all of us. And the sooner the better because it looks like this whole mess is going to blow up in our faces any minute. Jordan? Are you there?"

"Hang on a second." Heels clicked on a wood floor and a door closed. Jordan sighed irritably. "I've talked to the police. Twice, as a matter of fact. I don't see why I should talk to you about any of this."

"Because I know things the police don't. They might never figure out who killed Anna, but with your help, I might. Doesn't it bother you that you could be helping a killer stay free?"

"Keith did not kill Anna."

"All the more reason to give him an alibi. Because right now he doesn't have one. I happen to know he did not leave the house when he said he did. When the police learn that, he's going to be their number one suspect. A guy pretends to leave but doesn't. A girl gets killed. The guy doesn't come clean. That doesn't look good."

"Trust me, he couldn't have killed her."

"How do you know?"

"Because you're right. He was with me the whole time."

"From when to when?"

"From right after we got out of the hot tub until around three-thirty."

"Is that when he left for real?"

"Yes."

Sunny paused, thinking. "Okay, good. And do you happen to know how Marissa found out about you two?"

"Keith forgot to turn off his phone. It started ringing and she came to get it."

"She saw you together."

"Yes."

"What happened?"

"Nothing. She didn't say anything. She just stood there for a minute and then turned around and left. Keith left right after that."

"Who was calling him at three-thirty in the morning?"

"Oliver."

"Did he pick up?"

"No. I assume he called him back from the car. What exactly are you getting at with all this? Keith didn't kill her. He had no reason to kill her, and besides, he's the furthest thing from a violent person."

"He actually did have a reason. A very good reason. When I know what it all means, I'll call you."

Sunny hung up the phone and got out of the truck. The whole night was getting more and more confused. She told herself that maybe when she had a chance to talk to Sergeant Harvey and they put their heads together over everything she'd learned and whatever he knew that she didn't, it would all fit together and make sense. She checked her phone for messages. He hadn't called. Sunny looked at the front gate with its overgrown rosebushes sheltering her little house. It certainly looked sweet and safe and inviting, just like always. Last night she forgot to lock the front door. That was the only explanation. With the doors and windows locked, there was simply no way to get into the house without making enough noise to wake her, and the police could be here in two minutes if someone forced their way in. She would keep her cell phone with her in bed and it would be fine.

The sunset was over. The last of the twilight gold was gone and the sapphire blue at the horizon had faded to a grayish gloom just before dark. She closed the gate behind her and paused, lost for a moment in thought. A movement from the stoop attracted her attention and she froze when Andre said, "Hey."

She looked back at the street. His motorcycle was parked under the tree ahead of her truck and she hadn't even noticed. He was sitting in his biking leathers with his helmet next to him, as though nothing had changed.

"What are you doing here?" she said, her heart still racing.

"Waiting for you."

"Why? You're supposed to say something. You scared the crap out of me."

"Sorry. You haven't returned my calls, so I figured I'd stop by. What's going on with that?"

"What's going on with that?" She stood as though in a daze. "Um, can we talk about this later? I sort of have a lot on my mind at the moment."

"I think I have a right to know what's going on."

"Oh, really?" Sunny's eyes flashed. "That's interesting. Let's see, where do I start? How about this. How do you know Oliver Seth?"

"We met at Vinifera. He came in for dinner. He stayed late at the bar, we got to talking. The usual."

She waited. "Is that all?"

"He comes into the restaurant when he's in town. We're friends."

"Not business partners?"

"Maybe someday. Who knows? The guy certainly has enough cash to bankroll whatever I dream up."

"And you don't think it's odd you never mentioned that to me?"

"There's nothing to mention yet. I told you we were friends."

"Okay, fine," said Sunny. "I can see I'm not going to get anywhere with that. Next question. Why did you take rubber gloves from under the kitchen sink in Oliver's house the night Anna died?"

He looked surprised. "How do you know about that?"

"It doesn't matter. Why did you need gloves?"

He spread out his hands in front of her. For a cook, they were surprisingly smooth and soft-looking. Andre took the time and trouble to be well groomed head to toe. It was one of the things Sunny liked about him, and maybe one of the things she didn't like, too.

"Can't you guess?" he said. "I told you, we were having a spa night. I wanted to do a deep moisture treatment. You put lotion or Vaseline on your hands and then put on the gloves and get in a hot bath. It works great. You should do it. Let me see your hands."

"Andre, stop. And what did you ask Cynthia for?"

"When?"

"In the kitchen. Right before you got the gloves. You came into the kitchen and spoke to her and she left. That's when you took the gloves."

"Now you're freaking me out. What's going on?"

"Just answer me honestly for once in your life."

"What do you mean by that?"

"Before the gloves?"

"A nail file. I asked her for a nail file. Why are you interrogating me?"

"What did you do with the gloves when you were done?"

"I put them in the garbage. It's no big secret, if that's what you're worried about. I told the police about it. I'm not an idiot. I knew it would look suspicious to have rubber gloves in your room when somebody just got killed."

"What was Cynthia cooking at that hour, anyway?"

"Lemon meringue."

"That's right!" said Sunny. "I remember Oliver asking her about a meringue pie earlier in the day. I can't believe she decided to make him one so late at night."

"She waits on that guy like he's a prince. But you should talk. You're the original midnight baker."

"It is nice to bake at night when it's quiet and you can concentrate." She thought for a moment. "But we didn't eat a meringue pie. If she went to all that trouble, why didn't she serve it the next day? It wasn't exactly a festive atmosphere, but we were hanging around all day and she did feed us lunch."

"I wondered that, too. But she couldn't serve it. She froze it."

"She *froze* it? How do you know that?"

"I saw it in the freezer when I was putting ice in a pitcher."

"When?"

"On Sunday."

"But you can't freeze a homemade meringue pie."

"No, I didn't think so."

"You can't," said Sunny. "The texture gets all weird, and when you defrost it the peaks fall. You know that. I know that. Anybody who has spent years in a professional kitchen knows that, and Cynthia has been a cook for years."

"Maybe she knows something we don't," said Andre. "Or maybe she did it by accident. We were all upset that day. Maybe she was distracted and just wanted to get it out of the way. Like everybody else, she'd been up half the night. Who knows? Why do you care?"

"I just think it's very strange that a person would stay up until two in the morning making a special dessert for someone and then ruin it."

"Maybe she knew Oliver wouldn't feel like eating it on a day like that."

"Maybe. Still, it seems odd." She sat down on the stoop next to Andre. "It's odd to waste all that effort, you know? You stay up late making a pie, and then in the morning you decide to botch it. That seems odd, doesn't it?"

"Sunny, why are you obsessing about a pie? I'm sure someone ate it even if it wasn't perfect anymore."

Sunny turned and looked into his eyes for the first time.

"Wasn't it perfect? I mean, meringue is surprisingly hard to do just right. You know, with the good stiff peaks all golden brown at the tips, symmetrically arranged, with a nice, tidy edge. I can never get mine just right. Of course, I don't bake it very often."

"This one was pretty as a picture, at least when it started out. It got sort of crumpled in the freezer. Cynthia is an excellent baker."

"Crumpled. That's interesting," said Sunny. "Like maybe somebody handled it or something?"

"Who knows? Maybe she dropped it. It was sort of messed up. But you could see it had been good to start with."

"That's very, very interesting," said Sunny.

"I guess I don't find it as interesting as you do," said Andre. "I came over to talk about us, not Cynthia's abilities as a pastry chef."

She took her phone out of her pocket and checked the time. "Aren't you going to be late for work?"

"I was late an hour ago."

"Then why don't we talk later on, when we don't have to rush."

"Sounds good. But, Sun?"

"Yeah?"

"I'm going to hold you to it."

Sergeant Harvey didn't pick up his phone. Sunny stretched out on the couch and listened to it ring. At the beep, she left another message.

"Steve, it's me again. I mean Sunny. McCoskey. It seems like you've been pretty busy, but could you give me a call when you have a chance? It's Thursday evening. If you could call tonight, that would be best. It doesn't matter how late. I'll keep the phone by the bed. I know we talked about how sensitive the Anna Wilson case is, and how important it is that I stay out of it as much as possible, and, believe me, I completely understand that issue. I mean, I have the broken window to deal with. But you also said I should call you if I came across anything really significant, and it turns out that something significant has come up. A new piece of evidence. It might sound a little crazy, but I think there may be something to it. Just a hunch, but still, it might be worth checking out. Cynthia, Oliver's private chef, baked a lemon meringue pie late on the night Anna died. It might still be in the freezer in the kitchen at Oliver's house. If it is, we need to defrost it. I know it sounds a little crazy, but I am absolutely serious about this. Give me a call and I'll explain."

She hung up and lay on the couch wondering if Sergeant Harvey would follow through on her tip or ignore it. He obviously thought she was some kind of crackpot since he didn't even bother to return her last call. Still, she had to try. A breeze came in the open window and she savored it for a few seconds before she shut up the house like a prison. She closed and locked all the windows, drew the drapes where there were some to draw, double-checked the doors, and walked around a second time making sure every opening to the little cottage was as secure as possible. When she was done, she was satisfied no one could get in without crashing through a window or breaking in the door, and then at least she'd know they were coming. She stood in the kitchen and ate a banana absentmindedly, leaving the peel on the counter.

"Now for one last bit of unpleasantness," she said to herself out loud and picked up the phone again. She dialed information, asked for Oliver Seth's number, and waited while they connected her. Cynthia Meyers answered.

"Hi, Cynthia, it's Sunny McCoskey. I'm hoping to catch Oliver. Is he around?"

"Hi, Sunny. He's in his office. Just a second and I'll let him know you're on the line."

A moment later Oliver picked up. They spoke briefly about how he was doing, how long he planned to stay in town, and the latest news from the police.

"They're tight-lipped with me," said Oliver. "I gather from various sources that they seem to think she was killed, based on the autopsy, and that it wasn't the fall that killed her. Other than that, I haven't heard anything."

"That's why I'm calling. Some new developments have come up, and I'd like to talk them through with you. But I think we should do it in person, not on the phone."

"What's it about?"

"Given the situation, I'd rather not discuss it on the phone."

"Given the situation, I'm sure you can understand I don't have much patience with guessing games," said Oliver. "If you can't tell me what this is about over the phone, I don't want to hear about it in person, either."

Sunny took a moment to think.

"Well?" said Oliver impatiently.

"I'm just trying to think of the best way to explain the situation," said Sunny carefully. "It's just this. Think about who you talked to that night after the fight with Anna. Hasn't it occurred to you that someone is lying about where they were when she died? I discovered a couple of interesting new facts that I will have to share with the police soon. I don't have a choice. They're going to come to light eventually, anyway. I think it will be easier for everyone if you can help me get the pieces in the right order beforehand. It's up to you. You can talk to me now or wait and hear it from the police. Either way, it's time to face the truth."

"What kind of facts?"

"The kind of facts you get when you figure out how to control your fate."

"You figured that out, did you?" said Oliver.

"A girl named Europa helped me."

"Then I guess I have no choice. When and where?"

"I could meet you at seven tomorrow morning at Bismark's. I'll go over to the police station afterward."

"Fine."

He hung up and Sunny went to have a much-needed hot bath with plenty of lavender salts to put her mind at ease. Afterward, settled in bed, she picked up the volume of Mozart's letters she'd been reading for some weeks and retreated to a world preoccupied with concerts, lunches, long carriage rides, and silk-lined dress suits. No unexplained evil there, thought Sunny. Mozart didn't go around locking and checking his doors and windows before bed. Bureaucratic ineptitude, class snobbery, and entrenched greed, yes. Illness and sudden death, definitely. Unexplained evil? Not so much, thought Sunny. But could Paris in the 1780s be so much safer than St. Helena in the 2000s? Hardly. The old question came back to her again: Was she somehow, however accidentally, however unintentionally, inviting death—no, murder—into her life? She put the book aside and turned out the light. Despite a roiling mind, she was quickly taken by heavy sleep. She dreamed a jumbled montage of self-doubt and missed opportunities, arriving too late at a party, losing her footing as the car she was getting into pulled away, friends turning against her, a sudden fright that seized her and a scream that would not come. She jerked awake, heart pounding, alert to a new sound in the silent house. From the front room came the quiet scraping sound of a key as it found its purchase in a lock. Then the slide and thump of the dead bolt releasing, and the tiny creak of the front door as it opened softly.

19

Her first response was anger. Who would dare to wake me up in the middle of the night, let alone come into my house uninvited? she thought fiercely. Then came fear. Sunny ran through the possibilities in a frantic rush. Who had a key to the front door? Rivka. Her father. Wade. Andre. Would any of them arrive in the middle of the night without calling or even knocking and let themselves in without making a sound? Of course they wouldn't. Sunny listened, hardly breathing. For several long seconds, the house was completely silent. She hoped for a moment that she had been mistaken, that perhaps she had imagined the sound of a key in the lock and the front door opening. In a moment she could chalk it up to a bad dream and an overactive imagination, she thought with relief. She would read another page or two of Mozart and then go back to sleep. In the morning it would all sound so silly when she told Rivka about the fright she'd given herself.

All was quiet. She had nearly decided to turn on the light when she heard a sound like a soft footfall, followed by another, this time accompanied by the slightest creak of wood. The house always creaked in the quiet of night. It had its own nocturnal clicks and rumblings and sighs that were as familiar as a lover's. This was different. This was the unmistakable sound of a floorboard creaking underfoot. Sunny's heart thumped like she was running for her life. She made an inventory of the items within reach, considering each one's potential as a weapon. There was a carafe of water on the bedside table and a one-by-one stick on the windowsill, used to prop open the window on warm nights. The cell phone was under her pillow.

She crept out of bed and took up the stick, which was too light to be much use as a weapon but would have to do, and the phone and edged toward the bedroom door, stepping softly in bare feet. From the doorway, she could see most of the living room. The front door was closed. There was no one there. Everything seemed completely normal. The refrigerator ticked on and began to hum reassuringly. She advanced to the kitchen doorway. The place seemed perfectly peaceful. It was even tidy, except for the banana peel she'd left on the counter. She put the stick and the phone down, picked up the banana peel, and was just about to drop it in the container she used for compost scraps when someone cleared his throat behind her. She wheeled around and let out an involuntary shriek that seemed to rise from her toes and last half a minute. Andre Morales was standing in the hallway in his biking leathers, watching her. She picked up the stick and flipped open the phone.

"Sunny, it's me!" he said, stepping forward. "It's just me."

"What on earth are you doing here?" she said, sounding shrill and brandishing the stick. "What are you doing? Are you trying to give me a freaking *heart attack* or something? Oh my God. I can't breathe. Dammit!" She leaned forward and put her hands on her knees. "You scared me to death. How did you get in here?"

"Sunny, I have a key. You know that."

She stood back up. "But what are you doing here? Why did you sneak in here like that?"

"I was just trying not to wake you. I went in the bathroom to get a tissue. But then I saw you in the kitchen and I figured I'd better say something because I didn't want to scare you."

"Well, you did. You scared me half to death. But that still doesn't explain what you're doing sneaking around in the middle of the night."

"I wanted to see you. I told you I wanted to talk and you said we should do it later, so I figured I'd come by after work."

"I meant later as in someday when we felt like it. You can't just come in here without calling or anything."

He smiled at her sadly and took off his jacket. "I always come in after work without calling."

"Andre, don't bullshit me, please. Things have changed and you know it."

"Of course I do. I just thought if I came over we could, you know, relax and talk through whatever's on your mind and maybe get back to normal. Can't we do that?"

He stepped into the silver glow from the neighbor's porch light and Sunny studied his familiar face.

"I'm beat," she said, putting the stick and the phone down.

"So am I. What do you say we go to bed?"

He gave her the smile that had started everything months ago on their first date. She forced it out of her mind and shook her head. "I think we should, but not together. Not tonight."

She turned away and was astonished to see Cynthia Meyers standing in the hallway. She was wearing a tank top with jeans and little white Keds sneakers, as if she were headed out for a Sunday picnic. Strands of blond hair fell down from her ponytail across toned and muscular shoulders. Her face looked strained. Most surprising of all was the tiny pistol she held in one hand.

"Morales," she said, gesturing to Andre with the gun, "you are always turning up in the wrong place at the wrong time. Either you have very poor timing or very bad luck."

"What's this all about?" said Sunny.

"It's about a girl who couldn't leave well enough alone and got herself and her boyfriend killed."

"I don't understand."

"That's right, you don't," said Cynthia. "Which is why you should have stayed out of it. But it's too late now. Now you have to tell me why you wanted to meet with Oliver. And hurry up."

"You eavesdropped on our call."

"I'm bad that way," said Cynthia, smiling. "Now, why don't you tell me what you're going to tell Oliver tomorrow before I get impatient."

Sunny licked her lips and looked at Andre. His face was frozen in fear. She looked back at Cynthia. "I was going to tell him that I found out that Keith didn't leave the party when he said he did."

"Go on," ordered Cynthia. The hand holding the gun trembled. Sunny stole a quick glance at her face. The pale light bleached her skin and she looked gaunt and tired.

"Keith knew Anna had found out he and Oliver were propping up their new business with phony invoices," said Sunny. "She had threatened to expose them. That's what their big fight was about."

"And you think Keith killed her to keep her quiet," suggested Cynthia.

"That's the theory I was going to put across, yes," said Sunny.

Cynthia nodded, smiling. "I'm not an idiot. You have two seconds to elaborate convincingly or I will kill you both right now and go on my way."

"Yes, you're right, there is more," said Sunny quickly. "After I discovered Keith never left the house that night when he said he did, I figured it had to be him who killed Anna. My theory was that he pretended to leave, but instead he waited outside Oliver and Anna's bedroom window. After their fight, he climbed in the window, suffocated her, and pushed her out onto the concrete, hoping the fall would mask what really happened."

"Is that it?" said Cynthia. "A theory?"

Andre looked at Sunny with wide eyes.

"No, there's more," said Sunny. "It turns out a woman named Astrid in Rome was helping them. With the fraud. Oliver was in love with her. Anna found out about that, too. In any case, Anna may have been trying to blackmail Oliver. That's why Keith killed her."

"Trying to! She wanted everything," said Cynthia. "She wanted everything or she was going to ruin us all and send Oliver to jail. But you're wrong about one thing. He couldn't care less about Astrid. You think Oliver's world revolved around women like Astrid and your friend Anna. She always thought so, too. I'm the only one who knows the truth. She was nothing special to him. Neither of them were. Girls like Anna and Astrid come and go through Oliver's life all the time. Sometimes there wasn't even a whole day between when one of them left and the next one arrived. It's a form of entertainment for him. A game. But do you know who he always comes home to? Who the real constant in his life is? Me. It's been me for years. Everyone thinks I'm just the cook. I'm part of his business, part of his family, part of every aspect of his life. Whether things are good or bad—and believe it or not, even a man like Oliver Seth has bad days—I'm always there for him. He trusts me. He relies on me. He comes to me for everything. Oliver is my whole world. It doesn't matter what everyone else thinks. I've loved him for years. We've been as married as any married couple. Your little friend

Anna thought she would change all that by making him marry her, and when that wouldn't work, she decided she would destroy him."

Andre looked nervously at Sunny, then back to Cynthia. "I always knew you were more than just his personal chef. I could tell, couldn't you, Sun?"

"You, shut your mouth," said Cynthia, her voice raspy with emotion. "And you, finish your story. Hurry up."

"Would you like something to drink?" said Sunny. "You sound like you could use a drink. I have a bottle of wine open in the refrigerator."

"Very funny. Are you finished, then?"

"With what I was going to tell Oliver? Yes. But there's something else you should know. I've already told the police about the pie. They've got it by now. So none of this actually matters. It won't matter what anyone tells the police or Oliver anymore, or what they don't. It's over, Cynthia. Your DNA is going to be all over that pie."

"*The pie!*" said Cynthia, letting out a laugh that gave Sunny a chill. "I got rid of that days ago, *cherie*. That was the first thing I did when we got back into the house. Is that all you've got? Was that your big piece of evidence against me? That puts my mind at ease."

"Adding two more murders to the list is not going to help you," said Sunny nervously. "But if you leave now, maybe you can still get away."

"Not so," said Cynthia. "Two more murders will help me immensely. When you're gone, this whole nasty business will be over and I can go on my way."

"Why risk it?" said Andre. "Why get the police coming after you? You yourself said they have no evidence. And we certainly wouldn't say anything."

"Andre, I don't want to kill you," said Cynthia kindly. "With all my heart, I don't. I feel sorry for you. But you can see I don't have a choice. Your girlfriend had a choice. She could have stayed out of the whole business." She turned to Sunny. "What did it have to do with you, anyway? It was never any of your business."

"Anna's death was my business," said Sunny.

"In any case, I don't have a choice," said Cynthia. "I have to end this. I'll spend the rest of my life running, but I won't spend it in jail. And Oliver must never know the truth."

Cynthia brushed a strand of hair back from her face and set her mouth in a hard line. Sunny touched Andre's hand and he grasped her fingers gently. None of them spoke or moved and time seemed to stop as they stood watching one another, waiting for Cynthia's next move. Sunny thought at first that the flash of light that made them all turn toward the big front window in the living room must be the pistol shot she'd been anticipating, and in the split second that followed she half felt the searing burn of a bullet strike her flesh. At the same time, she knew it couldn't be that, since it came from outside the house. Next they heard an explosive pop like the sound of gunfire, followed by glass shattering. A man's deep voice shouted, "Freeze! Nobody move!"

That was the beginning. The next few seconds were such a blur of activity and loud noises, with so much happening at once, that afterward no one could be certain of the exact sequence of events, least of all Sunny. Later she was sure of just three things. First, that the towering figure of Keith Lachlan had crashed through the front door. Second, that there were gunshots and Lachlan crumpled and went down hard. And third, that Sergeant Harvey appeared in the doorway afterward, silhouetted in his patrol car's floodlights like the hero in an action film.

Around the same time, though exactly when was impossible to say, Sunny saw Andre lunge forward and knock Cynthia's arm upward, sending the shot she fired into the kitchen ceiling. The shrill whine of approaching police sirens filled the air. Keith groaned and thrashed from the vicinity of the front door. Sergeant Harvey charged into the kitchen. He looked at Sunny, immobile with shock, then Cynthia, whom Andre was holding with her arm twisted behind her. The pistol lay on the ground nearby. Sergeant Harvey kicked it down the hall and threw an elbow into Andre's side, doubling him over and setting Cynthia free. He crumpled to the ground and Sergeant Harvey stepped on his back and slapped a cuff on his wrist. Cynthia ran for the front door, slipped on a pool of Keith Lachlan's blood, and took a nasty fall down the steps. She was still groaning and cursing at the foot of the stoop when the second and third police cars screeched up to the gate.

Serenaded by birdsong, Rivka Chavez pedaled her bike up the sidewalk and dismounted at the gate, which was smashed and hanging by one hinge. Andre and Sunny sat on the stoop, huddled over mugs of hot coffee and watching the morning brighten.

"What happened to the gate?" said Rivka, holding out a white paper bag. "I brought morning buns. And what happened to your window!" She gaped at the jagged hole where the front window used to be.

"Tornado," said Andre. "Late last night."

Rivka glared at him, leaned forward to examine a red stain at the top of the stairs, and pushed past them into the house. She paused to run her fingers over the splintered door frame. They listened to her stomp through the house and come back out.

"There's a bullet hole in your kitchen ceiling," she said incredulously. "And somebody busted in your door. Would you mind explaining what's going on?"

"You might as well get a cup of coffee," said Sunny. "It's a long story."

"What about work?" said Rivka, looking at her watch. "It's seven o'clock already."

"Have a seat," said Sunny, patting the stoop next to her. "The restaurant is closed today."

20

The coals, gnarled old vine stock chopped into briquette-size hunks, glowed orange under a thin coating of silvery gray. Rivka arranged lines of herbed quail on the grill and stood guard over them with her tongs. A willowy figure strode past her toward the parking lot, the sleeves of her apricot kimono dress rippling behind her.

"Where is she going?" said Rivka.

Sunny paused on her way to the table. "Annabelle? Monty said she forgot her earrings."

"And she's going to go get them? Can't she do without, or send someone else? She can't leave her own engagement dinner. We're just about to sit down!"

"I know," said Sunny with a shrug. "You want to try to stop her?"

Rivka hung the tongs on the grill and crossed her arms indignantly. "She's going to miss it. These birds are going to be ready in five. I can't take them off now."

"I told her that. It's her party; she can miss it if she wants to."

Sunny carried the last of the salads out through the mix of friends clustered around Wildside's backyard and gave the table one last glance, moving a glass half an inch closer to a plate, tucking a flower a bit deeper into its vase. Search warrants, shattered windows, murder investigations—it was all behind them now, thought Sunny with satisfaction. Cynthia Meyers was in jail awaiting trial for homicide, among other charges. Wildside's waitstaff glided among the guests, offering pristine little shrimps, toasts with a smear of goat cheese, and diced ahi tartare with fresh ginger and blackened sesame seeds on rice crisps. A gloss of chatter floated over the scene, punctuated by laughter and mixed with the jazz string quartet playing acoustic off to one side.

Most of the restaurant's staff was on hand to help. That morning, they'd carried half a dozen four-tops out the back door of Wildside and set them up next to the garden, under the olive trees, and covered them with white linen to make one long table. Down the center were half a dozen candelabra and as many vases overflowing with roses from Sunny's yard and the rosebushes that grew at the end of each row of vines across the street.

It was a perfect night: still, warm, and golden. Monty Lenstrom was nervous. Already he'd had too much of the local bubbly and was standing by Rivka with a champagne flute in his hand, looking dazed in his linen summer suit. Wade Skord clapped him on the back.

"You finally did it. And before retirement," he said.

"I am in love with an extremely neurotic woman," said Monty. "And I'm going to marry her. That's what I'm doing."

Wade took the tongs and lifted a quail. "Looks like we're almost ready. I could eat about, oh, seven of these guys myself."

"You get one," said Rivka.

"You've gotta be kidding. That's a Scooby snack, not dinner."

"Relax, it's just the starter. Everybody gets a salad and a quail to start. Then bouillabaisse avec garden tomatoes, garlic, white fish, and whatever else Sunny threw in there with a big tasty crouton floating on top and a dollop of Mama McCoskey's spicy rouille. Nobody is going to go home hungry."

"Good. Then let's get this thing started, I'm starved."

Sunny came up beside them. "I think we're about ready. Annabelle back yet?"

"Of course not," said Rivka. "She's probably still gassing up the car and having her nails done. It's fifteen minutes each way at least."

"Well, we can't wait. We'll just have to start without her. Everyone knows how she is, anyway." Sunny glanced at Monty. "I mean, I'm sure she'll be back soon. What do you think?"

"Let's do it. I don't want people eating cold bird. We can make a toast when she gets here," said Monty.

"Is that who I think it is?" said Wade, pointing a shrimp tail at the parking lot, where Franco Bertinotti and Keith Lachlan were getting out of Oliver Seth's convertible BMW. "That guy must be, what, seven feet tall? Where did he find a suit that big?"

"Not quite, but tall enough," said Sunny. "It's good to see him walking again. It's funny to think what might have happened if he hadn't shown up that night. I might not be here."

"She wouldn't have done it," said Monty. "There's no way she would have gone through with it."

"Of course she would have," said Rivka. "After you've smothered someone in their sleep, pulling the trigger on a gun is nothing. Besides, she had no choice. What's she going to do, just walk out and go home? Once you break into somebody's house and pull a gun on them, you're sort of committed."

"Steve was right behind him," said Sunny. "But he might have been too late."

Franco and Keith walked toward the group. Sunny was the first to greet them. "How is the leg?" she asked, standing back. "Looks okay from here."

"It's healing up pretty well," said Keith. "I can't complain. I'll never model with that leg again, but I still have the pretty face."

Sunny turned to Franco and let him pull her to him for a kiss on each cheek. "I'm glad you decided to stay. I was hoping you would," she said.

"Had to," said Franco, winking at the others. "I have to finish hammering out the deal with the new boss."

Monty and Wade looked at Sunny.

"We are considering . . . *I* am considering," she said, "the *possibility* of potentially, if all the details are exactly right, taking on a financial partner so we could expand the business, *if* that's what we decide to do, and we may not. There are still a lot of details to work out."

"You've got talent and guts," said Franco, "not to mention a great team." He nodded to Rivka. "With a little backing, Wildside could expand into a nice little franchise."

"It's already a nice little franchise," said Sunny.

"But we're ready to grow," said Rikva, leaning into her.

"We're ready to consider it," said Sunny. "I've always handled the business on my own, on my own terms. It's not an easy thing to give that freedom up."

"Sometimes you have to trust your fate," said Keith. "Everything is negotiable."

Rivka beamed. "Look out, Andre Morales, here we come."

"It's about time," said Wade. "You know," he said, pausing to finish chewing a shrimp, "I find it ironic that the person who wasn't looking for a backer found one and the person who was looking for one lost one."

"You mean Andre?" said Keith. "Oliver may still do something with him. It might just be on a slower time line."

"You mean he'll have to fit it in in between federal corruption investigations?" said Sunny. "He's going to be busy with his lawyers for a while. Oh, sorry. I guess you're caught up in that whole mess, too."

"Not me. I had no part in any of it," said Keith, raising his hands. "I just execute the contracts, I don't vet the strategy. That's his boat to sink. I'm just the lawyer."

"Come on," said Sunny. "You're not named on any of the indictments?"

"Oh, I'm named, all right. Everyone is named. Even this guy." Keith jerked his thumb at Franco. "But Seth and Taurian will bear the brunt of it. It'll be fine. This is a problem money can fix."

"Are you sure?" said Sunny. "Won't he go to jail?"

Keith looked incredulous. "Oliver Seth? No way. He might pay a hell of a fine and a fortune in legal fees, but he can afford it. He's made way too many people too much money to go down for something as minor as doctoring the books."

"But wasn't it more than that?" said Sunny. "Cynthia was sure it would ruin him."

Keith turned his hands up as if to say there was nothing he could do. "Inconvenient, certainly. Expensive, definitely. Embarrassing? A little. Ultimately not that big a crisis. He'll live to deal again. Or at least retire somewhere hospitable."

Sunny frowned and was about to say something, then decided it was a good time to call everyone to the table.

———————

In the deep blue of late twilight, the last of the rusty orange bouillabaisse was ladled out and the last of the dinner wines poured. Ripples of laugher rose up, and happy shouts punctuated the coming of night. Wraps appeared on bare shoulders and Monty emerged from the kitchen with his arms full of fresh bottles.

Decades earlier he'd started buying ports from the best years to shore up against future celebrations. He smiled knowing those days were here at last.

"I've been meaning to thank you," said Keith, taking the seat next to Sunny.

"For letting you come to my rescue?"

"I guess you didn't know the police had an arrest warrant out for me that night. If it weren't for you, I might have gone to jail for Anna's murder."

"How do you know?"

"The guy who put the bullet in my leg told me."

"Back up, folks," said Rivka. "Sunny keeps telling me she doesn't remember exactly what happened that night. It's all some kind of blur to her. But you were there. What exactly happened, anyway?"

"And while you're at it," said Sunny, "why don't you explain how you ended up at my house in the first place. I've been wondering about that."

"It's pretty simple," said Keith. "I was at Oliver's house when you called. I saw Cynthia listening in, and when she took off right afterward, I figured I'd follow her and see what she was up to. I knew things were getting thick. Jordan had already called me after you talked to her, so I had my suspicions about what was going on.

"I followed her over to your place and watched her jimmy the bathroom window. Trouble is, I didn't have a plan. I figured she had some kind of weapon. Nine-one-one would have been too slow. Then I remembered something this guy told me about." He grabbed Franco as he walked past. "The trusty old Sicilian paper-bag trick."

"You are insane. I still can't believe you actually used the paper-bag trick," sputtered Franco, choking on a mouthful of bread and wine.

"What is the Sicilian paper-bag trick?" said Rivka.

"It's absolutely nothing," exclaimed Franco, taking a seat. "That is the insanity of it! I told him a little story of something funny that happened when I was a boy in the countryside in Sicily. How one of my cousins hid outside an uncle's house who was a notorious hothead and pretended to be an angry neighbor on attack. He had a paper bag that he blew up with air and then popped to make a sound like a gunshot. It worked just the same way as for Lachlan, here." He laughed breathlessly. "Ha! Only my cousin got buckshot in his behind, not a bullet in the leg."

"It was that or nothing," said Keith, his face lit by candlelight, the long fingers of his big, graceful hands interlaced on the table. Overhead, little Moroccan tin lanterns filled with tea lights flickered from the olive branches.

"So you're outside Sunny's house," said Rivka, "and you see Cynthia climb in the bathroom window and you decide there isn't time to call for help."

"No, I called. I just figured it would be too late by the time they came. I knew I had to do something in the meantime. There was an old McDonald's bag in the car. I decided that was the best I could do. So I take it and go up to the front door and I listen. I can hear them talking inside, which is better than not hearing anything, but I figure I'd better get on with whatever I'm going to do or it's going to be too late. So I blow up the bag and yell something like, 'Freeze! Police!' Then I pop the bag and hit the door with everything I've got. At first I thought a splinter from the door must have got me. One of the shots—I don't know if it was the cop's or Cynthia's— shattered the front window. There was glass everywhere, then the cops stormed the place. The next thing I know, Cynthia was running toward me and then *bam!*, she goes down. Then Morales gets the sucker punch and he's down. You know the rest. Cynthia goes to jail. I get seventy-eight stitches in my thigh."

"Andre and I spent the next three hours explaining everything at the police station," said Sunny.

"But I still don't get how you knew to follow Cynthia in the first place," said Rivka.

"The same reason Sunny knew it was her who killed Anna. Because I knew it wasn't me. I had a general idea I was about to get set up, but I didn't realize how close I was until I saw Oliver's face after he hung up the phone. I knew then he thought I did it. I started thinking about that night. Oliver and I had spoken, late, about what Anna had found, and how she was threatening to go to the press with it. He was upset and concerned. To tell the truth, part of me always thought maybe *he* did it. I didn't want to think that, of course, but who else could it have been? No one else knew what was going on. No one else would care enough about Anna to go to the trouble of killing her. Then when I saw his face, I knew he felt the same way. He'd been thinking maybe it was me who killed her. Then it hit me. The only other person Oliver really trusted was Cynthia. All of a sudden I knew what had happened."

"That's exactly how it was with me," said Sunny. "At first I thought it had to be you. That Oliver confided in you and you decided to take care of the problem yourself, to save your own skin as well as his. When I found out all that business about the pie, I realized it could have been Cynthia, too. You guys were like a family. You, Oliver, Anna, and Cynthia. It had to be one of you. I wanted to see Oliver to find out if he had told Cynthia about what happened with Anna."

"But even if he told her, it wouldn't prove she did it," said Rivka.

"That's right," said Sunny. "That's why I told Sergeant Harvey to go up to Oliver's and get the pie."

"Which she had already disposed of," said Keith.

"What pie?" said Monty.

"Cynthia was making a pie that night. She wore rubber gloves when she killed Anna, and covered Anna's mouth with duct tape. Afterward she needed to stash them somewhere, so she put them in the pie and put it in the freezer. It was gone by the time I figured it out."

"So if she hadn't panicked and come after you that night, she might have gotten away with it," said Rivka. "Keith might even have been accused of Anna's murder."

"And it would have been ugly. As it turns out, I was driving down the hill about the time Cynthia killed Anna. I wouldn't have had an alibi. In fact, I would have been in exactly the wrong place at exactly the wrong time, and what's worse, I'd already lied about it."

"That is extremely ironic," said Wade, waggling a forefinger. "The real killer gets caught because she's trying too hard not to get caught. And the guy who everyone thinks is a killer turns out to be the hero who saves the day."

"It might be ironic, but it didn't have to happen at all. If you'd gone to Wade's house like you said you were going to," Rivka said to Sunny, "none of it would have happened. The police were getting close. They probably would have tracked the murder back to Cynthia eventually."

"While I waited in jail," said Keith.

"Sometimes you have to be bad to be good," said Sunny.

"Don't be cocky. You thought it was Keith or Cynthia," said Rivka, "but it could have been anyone, really. The guy who found her, our friend Franco here, even Andre."

"No," said Sunny, "it had to be someone who knew about what Anna had discovered. Somebody who would lose as much as Oliver or more if Anna made what she'd found public. I didn't think Anna told anyone that night other than me. She said I was her insurance policy in her e-mail. That left Oliver. I found out he'd called Keith, and that Keith had lied about where he was when Anna died. But he'd already lied about leaving the party *before* he found out about the fight. That was too much of a coincidence. Molly was thoroughly occupied the whole night. The only other person Oliver might have told was Cynthia. And if he went down, she definitely went with him. He was her landlord and her employer, and she was in love with him besides. It all fit perfectly. After the fight with Anna, Oliver turned to the only shoulder he could cry on. He went to see Cynthia at her house, confided to her what had happened, and went back to his house. Then he sat in his car in the garage the rest of the night and fiddled with his phone. By morning, Anna was dead.

"All of that made sense. My mistake was assuming Cynthia thought she got away with it." Sunny looked around the table. "Now that it's over, we think we know exactly what happened, but I'm not sure we do, or ever will."

"What do you mean?" said Rivka.

"The biggest question of all," said Sunny, turning to Keith. "When Oliver told Cynthia, and even you, about Anna's threats, was he just confiding his troubles, or was he giving implicit instructions to prevent a disaster at all costs? Did part of him want her, or you, to kill Anna? Was that his intention in disclosing what had happened?"

Keith nodded solemnly. "I've wondered that, too. There is no way to know for sure. He probably doesn't know himself."

"He couldn't have been blind to his power over Cynthia," said Sunny. "He knew she worshipped him."

"Oliver is, shall we say, conflicted about women," said Keith.

"I don't think it's about women so much as power," said Sunny. "He simply wants what he wants and he doesn't care what happens to other people in the process. He's like a spoiled kid with endless means."

"That's not spoiled," said Rivka. "That's much more serious than spoiled. It's evil. It takes a dark heart not to care how your actions affect others."

"You mustn't go too far," said Franco. "Oliver Seth is anything but evil. He's one of the kindest, most generous, hardworking people I know. It is true that he can be, on occasion—particularly when it comes to the enjoyment of women—excessive. Oliver likes to have a good time and he has no regard for what other people think of him. There are worse things. I would go further and say that he also understands, from experience, that people can be bought. This is something only a very few people experience. Everyone likes to say, and believe, that there is no price, but he has done it often enough to know that the price is simply much higher than most people imagine. This is a corrupting experience. And yet I think he genuinely loved Cynthia in a certain way. In his way. He respected her talent as a cook, that is certain, and he was very close with her as a friend, but essentially he saw her as an employee, not his wife, which is perhaps, I would dare to say, a far narrower distinction in his case than one would like to admit. If they slept together occasionally, that was simply something that happened. A perk, even, I'm sure is the way he imagined it. And of course it goes without saying that Cynthia was extremely well-paid."

"How can you go on making excuses for him? He knowingly played all those women off each other," said Rivka. "This girl Astrid. Anna. His live-in mommy surrogate and occasional lover. And Anna died because of it, not to mention the fact that Cynthia will spend the rest of her life in jail. He should be made to take at least partial responsibility for driving her over the edge. It's not fair he gets to just walk away and say, 'Oh well, at least I had a good time.'"

Sunny glanced approvingly at Rivka and watched Franco carefully.

"That is hardly what he is saying," said Franco. "On the contrary, I think it is an extremely difficult time for him. He's lost Cynthia as well as Anna, not to mention 'this girl' Astrid, who I have instructed to find other employ and entertainment immediately."

Sunny raised her eyebrows. "How can you instruct her to do that?"

"I can't. She is a grown-up woman of twenty-two years old. But as her father, I can make a suggestion and hope she listens to me. Astrid is a remarkable young woman. She's talented, beautiful, well educated, and capable. She is also impetuous and reckless. But this time it was me who was reckless, by introducing her to our friend Mr. Seth. To think it could have been her on the ground that morning!"

"But he had her arranging meetings in Russia," said Rivka, "and setting up new companies. She's just a kid."

Franco made a gesture of innocence with his hands. "As I said, she has had a very good education. She studied business in Germany. Astrid's mother is Russian and her current husband is a rather high-ranking member of the Russian Parliament, so Astrid is fluent in the language and rather well connected in the business community. In any case, it hardly matters now. She is young, so there is plenty of time yet to find another job and a lover she can tell her father about."

"I don't see how you can be so nonchalant about your daughter and your boss getting together," said Rivka. "Especially given the circumstances."

Franco chuckled. "I suppose I don't think of Oliver Seth as my *boss*, first of all. And second, we are not so concerned about such things in my part of the world. What Astrid does with the intimacy of her heart is her business. Besides, we cannot know the answers to these kinds of questions. The secret pacts formed between lovers are beyond the scrutiny of outsiders, aren't they?"

Monty smiled to himself.

"But did he love Anna or your daughter?" insisted Rivka.

"*Boff.* Who knows? Both, neither—it doesn't matter. It's time to move on. It's time to celebrate this man's upcoming wedding, not mash our teeth through this old business that's in the past. But I'll make one point before I let it drop." He looked at Sunny. "All the times when I saw him most happy were when he and Anna were getting along well. I thought for a moment they would be happy together."

Wade Skord waggled a finger. "In trying to help the man she loved, Cynthia inadvertently took away the only woman who ever made him happy."

Sunny gave him a heavy look. "Skord, you have got to stop."

Monty ran his hands over the mottled skin of his domed head and resettled his glasses. "Hang on, hang on. We have to go back again to that night at Sunny's place. Andre was there to hook up. Cynthia was there to stop Sunny from blabbing. Keith, you were there to see what Cynthia was up to. How did Harvey happen to be there? Did he get Keith's nine-one-one?"

"He got my messages from earlier that night," said Sunny. "He came by to see if I was home and he saw Keith lurking around outside. Then he heard gunfire and saw Keith storm the door, so he shot him."

"That guy is one hell of a cop," said Wade.

"I don't know about that," said Sunny. "He told me he saw the pie Cynthia made in the freezer that Sunday morning and didn't think anything of it."

"So?"

"Meringue in the freezer? If that's not fishy, I don't know what is."

"Come on, he can't know everything," said Wade.

"All I'm saying is he'd catch a lot more murderers if he learned a little something about cooking," said Sunny.

Annabelle came over and settled gracefully next to Monty in her peach silk dress with its butterfly sleeves and wide sash. A cascade of tiny gold discs dangled from each ear. "That was a marvelous feast," she said, taking up Monty's glass.

"Did you actually eat?" asked Rivka.

"Of course!"

"Human portions, or are you still doing the calorie-restriction thing?"

Annabelle shook her head slowly. "No more starvation rations for me. Monty convinced me the extra years weren't worth the grief."

"They get tacked on the end of your life when you're already half dead, anyway," said Monty. "Who needs that? *Carpe diem.* Besides, if we drink enough red wine, the resveratrol will keep us young."

"I'll drink to that," said Wade. "Speaking of toasts, isn't it about time we made one?"

Monty held up a hand to silence him. "Later. I want to finish this other business first. Annabelle and I were going through the whole Anna Wilson affair last night, and I need a few more things cleared up before we get off track with all the wedding stuff. For example, I still don't understand how Cynthia managed to break into Sunny's house and take her picture without waking her the night she left the note on the truck. Or even why she would go to the trouble. You didn't have anything on her at that point, did you?"

"No, but it didn't matter because it wasn't Cynthia, and they didn't break in," said Sunny. "Remember when I ran out of gas coming home from Wade's house and Molly Seth stopped to help me? She had Mike Sayudo, the gardener who found Anna's body, make a copy of my key when he went to get the truck."

"But why?"

"She was trying to protect her brother. I think she was worried he might have actually killed Anna. She wanted to make sure I kept my mouth shut if I found out anything about him. Steve told me all about it just a couple of days ago."

Annabelle wore a knowing smile. "When Monty told me this story, I knew immediately it had to be either the sister or the cook."

"What makes you say that?" asked Sunny.

"Women are territorial. A long time ago, before I met Monty, I dated a guy who had a housekeeper who'd been doing his laundry, making his bed, and fixing his dinner for twenty years. Once she locked me out of the house and tried to pretend it was an accident. Finally I told him he should propose to her and get on with his life."

"That is such baloney. You told me you thought the artist did it!" said Monty.

"No, I told you he was third on my list. I said the sister or the cook or else the jilted artist lover."

"Troy? Hardly," said Franco. "I think in general he would prefer Molly's friend Jared Bollinger, from what I hear."

"He's gay? Since when?" asked Sunny.

Franco waved a hand. "These things are not always as clear-cut as one imagines."

"Maybe we should introduce him to Bertrand," said Sunny. "They'd make a perfect couple."

"Matchmaking," said Rivka. "Now, that's a nice, safe hobby. I like it. I like it better than waiting for crazy people with guns to come and kill you in the middle of the night."

Sunny looked at Wade. "That reminds me of something I've been meaning to tell you. You'll never guess who was in the restaurant the other day. Bertrand was atwitter."

"Who?"

"The president of NASCAR."

"Mike?" said Wade. "Good, I told him lunch at your place was a sure bet."

"You know him?"

"Don't look so surprised. Even we vulgar plebs have our connections."

"The important thing," said Monty, looking at Sunny, "is that the bad guy—I mean, bad girl—is behind bars. Our tranquil valley is free of malice and violence once again."

"As far as we know," said Sunny.

"Ever the pessimist," said Monty. "You'll be out hunting for the next bloodthirsty maniac tonight as soon as everyone else is in bed."

"No chance," said Sunny. "All I want to do from now on is cook. Just cook. I want to cook at the restaurant. I want to cook at home. I may even travel somewhere and cook."

"I'm so glad to hear you say that," said Monty. "For weeks I've been wanting to ask you to cater the wedding, but I was afraid you'd say you're too busy. But now it sounds like you'd like nothing better!"

Sunny gave Rivka a resigned smile and told Monty, "I would be honored."

It was dark when Rivka and Sunny carried out sheets of peach tart warm from the kitchen and served it with homemade burnt caramel ice cream. The band had packed up and Wade had gone to his station wagon for his guitar, which he now strummed softly, sitting on a chair under an olive tree.

Headlights swung across the table of friends in the deepening night and a few minutes later Andre Morales crunched toward them across the gravel. Sunny watched him make his way past the garden with Mount St. Helena as a backdrop. He kissed Sunny and Annabelle on the cheek and shook hands with Monty. The party fell silent, with half a dozen conversations suddenly hitting a lull as if by prior agreement. In the quiet, Andre nudged Sunny up from the table. They strolled toward the vineyard, admiring the spray of stars in the velvety blue sky. Sunny looked back and saw Rivka's boyfriend and Keith Lachlan knock knuckles and heard their big, throaty laughs. At the long table, Monty and Annabelle were squeezed together, hands intertwined, their faces lit by candles burned low.

"So you think we can get through this?" Andre said, squeezing her hand.

"I warn you," said Sunny sternly, "I will not be charmed."

"I'm not trying to be charming. I'm trying to reopen negotiations. Someone once told me everything is negotiable."

Sunny narrowed her eyes. "Some things are nonnegotiable."

"Right. Well, then, forget negotiation. Why don't you just tell me what you want and I'll agree to it."

"I think I'm going to need some time to consider that offer," said Sunny, turning back to the party.

They rejoined the others just in time to drink another toast, the final toast, to Monty and Annabelle, the beautiful night, good friends, the peace and tranquillity of the valley. Tonight Sunny would sleep with her windows open and her door unlocked, as if none of it had ever happened.

Acknowledgments

Purists will note that one cannot see Mount Tamalpais from the steps of the Mission San Rafael in Northern California. A large and not terribly handsome building has been constructed in front of the chapel, entirely blocking the view. From the street above, Mount Tam rises up like a great maternal guardian, bottom-heavy and protective. It felt good to restore, if only in fiction, what must have been an inspiring setting.

Some books take longer to write than others. My editor, Jay Schaefer, showed superhuman patience in waiting for this one. For that and many other kind gestures over the past decade and more, he has my gratitude, as well as my friendship.

The people closest to me did much to make the writing of this book possible, chief among them Judy B. and Randy Brown, who lent continuous encouragement, read manuscripts, offered advice, babysat, and let me ravage their refrigerator with merciless frequency. I also depended on the ever-capable and delightfully cheerful Nai, her sidekick Mimi, and that adjacent triumvirate of good company, Rachel, Ted, and Savannah. For inspiration, there is no one like Ivan, whose fresh perspective on the world is a constant source of pleasure, unless it is the Good Twin, even *in absentia.*

A number of friends with expertise in food, wine, and good living (lucky them!) read manuscript versions of *Lethal Vintage*, generously offering not only their time but their valuable opinions and insights. These included Jonathan Waters, Suzanne Groth Jones, Rebecca Carter Harrach, Adam Browning, Andy Demsky, Lisa and Jerry Niess, David Strada, David Polinsky, and Andrew Stern. I would like to thank them for their contributions, and point out that any errors or oversights that remain are mine despite their guidance, not due to it.

—NG